prlg

D1478964

10/23

The Plot
Thickens

Center Point
Large Print

Also by Susan Page Davis and available from Center Point Large Print:

Fort Point
Found Art
Heartbreaker Hero: Eddie's Story
The House Next Door
The Labor Day Challenge
Ransom of the Heart
Breaking News
The Rancher's Legacy
Blue Plate Special
The Corporal's Codebook
Ice Cold Blue
Cliffhanger
Persian Blue Puzzle
The Sister's Search

The Plot Thickens

Skirmish Cove Mysteries – Book Two

Susan Page Davis

CENTER POINT LARGE PRINT
THORNDIKE, MAINE

This Center Point Large Print edition
is published in the year 2023 by arrangement with
Scrivenings Press.

The text of this Large Print edition is unabridged.
In other aspects, this book may vary
from the original edition.
Printed in the United States of America
on permanent paper sourced using
environmentally responsible foresting methods.
Set in 16-point Times New Roman type.

ISBN: 978-1-63808-686-4

The Library of Congress has cataloged this record
under Library of Congress Control Number: 2022951683

FIRST STORY — NOVEL INN

TO BLUFFS OVERLOOKING BEACH ⇧

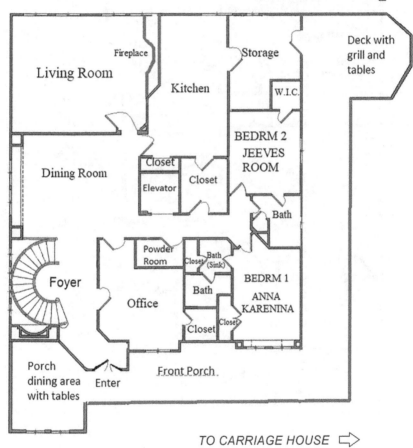

Living Room

Fireplace

Kitchen

Storage

Deck with grill and tables

W.I.C.

BEDRM 2 JEEVES ROOM

Dining Room

Closet

Closet

Elevator

Bath

Foyer

Powder Room

Closet

Bath (Sink)

BEDRM 1 ANNA KARENINA

Office

Bath

Closet

Closet

Porch dining area with tables

Enter

Front Porch

TO CARRIAGE HOUSE ⇨

SECOND STORY — NOVEL INN

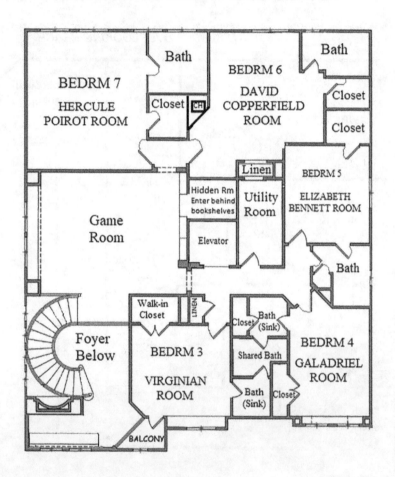

THIRD STORY — NOVEL INN

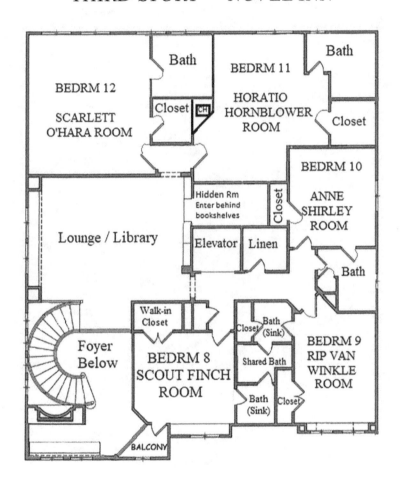

BEDRM 12

SCARLETT O'HARA ROOM

Bath

Closet | CH

BEDRM 11

HORATIO HORNBLOWER ROOM

Bath

Closet

BEDRM 10

ANNE SHIRLEY ROOM

Lounge / Library

Hidden Rm
Enter behind
bookshelves

Closet

Elevator | Linen

Bath

Walk-in
Closet

Foyer
Below

BEDRM 8
SCOUT FINCH ROOM

Closet | Bath (Sink)

Shared Bath

BEDRM 9
RIP VAN WINKLE ROOM

Bath (Sink) | Closet

BALCONY

Chapter 1

Jillian Tunney left the Novel Inn under her sister's capable supervision and walked briskly into the heart of Skirmish Cove. She loved the little town on the bay's edge, where salt permeated the air and small businesses lined the sidewalks. Snow hadn't fallen for nearly a week, and the sky formed a brilliant blue canopy. The air was warm enough to start shrinking the snowbanks left by the plows.

When she reached the snug little Book Rack, she pushed open the door and greeted the owner with a big smile.

"Good morning, Carl."

"Jillian! How are things going at the inn? January slump?"

"No, actually. We're nearly full right now."

"Ah, the Winter Carnival?"

She nodded. "It's only two days away. This weekend, we're booked solid."

Carl Roofner looked around his store, where only one customer browsed that morning, and arched an eyebrow. "It's winter slow in here. I hope some of the carnival goers decide to go book shopping."

"I'm sure they will." Jillian pointed to the end cap. "I see you have all the local interest books displayed."

"Yes, to showcase our Maine authors. Stan is coming in to help tomorrow and Saturday. We're hoping for a blitz."

"What about Eric?" Carl's son worked part-time at the store as well as Stan Chappell. Jillian was sure Stan must be nearing retirement. He looked a decade older than Carl, though neither of them was young.

"Oh, Eric's going to Clifton for a snowmobile rally."

"What? On carnival weekend? Won't there be snowmobile events here?"

"Not as many or as interesting, I guess." Carl shrugged. "He doesn't think we'll get that much traffic in the bookstore this weekend. What can I do for you this morning?"

"I'm thinking of redecorating one of the rooms at the inn."

His face lit with interest. "What's the theme? No, let me guess. A Maine story, maybe? Something by Stephen King?"

Jillian blinked. "I hadn't even considered that. I mean, how many people want to sleep in a room with horror décor?"

"True, true."

"No, it's an old classic. *Around the World in Eighty Days*. I thought a Phileas Fogg room would be fun."

Carl nodded slowly. "I can see it. Some sort of elephant artwork, perhaps." He eyed her keenly.

10

"Not the most politically correct story for these times."

"I know," she said with a little grimace. "The British Empire and all that. Maybe I should reread it first—it's been more than twenty years for me. I don't think the movies they've made have been exactly accurate."

"I'm certain they're not. But, Jillian, you can order it online so easily. Why here?"

She smiled and leaned on the counter. "You know me, Carl. I like to support the local businesses. Besides, I want an original copy."

The older gentleman's eyebrows rose.

"Oh, I don't mean a first edition—I can't afford that. But an old one, leatherbound, illustrated maybe." Jillian shared her vision with a sweep of her hand. "We'd put it in a glass display and have pictures of book covers or movie posters on the walls. And curtains that smack of the Orient."

"Sounds interesting." Carl leaned toward his computer and clicked away on the keyboard. "Let's see . . ." He squinted at a distributor's catalog listings. "Here we are. *Around the World in Eighty Days*. Hmm. There are about a million versions."

Jillian waited patiently. As a small business owner, she sympathized with the older man. Carl was widowed and in his sixties. Keeping the shop open couldn't be easy, especially in the slow winter. But she admired his tenacity.

"I see an 1880 version, published in London. That's the oldest one offered in English. Now, if you want it in French . . ." Carl turned the monitor so she could see the screen.

"That's beautiful." She peered over his shoulder at the computer's screen.

"Illustrated."

"Yes." She blinked at the price. She could just hear her younger sister Kate's response when she learned Jillian had spent over four hundred dollars for an antique book.

He clicked a few keys. "And this sheet music from the Michael Todd film's theme would make an excellent wall decoration. You could have it framed."

Jillian nodded. At twelve dollars and fifty cents, the sheet music was a bargain. "I'll take the sheet music. Will you do a little more research for me when you have time and see if you can find another copy of the book that old for just a little bit less?" She formed a half-inch measure with her thumb and index finger.

"Sure." Carl brushed his graying hair back off his forehead and worked on his keyboard some more.

"And why don't you get me an inexpensive paperback copy too. I don't think I'd want to handle the antique one very much, especially if I decide to spend that much."

"I'm pretty sure we've got it in the classics

section." Carl didn't look up from his work. "I know we have a children's adaptation."

Jillian almost discarded the idea of purchasing a children's version of the book, but it might be good to have on hand for families who stayed at the inn. Two women came through the door, greeted Carl, and headed for the discount table.

"I'll go take a look." Jillian walked farther into the store, taking in the colorful book covers face out on the shelves. So many enticing images.

Reluctantly, she moved past the mystery section and made her way to the classics. Stan was working at the end of the aisle, gently taking nature guides and books on astronomy from a carton and arranging them on a rack under a sign reading "Science and Nature."

"Hi, Stan."

"Hello, Jillian. Looking for something special?"

"Thought I'd revisit *Around the World in Eighty Days*. It's been . . ."

"More than eighty days, eh?" Still spry, Stan moved quickly to her side. "You're almost there. Here we go." He stooped and took a copy off a bottom shelf.

"Perfect. And now for a children's version."

As usual, Stan knew exactly where to find the title she requested. She left the Book Rack ten minutes later with a warm feeling of friendship. Both the paperback of Jules Verne's novel and a colorful picture book nestled in her bag. Those, with the sheet music Carl had ordered, had set her back almost forty dollars—plus tax—and she had yet to convince Kate that she wanted to redecorate one of the rooms. Surely the exotic locations and action in the story would sway her sister.

"You really want to redo a whole guest room?" They'd discussed the possibility before, but Kate was still surprised Jillian decided to move forward without consulting her first.

"I think it's time." Jillian turned a row of bacon slices on the griddle. "Think about it. Nobody reads *The Virginian* anymore."

Kate scowled. "They remember the TV show."

"Only people my age and older. Anyway, I put in an order for an illustrated, leatherbound edition. Carl Roofner at the Book Rack is ordering it for me."

"Why?" Kate asked. "You could just order it online."

"I know, but we like to support the local businesses."

"True."

Jillian smiled. "We can display it in the room. It's an 1880 edition, and he found one for a pretty good price."

"What else do you plan to use for decorations? A balloon?"

"That wasn't in the book."

Kate loaded a tray with a can of coffee, filters, and metal containers of silverware. "It wasn't?"

"Nope. Only the movie and TV mini-series versions. Verne did write a book called *Five Weeks in a Balloon*, though, so I guess the screenwriters figured it was okay."

"They always change stuff." Kate hefted the tray and went into the inn's dining room to set up for the breakfast crowd. She wasn't completely against the idea, but usually they made these decisions together, as joint owners of the inn. She checked the small refrigerator in the dining room. No almond milk. They had a couple of vegan guests, so she needed to put a fresh carton out.

She was still mulling Jillian's decision to spend almost two hundred dollars on an old book. Even though she insisted Carl had found a bargain, Kate wasn't on board with the idea.

"Morning, Ms. Gage!"

"Oh, hi," Kate said with a smile as two of their guests entered the dining room. "Call me Kate. We're just about to bring out the hot dishes."

When she returned to the kitchen, Jillian had three egg cartons open on the counter and was cracking eggs like a shell-hating robot. Three dozen seemed excessive, but Kate remembered the Novel Inn was full this weekend for the Winter Carnival, so it might not be too much. And if their brother dropped by, he'd help clean up the leftovers.

Skirmish Cove was determined to earn a spot with vacationers as more than a picturesque summertime venue. Outdoor activities were set up for adventurers—snowmobile tours, snow-shoeing, and cross-country skiing. A small pond near the library had been turned into an ice skating rink, and a hill behind the town hall was designated for sledding and tobogganing. Contests throughout the carnival included snow-man making and skating relays. Restaurants and gift shops were in high gear, and so was the inn.

Kate grabbed the almond milk and several containers of Greek yogurt. "Can you believe the snowmobilers in David Copperfield are up already? They're starting on coffee and muffins, but I told them bacon and eggs would be right out."

Jillian looked at the clock hanging over the dishwasher. "Breakfast doesn't officially start for another ten minutes."

"Yeah, I think they want to hit the trails early." Kate went back to the refrigerator. "Do we have more individual butter servings?"

"In the second freezer."

"I think I'll miss having a western-themed room." Kate glanced at her sister, half hoping she'd immediately give up her plans for change. "Maybe we should redo Anna Karenina instead. Nobody reads Russian novels anymore."

"Says you." Jillian carefully poured her mixture

16

for scrambled eggs into the pan. "Besides, we'd have to give it a feminine theme. What woman would we use?"

"Annie Oakley?"

"She was a real person."

"Right. Let me think about it." Kate headed for the storage room behind the inn's kitchen, where they had two upright freezers. She found the butter easily. Back in the kitchen, Jillian loaded a pan with crisp bacon while the eggs cooked.

"How about Cinderella?" Kate asked.

"Well . . . I guess that's a possibility, but it's not a novel, and we're the Novel Inn." Before Kate could accuse her of being too picky, Jillian said, "Here, the bacon's ready."

Kate lifted the pan and carried it out to the dining room, where she put it into a slot on the serving counter.

"Good morning, folks. Eggs will be right out."

The couple already seated greeted her cheerfully, and another duo came in the door.

"Hello," Kate said cheerfully. "You're just in time. Here comes my sister with the scrambled eggs."

The Novel Inn had become a way of life for her and Jillian. Along with their brother Rick, they'd inherited it from their parents the previous spring. It had taken them a few months to master some aspects of the innkeeping business, but they'd made huge strides. They'd spent a lot of time in the fall figuring out how to draw in wintertime guests at a literary-themed inn on the Maine coast.

Finally, their efforts were paying off. Reservations were coming in weeks and even months in advance. The house was full most weekends, and they had a respectable number of rooms filled during the week.

"You know," Kate said as she returned to the kitchen, "I was serious about the western theme. A lot of people like it, especially people with kids." She scrutinized Jillian's face. "No? I guess you're set on Phileas Fogg."

"Kind of."

"How about Nancy Drew?"

Jillian frowned. "I'm going to do more bacon for the late risers. What about oatmeal?"

"We've got the instant kind out there."

"I know, but it's winter. People want hot stuff."

"There's the waffle maker, and bacon and eggs."

"I'll do some link sausage, too."

Kate let out a big sigh. "You sound like Mom. Better too much food than not enough."

"You know it's true. We've got about twenty more people who aren't even in the dining room yet."

Jillian might be exaggerating, but not by much. Their twelve rooms had housed twenty-two guests overnight. The largest rooms, Hercule

Poirot and Scarlett O'Hara, held families, while the others had couples or singletons. And more than half of those would be here another night.

"Relax, Jill. They have the toaster, and there are muffins, bagels, Danish pastries, and several varieties of whole-grain bread."

"Okay, you're right. But can you get me two more pounds of bacon from the fridge?"

The carnival was in full swing Saturday, and the inn emptied by nine in the morning. They didn't serve lunch or dinner unless by special request, and Jillian and Kate expected most of the guests to stay out all day.

After a leisurely brunch together, Kate ventured out to enjoy the carnival attractions. Jillian sat in the office, happily analyzing the profits for the month. The phone rang, and she answered it almost on auto-pilot.

"Jillian? It's Carl Roofner. Your special order book is in."

"Already? That was fast! You just ordered it Thursday."

"It sure was. You can come get it anytime."

"Well, Kate's not here, so I can't leave right now. I'll probably come over this afternoon."

Knowing the book was waiting for her at the Book Rack distracted Jillian. She wrote checks for the two night desk clerks and the part-time maid and put away her ledgers. When Kate got back, bubbling with reports on the carnival, Jillian was eager to go out and take it in for herself.

"You've got to see the snowmen in front of the library." Kate unwound the knitted scarf from her neck and pulled off her gloves. "The contest doesn't close until four, and they'll do the judging and hand out prizes then."

"When's the skating relay?"

"That was this morning."

"Who won?" Jillian was a little disappointed she hadn't been on hand to watch.

"A team of high school boys. Jeremy Tilton was on it."

"Sandra's son? Wow, I'm so happy for him!" The teenager was a major *Lord of the Rings* fan and had visited on a slack day last summer to view their decorations in the Galadriel Room. "What was the prize?"

"They all got trophies and gift cards for pizza and ice cream."

Jillian shivered. "Ice cream in January?"

"Hey, that's what was donated. I saw Sandra. She says hi." Sandra Tilton, a volunteer firefighter, was a friend of Jillian's.

"Great. Well, as soon as I get a bite to eat, I'm heading for the Book Rack. My copy of *Around the World in Eighty Days* arrived already. I may go by the library after and watch the snowman judging."

Kate peeled off her parka. "Take your time. I doubt any of our guests will come back for at least another hour. Some of them will pop in before they go out for supper, but it should be a quiet evening."

They ate sandwiches for lunch in the inn's kitchen. Jillian wasn't very hungry, and she knew treats would be on sale at booths throughout the carnival area and downtown. She put on her winter jacket and matching hat and gloves. In the doorway, she paused. "If anyone calls wanting to make a reservation, check the list carefully. We don't have many vacancies over the next couple of weeks."

"Got it." Kate was already settling in at the front desk with her iPad.

Since it wasn't too cold, Jillian decided not to drive. No doubt traffic would be heavy near the library, and a block near the skating pond was barricaded to keep out vehicles during the weekend events. She didn't want to add to the congestion, so a brisk walk was in order.

When she came near the library, a few snowflakes were falling. According to the TV weatherman in Bangor, that wouldn't last long or accumulate, but it added a lovely touch to the festivities.

The sidewalk near the snowman contest on the library's lawn was packed with spectators. Jillian wended her way between the onlookers and found a spot where she could see without standing in a foot of snow. At least a dozen of the entries were finished, and five teams were still working on their masterpieces. The competitors were allowed to use extra props for facial features, as well as hats, scarves, and up to two more items.

Jillian got a good laugh out of the firefighter snowman, who had a snow Dalmatian sitting patiently beside him. Another entry was composed of a carefully sculpted Statue of Liberty, but the team was having a hard time keeping the upraised arm with its candleholder torch from collapsing.

After watching the action for ten minutes and greeting several acquaintances and two of the inn's guests, she walked on to the bookstore. She hoped Carl had seen a lot of customers today, but pedestrians were sparse in this section of the downtown.

She pushed open the door expecting a vibrant greeting from Carl. Instead, the whole store was silent. Stepping inside, she let the door swing shut behind her and peered toward the counter. No one. The cash register and the stool at the computer were both empty. She scanned the room but didn't see any graying heads above the rows of bookshelves. Carl must be out back.

She stepped toward a rack of inspirational romance and stopped.

Scuffed, brown oxfords stuck out beyond an end cap full of Gerry Boyle novels.

Heart pounding, Jillian stepped forward. Between the racks of merchandise, the pair of feet remained motionless. She pulled in a shaky breath and inched closer.

Stan Chappell lay sprawled on the floor, his head turned to one side. His eyes stared vacantly at a row of Maine travel books.

Chapter 2

Rick Gage shoved open the door to the Book Rack. His sister Jillian was sitting behind the store's counter, talking to Officer Dave Hall, who'd beaten him to the scene. Dave frantically jotted notes as Rick approached.

"Jillian, are you okay?" Rick asked.

"Yeah, I . . ." She stopped talking and looked to her right, deeper into the store.

Rick followed her gaze. He took a few steps and found the body. The dispatcher had told him someone had been killed in the store but hadn't identified the victim. He stared down at the older clerk. He'd expected to see the owner lying there, but this was definitely not Carl Roofner. Kneeling carefully to avoid the blood that had seeped from the body, he put his hand to the man's throat. As he'd feared, nothing.

He sensed movement and turned his head. Jillian and Dave stood beside him.

"It's Stanley." Jillian's voice had a husky note.

"Yeah. What's his last name?" Rick asked.

"Chappell. Stan Chappell. He's worked here a long time."

"Where's Carl?" Rick didn't visit the bookstore often, but he made a point of knowing the business owners in town.

"I don't know. The store was empty when I came in. Except . . ." She stared bleakly at the body.

Rick looked at Dave. "Get a number for Carl Roofner and call him."

As Dave stepped away, the door opened and another uniformed officer, Geordie Kraus, came in.

"Call Sgt. Watkins first," Rick told Dave. "Tell him the team is you, me, and Geordie. We don't want to take the rest of the officers away from crowd duty." Since the first policeman on the scene was their rookie, Rick had no qualms about taking charge. Dave did his bidding without a blink.

"Hey, Geordie," he said as the other officer drew close. He and Geordie had worked together for several years. They understood each other's methods and made a good team. "This is a store employee."

Geordie looked down at the deceased man. "I know him. Stan Chappell."

"Right." Rick looked up at Jillian. "You found him just like this?"

She nodded.

"Did you touch him?"

"No. Well . . . just his wrist. I couldn't . . ."

"It's okay." Rick stood and patted her shoulder. "Why don't you go sit down where you were. I'll come over there if I need to ask you anything." He turned to the rookie. "Officer Hall, is there any sign of tampering with the cash register?"

Dave snapped to attention, accepting his cue for a little more formality than usual. "I don't think so. I inspected around the counter area before you arrived. It didn't look like a robbery."

"Okay." As Jillian made her way to the counter, Rick did another visual sweep of the space. He spotted a camera above the street door, aimed toward the counter, and tucked the information away.

Dave came to his side. "I checked the body when I first got here. No question he was dead, so I didn't call an ambulance."

"Did you call the medical examiner?" Rick asked.

"No, there wasn't time before you came in, but I just told the sergeant that we need him."

"Good. What else can you tell me?"

"Well, it looks like a gunshot wound."

Rick nodded. "The M.E. will have to say for sure."

"I spotted a shell casing over there." Dave pointed.

Squinting at the floor, Rick saw the shell lying about eight feet away, in the shadow of a row of shelving. The shooter hadn't policed his brass. That might be helpful.

"Good job. Put out a marker and bag it."

Dave nodded. "I was on foot this afternoon, patrolling the downtown."

Rick tossed Geordie his car keys. "Go out to my SUV and get some evidence markers and bags. Gloves. Whatever else we need. It's all in the back."

"Sure thing."

Turning back to Dave, Rick said, "Why didn't it smell like a robbery to you?"

Dave gritted his teeth and slowly shook his head. "Honestly, there didn't seem to be anything wrong near the cash register. And Mr. Chappell still has his wallet in his pocket. It's almost like somebody came in, shot him, and ran out."

"What about Roofner? Did you get him on the phone?"

"Not yet. They're working on it at the station. Oh, and Rick, Sgt. Watkins said we'll have to call the S.P. in."

Rick scowled and clamped his jaws tight. It was standard procedure in Maine to let the state police handle murders outside the two biggest cities, Portland and Bangor. He didn't like it— by the time an S.P. detective got there, valuable evidence could be lost. He decided to keep on the way he would if the case wasn't about to be yanked away from him. When the detective arrived, he would hand over what he'd learned. In the meantime, he'd make sure they weren't sloppy.

From her post a few yards away, Jillian said hesitantly, "Rick, I have Carl's number. Do you want me to call him?"

Rick walked toward her frowning. "You have his personal number, not just the store?"

"Yes, we've gotten quite chummy." She shrugged. "I'm a book lover."

That was true. Jillian was a former English teacher. Rick couldn't remember a time, even when they were kids, when she didn't have her nose in a book.

"Don't call him, but give me the number."

He entered the number Jillian read him into his phone and stepped aside to make the call. After five rings, he heard a gruff "Hello?"

"Mr. Roofner?" Rick asked.

"Yes."

"This is Officer Rick Gage. Can you come to your store right away, please? There's been an incident."

"What—what kind of an incident?"

"Just please get here as soon as you can."

"All right. I had run up to Bangor for a book fair, but I'm nearly home now. I should be there in about fifteen minutes."

"That's fine. Thank you." Rick closed the connection.

"Now you've got him all upset," Jillian said. "He'll probably have a heart attack before he gets here."

Rick shot her a dark look. "You sound just like Mom."

When Jillian's face quivered, his conscience berated him.

"I'm sorry. I shouldn't have said that."

She swiped at a tear that ran willy-nilly down her cheek. "No, I just—"

Rick went to her and slipped an arm around her shoulders. "I'm sorry, sis. This has been a shock for you."

With a sniff, she burrowed her face into his shoulder for a moment then pulled away. "I'm okay. Really."

He gazed keenly into her eyes for a moment. Jillian was the strong one, the one who'd held the family together since their parents died. She didn't crack unless something really bad happened.

Brushing her cheek with his knuckles, he whispered, "I'm sorry." His common sense told him that repeating the words wouldn't make them more powerful.

"Hey, Rick?"

He turned. Geordie had brought in his fingerprint kit and a canvas bag of miscellaneous equipment. Dave was placing a yellow plastic marker with a 1 on it precisely where the shell casing had fallen.

"There should be video," Geordie said.

"Right. Mr. Roofner's on his way in. I'll ask

29

him about it. Look around and see if you find any other cameras besides that one." Rick pointed to the one over the door. "There may be one outside too."

The door opened, and a woman started to enter then stopped when she saw the uniformed officers. Rick recognized the woman who owned his favorite seafood restaurant with her husband and hastily stepped forward.

"Hello, Mrs. Sheldon. I'm afraid the store is closed at the moment. You'll have to come back tomorrow."

"Is something wrong?"

He hesitated. "Well, yes, but please don't broadcast it."

"Carl—" She stood on tiptoe, trying to see past him into the store.

"Carl's fine," Rick said as gently as he was able. "He's on his way here now. It's best if you leave and let us do our job."

Her gaze met his. She drew in a deep breath and nodded. "All right, Rick. I'll send up a prayer."

"Thanks." He closed the door and turned the metal lock knob. A small CLOSED sign hung inside the other half of the double panel. He flipped it to face outward and glared toward the two oblivious officers. "We need to keep customers out."

"Right," Geordie said evenly, though he was the last man to use the door.

Dave opened his mouth then closed it.

Jillian stirred. "Rick, what about Stan's family?"

"Do you know them?"

She shook her head. "I know Stan's married. I'm not sure about children."

"Okay, we'll see if we can get an address."

"If not, Carl will be able to tell you," she said. "Somebody should go and tell Mrs. Chappell in person."

"Of course."

The officers continued to search the floor, from the front door on back. After a few minutes, Rick found himself near Jillian again.

"Am I in your way?" She stood and moved aside. "I'm sure you want to look at everything back here, behind the counter."

"Why don't you go home, Jill? I can come by the inn later and tell you what progress we've made."

"I thought I'd stay until—"

At that moment Carl appeared at the door. He gave it a futile tug then fumbled with his key ring. Dave hurried to let him in.

"Mr. Roofner." Rick strode toward him. "I'm Officer Rick Gage, and this is Officer David Hall."

"What's going on?" Carl looked from Rick to Dave and back. "What happened?"

"I'm sorry to tell you, sir, Stanley Chappell is dead," Rick replied.

Carl's face went white. He staggered to the counter and leaned on it.

From behind it, Jillian reached a hand toward him. "Carl, I'm so sorry."

"What happened? Was it a heart attack? I thought Stan was in pretty good shape."

Jillian looked to Rick, and he stepped forward. "No, Mr. Roofner, it wasn't a heart attack. Maybe you can sit down for a minute on the stool where Jillian is sitting. I have a few questions I want to ask you."

Jillian moved aside as the older man walked slowly around the end of the counter, his face ashen. When Carl was seated, she laid a hand on his shoulder.

"I'm so sorry, Carl."

Rick considered telling her flatly to leave, but Mr. Roofner was about to go through a harrowing time. It might be better to have someone he considered a friend near at hand.

"Geordie," he murmured, and the patrolman understood and moved closer with his notebook and pen out.

"Mr. Roofner, what time did you leave the store today?" Rick asked.

"It was . . . about eleven thirty, I think. I opened the store and was here alone for a couple of hours." Carl glanced up at Jillian. "I called Jillian this morning."

She nodded.

"Why did you leave?" Rick asked.

"There was a book fair in Bangor this weekend. They had a lot of authors there, and we can go in as buyers and meet them. They give away samples of new books and . . . well, anyway, I thought I was going to miss it, but business was slow here. Stan assured me he could handle things alone if I wanted to run up there for an hour or so."

"So Stanley was in charge here while you were gone?"

Carl nodded.

"Where was the book fair held?"

"At the high school gymnasium, on Broadway."

"What time did you get there?"

"I stopped for a sandwich. I guess it was maybe a quarter past twelve."

Rick didn't like the slight wiggle room in the timeline. "Did someone see you come in?"

"Yes, they give you a ticket." Carl fumbled in his pocket and pulled out a small piece of card stock.

Rick took it and studied it. Good. It was time-stamped. "May I keep this, Mr. Roofner?"

"Of course."

"Did you see people you knew at the book fair?"

"Sure." Carl named off a few. Most were owners of other independent bookstores.

"Do you live alone, Mr. Roofner?"

"No, I live with my son, Eric."

Rick nodded.

"My wife passed away," Carl added.

"Were you on your way home when I phoned you?"

"Yes, I'd started out about fifteen minutes earlier. I had stopped for gas when you called."

"Where was that?"

He gave Rick the exact location of the fuel station and pulled a receipt from his pocket.

"I—Please, what happened to Stan?"

Rick hesitated, but he couldn't see much point in delaying any longer. Carl's movements accounted for the time span within ten or fifteen minutes, and the sandwich took care of that. "Do you have a receipt for the lunch you bought on the way?"

Carl gulped. "I guess I threw it away with the bag. But there's a paper cup from the Wendy's in my car's cup holder."

"Is your car locked now?"

"Yes."

"May we borrow your keys for just a minute?"

Carl stared at him, obviously baffled, but handed over a key ring.

Rick turned and placed it in Dave's hand, murmuring, "Go check on the drink."

Dave asked Carl what his car looked like and where it was parked. Carl started to rise, but Rick held out a hand.

"It's all right, Mr. Roofner. Just sit still. We'll take care of it."

Carl looked anxiously up at Jillian.

She patted his shoulder. "It's okay, Carl. They're just making sure."

"I—it's right out front. I usually park in the alley, but—" He shook his head and described the car.

Rick nodded at Dave, and the patrolman hurried outside.

Rick turned back to the old man. "I'll tell you what we know so far. It appears someone came into the store with a gun and shot Stan."

With a moan, Carl crumpled and leaned heavily on the counter. "I don't understand. Who would . . ." He looked around. "Where is he? Did an ambulance come?"

"No," Rick said gently. "He was already dead when he was found. He's still here, and the medical examiner is on his way. He should be here very soon. Is there a better place where we can talk quietly?"

"I—yes. Out back. I have a desk out there and a couple of chairs."

Rick nodded. "Let's go back there and continue this. But first, could you give us Stanley's address and home number? I'd like to send an officer there to break the news to Mrs. Chappell. We don't want her to hear it from someone else."

"Oh, no, of course not. Maybe I should go along when they tell her."

"I need to get some more information from you first." Rick glanced at Jillian. "Why don't you go on home, Jill? You can tell Kate, but other than that, please keep this to yourself. It will be public knowledge by tonight's newscasts, I'm sure."

She nodded, and his confidence ticked up just a notch. Jillian was dependable. She and Kate had gotten a little excited last summer and started questioning people connected to his case before the police could get to them, but she knew better now.

Dave came in through the front door and held it for Jillian. When she was out, he relocked it and nodded at Rick. "The cup's there with some ice still in it, and the receipt was in the cup holder, sticking out from under the cup." He held out a slip of paper encased in a plastic bag.

"Thanks." Rick touched Carl's arm and led him toward the back of the store. He was nearly certain that Carl had told the truth about his activity that day. He made sure the older man was on the side of the aisle farthest from the body. As they passed it, Carl caught his breath, and his step faltered.

"Easy," Rick murmured. "Let's go sit down."

Soon they were settled in a crowded stockroom.

Carl sat at the untidy desk, and Rick took the only available side chair, after Carl moved a stack of books off it.

"I want you to think about Stanley's acquaintances," Rick said. "Do you know of anyone who was angry with Stanley or held a grudge against him?"

"No. Everyone liked Stan. He . . . he was easygoing, very likeable. Always on time for work, and he'd fill in for me whenever I needed him." Carl ran a hand through his hair. "I'd have been here today—well, I *was* here this morning—except for the book fair. I was afraid I wouldn't be able to get away, with the carnival and all, but it wasn't too busy this morning."

"Yeah, it's okay," Rick said. "You couldn't have known. And I'm told your son also works here?"

"That's right." Carl threw anxious glances toward the interior of the store. "He would have been here today, but he wanted to go to some snowmobile rally in Clifton. He's part-time. I can't force him to work when he doesn't want to. I tried to talk him out of the rally, in case Stan needed help, but . . . well, he insisted." Carl shook his head. "I wish he cared more about the store."

"I see." Rick pulled out his pocket notebook and made a note to verify Eric Roofner's whereabouts. "Do you have other family?"

"Not close. Eric was our only child."

Rick nodded. "Now, tell me about the security camera over the door. Is that the only one?"

"Yes. It covers the checkout area. I figured that's most important."

"All right, we're going to need access to the video from that."

"Of course. But Anita—Mrs. Chappell. We really should tell her."

Rick sighed. "I need you here for a little while longer, Mr. Roofner. Let me send Officer Kraus to her house. You can go when we're done here." Carl's jaw tensed, and he added quickly, "I promise I won't keep you more than half an hour."

"I . . . all right."

After issuing instructions to Geordie, Rick touched base with Dave, who had found nothing else suspicious so far. He returned to the back room and sat down.

"Now, about that video, Mr. Roofner. Do you access it here at the desk?"

Carl showed him the system and transferred a copy of that afternoon's camera video to the police station's network.

"I'm sorry, Officer Gage, I should have offered you coffee." Carl waved vaguely toward a coffeemaker on a side table.

"Don't worry about me," Rick said, "but if you want some, go ahead."

"No, no."

"Just a few more questions. I wondered if you could give me your son Eric's phone number."

"Sure, but he might not hear his phone ring if he's off on a snowmobile trail."

Carl wrote the number on a slip of paper and handed it to him.

Rick punched in the digits on his cell phone and waited. After several rings, he got a voice mail message.

"This is Officer Rick Gage, in Skirmish Cove. Could you please return this call as soon as possible? Thank you." He closed the connection.

"Who would want to do this to Stan?" Carl asked. The tragedy was sinking in, and the older man's face was ashen.

"That's what we need to find out," Rick said. "Are you sure you don't want that coffee?"

The desk phone rang, and Carl snatched it up. "Eric? Is that you? Yes, that was Officer Gage. He's right here with me, at the store. We've had a—" He paused and looked at Rick. "We've had an . . . incident here at the store."

Rick gritted his teeth, wishing Eric had followed instructions and called him, not his father.

Carl threw him a nervous glance. After a short pause, he went on, "The police are here."

"May I speak to him?" Rick reached for the receiver.

Carl handed it to him with a shaking hand.

"Eric? This is Officer Rick Gage. I think we've met before."

"Sure," Eric said. "What's going on there? Is my dad okay?"

"He's a little shaken, but he's fine."

"Should I come home? Does he need me to stay at the store?"

"Uh, he'll probably close the store for the rest of the day while we do our job here. But it might be good if you were close by for your father."

"What happened?"

"I need to speak to you in person. Can you come to the store right away?"

"Uh . . . it will take me a while to get there. I had some engine trouble with my machine. A buddy's helping me with it, but it might take a while to load it."

"How long do you think it will take you to get here?" Rick asked.

"Oh, let's see, an hour and a half, maybe? Two hours."

"All right. Come straight to the Book Rack, and I'll see you here."

Eric swore. "Are you sure my dad's okay?"

"I'm sure. See you later." Rick ended the call. It would be good for Carl if his son was close by until he got over the shock of losing his friend in such a grisly manner. But he didn't like Eric's fuzzy timeline. He might be in Clifton, or he might not.

"Do you know who organized the snowmobile rally your son's at?"

Carl looked at him blankly. "I'm not sure. Probably some local sled club."

"Okay." Rick took a business card from his pocket and laid it on the desk. "My cell number's on here. You can go to Stan's house now if you want, but please let me know if you go home. We need for you to stay where we can find you for the rest of the day."

"Thank you. You understand, Stan was much more than an employee. He was my best friend." Carl pocketed the card and stood unsteadily.

"Are you okay to drive?" Rick asked. "We can have someone take you there."

"I'll be all right." Carl walked slowly to the doorway and turned. "The store . . ."

"We'll keep the doors locked while we work," Rick assured him. "You won't be able to reopen today, but we should be able to wrap up before tomorrow."

"We're closed Sundays."

"You can reopen Monday then. I'll let you know if it's not all right."

"Thank you. I may just stay closed until after . . . I'll see what Anita wants for arrangements."

"I'm sure Officer Kraus has explained to her that the body might not be released right away."

With tear-filled eyes, Carl nodded and went

out the door. He moved like a ninety-year-old, Rick thought, though he couldn't be much over sixty-five. This was the hardest part of his job— dealing with the people who suffered after a crime. He turned with relief to the part he liked best—putting the pieces together to find out who caused all that pain.

Chapter 3

"What's up?" Kate asked when her sister trudged into the inn's kitchen. "You took your time."

"Yeah, sorry."

Jillian's face looked positively ghastly, and Kate thumped the can of raisins down on the worktop, where she was mixing bran muffins for the morning buffet.

"What's wrong?"

"You're not gonna believe it."

"Try me." Kate stepped around the island and walked over to Jillian, studying her dismal expression for clues.

"It's Stan Chappell," Jillian said.

Kate frowned. "Is that . . ."

"You know, at the bookstore."

"Oh, right."

"He's dead. Murdered."

Kate froze. "What?"

Nodding miserably, Jillian sank onto a stool. "I found him lying there when I went to get the book I ordered."

"*Around the World . . .* ?"

"Yeah, but I didn't get it. I walked in, and Stanley was just lying there on the floor, and there was nobody else in the store."

"Oh, man! Did you call Rick?"

"I called 911. Rick's there now. Dave Hall got there first."

"He's only been with the department, what? Six or eight months?"

"Rick came right away, and Geordie too. I think Geordie's gone to tell the family now."

"Was it totally horrible?"

"Yes. I checked for a pulse. There wasn't one."

"Do they know what happened?" Kate asked.

"Looks like he was shot. I tried not to look, but . . . Rick sent for the medical examiner, but he hadn't arrived when I left."

"Wow. He's probably got to drive down from Bangor." Kate let it sink in for a moment then snapped back to the present. "I'll get you some iced tea."

"Thanks."

"I've been baking. Everyone's out at the carnival. I made blueberry muffins earlier, and now I'm making bran. Want one?"

"I'm not sure I can eat, but the tea sounds good."

Kate poured two glasses and gave one to Jillian. "I'll join you as soon as I get a pan of these in the oven." Quickly she measured out the raisins, stirred them into her batter, and scooped a blob into each muffin cup.

"We're not supposed to tell anyone yet," Jillian said after a sip of her tea. "Rick says it will probably be on tonight's news, but he was concerned about family members hearing about it before they were told officially, so it's just between you and me for now."

"Okay." Kate retrieved her iced tea and sat down near her sister. "Wasn't Mr. Roofner there?"

"No, apparently he'd gone to Bangor this afternoon. His son wasn't there either." It did seem a little odd, since Carl had told her he hoped for a lot of traffic in the store during the carnival, and he hadn't mentioned the book fair when he'd called her that morning. They both sat in silence for a moment. Jillian took another swallow of tea and looked up. "Any new reservations?"

Kate shook her head. "The only person I've seen all day is Mindy."

Mindy Nelson, their part-time maid, walked in as if on cue. As usual, she wore full makeup, but her lipstick looked a little worse for wear. She stripped her bandana from her shoulder-length brown hair. "Hey, Jillian."

"Hello." Jillian managed a smile that didn't look forced.

"All done?" Kate asked.

"Yeah, finally," Mindy said. "It took me a long time to clean all the rooms today."

"Well, we're full to bursting. You want some tea?"

"No, thanks," Mindy said. "I think I'll head home. My mom's with the kids, but it's been a long day."

"Thanks so much for coming in on a Saturday," Jillian said.

"I'll be back Monday morning, if you two can handle towels and trash in the meantime."

"Sure we can," Kate said.

Mindy smiled then sobered. "Oh, I meant to tell you—you know that guy in Rip Van Winkle?"

"Yeah." How could Kate forget the thirty-something man who'd taken the small front room on the third floor two days ago? As if his dark eyes and windblown hair hadn't been enough, he had a killer smile and a day's worth of stubble on his chin. She'd had to scold herself for staring. "His car has a New York license plate."

Mindy shrugged at this bit of data. "He's had his Do Not Disturb card on the doorknob since Thursday. I knocked and asked if he wanted cleaning, but he said no, so I left him alone."

"Some people just want a quiet getaway," Jillian said.

Kate nodded. "He came down for breakfast this morning after everyone else had left for the day. In fact, I was putting stuff away. All the bacon was gone, but I offered to fix more. He said, 'Don't bother.' But he took some of the sausage and finished up the eggs in the warmer. And I think he took a doughnut and a muffin up to his room with his second cup of coffee." She stopped to take a breath. Mindy and Jillian stared at her.

"Well, I guess we know he's not going to

starve," Mindy said. "Tell me, what was he wearing?"

"Yes," Jillian said. "And what color are his eyes?"

Kate flushed and stood. "You guys are mean."

Their laughter echoed in the spacious kitchen.

"On that note, I'm going. Just remember to ask him if he needs anything if you see him again." Mindy waved and went out through the dining room.

"So, we have a mystery guest." Jillian drained her iced tea.

Kate took the tumbler from her and headed for the dishwasher with both glasses in hand. "Maybe he's a writer. They like peace and quiet."

"You could be right." Jillian leaned back and peered through the dining room door. "I thought I heard—yep." She jumped up, and Kate heard it too. Someone had come in the front door. "I'll get it." Jillian disappeared toward the lobby.

Kate heard animated voices as she loaded their glasses and a few other dirty dishes then checked on her muffins.

"That was the Andersons," Jillian said as she returned. "They saw the police cars downtown and came home with a rumor that someone had died at the bookstore."

"What did you say?"

"Nothing much. Just, 'Oh, that's too bad.' "

47

Jillian drifted out to the office. By the time Kate finished the cleanup from her baking session, guests were filtering back and forth through the lobby. Most were going out again for dinner.

"Let's stay in tonight," Jillian said.

"Sure. Do you want me to go down to the house and fix us some supper?" The sisters lived behind the inn, in the converted carriage house that was once their parents' home.

"Okay. I'll stay near the front desk until Wayne gets here."

Kate shrugged. "I may keep you company."

"You don't want to go to the concert at the school tonight?"

"I don't think so. Let's play a game or something."

They spent a peaceful evening until ten minutes to ten, when Wayne came in.

"Man, you're busy this weekend. The parking lot's crowded." He stamped snow from his boots on the doormat just inside the lobby.

"We're full up," Kate said, gathering the Dutch Blitz cards off the desk where she and Jillian had been playing.

"Anything I need to know?"

"Everyone's in for the night except the David Copperfield Room." Jillian pushed her chair back and stood. "I expect they'll be in soon. If anyone asks, we're serving a full breakfast in the morning."

48

"Right. Dining room opens at seven on Sunday." Wayne grinned at her.

At fifty-two, Wayne had been glad to pick up some weekend work over the winter. He and his wife ran a seasonal business, renting out six cottages on their property from Memorial Day through the fall foliage season. Any extra income during the off-season was welcome. Kate and Jillian had a regular weeknight clerk, Don Reece, but the student who'd filled in on weekends over the summer had left them when he returned to school before Labor Day.

Kate brought her parka and Jillian's from the office.

"Have a good night, ladies," Wayne called as they headed for the back door via the kitchen.

The next morning, breakfast was busy between seven and eight. Another wave would hit later. The late sleepers always came down to eat before the kitchen closed and the hot foods were put away.

"I think enough people have eaten that I can handle the rest on my own," Kate told her.

"Are you sure? I'd like to go to church this morning."

"Yes, go," Kate said. "I'll go to the evening service."

Jillian went out the back door to get ready. Not long after Kate heard her car go up the driveway from the carriage house, the couple staying in the Scarlett O'Hara Room came down with their four-year-old daughter in tow.

"Good morning," Kate called out. She made sure the coffee and hot water container had plenty to offer the guests.

"Hi." Mrs. Durant was fixing a plate for her daughter while her husband put a booster seat in a chair and strapped it in place.

"Can I get anything for you, Mrs. Durant?" Kate asked.

"It looks like you've thought of everything. And call me Sheila."

"Okay." Kate smiled. "Did you enjoy the Winter Carnival yesterday?"

"Yes. The snowmen were so funny. I think that contest was the highlight for me."

"Who won?" Kate asked. "They were just getting started when I was there."

"A group of women, actually. They called themselves the Book Worm Club."

"Oh, I know most of them." Kate grinned. "It's a monthly book club, but I think they spend more time on tea and gossip than they do on their reading selections."

"Well, their snowman—snowperson—was a very cool librarian with an icy book in her hand. They said it was Shakespeare's *A Winter's Tale*."

"That's appropriate. Did the Statue of Liberty place?"

Sheila grimaced. "Unfortunately, by the time the judges got to her, her arm had collapsed. I think it just got too warm, although that made it more pleasant for those of us who were watching. Second place went to a dinosaur, and third prize was for a classic Frosty."

Mr. Durant took a banana and peeled it for his daughter. "I think Gabby liked the skating pond best, although she fell down about a gazillion times."

Sheila laughed. "It was her first time ever on skates. I was surprised they had some small enough for her."

"I think the parent-teacher group at the elementary school collects them," Kate said. "They get them out every year at carnival time, for visitors and kids who just don't have their own."

"Well, she loved it," Mr. Durant said. "Right, Gabby?"

The little girl smiled and nodded vigorously, her mouth full of banana.

"Say, we heard about someone being killed in town—at a bookstore." Sheila's face wrinkled. "It was on the morning news."

Kate shot a swift glance at Gabby, but she seemed more interested in the scrambled eggs and sausage her dad had placed in front of her than the conversation.

"Yes. One of the employees at the Book Rack."

"Did you know him?" Sheila asked.

"Only slightly. My sister knew him better. The bookstore is one of her favorite haunts."

"Such a shame." Sheila picked up a plate.

Another woman had come in while they talked, and she paused with a mug in her hand. "I was in there yesterday."

Kate turned to her in surprise. "Really?"

"Yes, I bought a book about hiking trails in the area. I thought we might come back in the summertime. It must be beautiful here then."

"It is, and we'd love to have you come back," Kate said. "What time were you at the bookstore?"

"It was in the morning, before some of the activities started. My husband and I thought it would be a good time to stroll through town. The downtown is so quaint."

Kate nodded. "Well, the . . . incident took place in the afternoon, or at least that's my understanding."

"Good thing we weren't in there then." She strolled along the buffet counter, picking out her breakfast dishes.

"Did anyone else come in while you were there, Mrs. Hoban?" Kate asked.

"A few people. It wasn't really busy though." The woman seemed very serious as she considered the pastry display.

"Maybe you should talk to the police officers

investigating the crime. My brother's one of them."

"Oh, really?" Mrs. Hoban perked up a little. "Sure, we can talk to him if you think it would help, but we were probably long gone before— you know." She shot a glance at the Durants, who sat at a nearby table.

"Right. Well, I'll be in the office if you need anything. Would you like me to tell Officer Gage you were in the bookstore yesterday? They'd probably like to talk to anyone who was there."

Mrs. Hoban took one of Kate's bran muffins, as well as a cruller. "Sure. Why not?"

Kate smiled. "I'll let my brother know. Will you be out today?"

"Yes, but we'll be back this afternoon, probably by four or so."

Kate nodded. "If you can remember any details about the other people in the bookstore, you might want to jot them down. Enjoy your day."

Chapter 4

Jillian went straight home after the church service and had lunch with Kate. All of the guests were eating out, so she anticipated a quiet afternoon while Kate went downtown and enjoyed the carnival activities.

She checked in a new couple, but otherwise things were quiet. Around two o'clock, her cell rang.

"I'm at the bookstore," Kate said. "Carl's a disaster. Can you come down here?"

Jillian hesitated. "I can't really leave the desk unattended, and I can't lock up."

"Yes, you can. The guests have key cards, remember?"

"All right. But what's going on there?"

"Nothing. The police told Carl he could reopen tomorrow, but it's a mess from where the cops did their thing. You know, fingerprint powder, stuff like that. And there's blood on the floor, I guess where Stanley died. Carl can't handle it. He's gone all to pieces."

"I'll be right there." Jillian grabbed her coat and purse.

After checking that the back door was locked, she hurried out and drove her red Taurus to the Book Rack. Traffic moved slowly because pedestrians thronged the streets. She was glad a lot of people had turned out but frustrated by the inconvenience.

She parked across the street from the Book Rack. The CLOSED sign still hung in the glass door, but Kate was just inside, watching for her. She turned the lock as soon as she saw Jillian and let her in.

"Thank you." Kate gave her a quick hug and whispered in her ear, "He's crying. I tried to talk to him, but he's just broken."

"Okay. How did you get in here? Did he let you in?"

"The door wasn't locked, even though it said 'closed.' I glanced in and saw him just sobbing away, so I came in."

"I'm glad you did." Jillian unzipped her parka and walked around the end of the counter. "Carl." She laid a gentle hand on his shoulder.

He looked up at her with bloodshot eyes. His eyelids were puffy, his face awash with tears.

"Carl, I'm so sorry." Jillian folded him in a hug. "Let Kate and me help you clean up."

"I don't know where to start." His voice quivered. "There's dirt everywhere, and Stan . . ."

"We'll take care of it." Jillian gazed at Kate, who gave her a firm nod.

A box of tissues had sat under the counter the previous day, Jillian remembered, and she

55

reached for it now. Carl took one and wiped his face.

"Thank you," he said thickly.

"You shouldn't have come down here alone," Jillian said softly. "Where's Eric? Did you ask him to come?"

Carl shook his head.

She looked around and made a quick decision. "Let one of us take you home. If you give us the store key, we'll clean things up, and you'll be ready to open tomorrow, when you feel better."

"Are you sure?"

"Yes."

In slow motion, he reached into his pocket and pulled out a key ring. Jillian accepted the key he gave her.

"Good. We'll make sure it's locked up tight when we're done and bring the key to your house."

"I have another one at home. Just . . . just leave it in the drawer under the counter."

"Okay. Now, where's your coat?"

A few minutes later, Carl was out the door with Kate, who had instructions to take him home in Jillian's car and then return to the Novel Inn. With any luck, none of the guests had noticed they were both absent for a short time.

Jillian hurried to the back room to get out Carl's cleaning supplies. After surveying the

56

contents of the closet, she phoned Mindy Nelson and explained what had happened.

"I know it's your day off, Mindy, but Carl Roofner's having a hard time. I'm going to do some cleaning at the store for him, so he can reopen tomorrow. I don't suppose you'd be able to come help?"

"Well . . . I was going to spend the whole day with the kids, but maybe my mom could come over while Annabeth has her nap."

"I'll pay you double wages," Jillian said quickly.

"You don't have to. Let me call Mom and see if she's up to it. If she is, I'll come right over. Otherwise, I'll call you back."

"Thanks, Mindy. And if you've got something for blood on a hardwood floor, bring it."

"Ew. I'll check online."

"You're the best." Jillian put her phone away and took a bottle of spray cleaner, a rag, a dust mop, and a sponge from the closet. The only floor-specific product in there seemed to be a one-step cleaner and polisher. She decided to see what Mindy brought along. While she waited, she concentrated on removing all the fingerprint powder around the door handles, cash register, and counter.

Twenty minutes later, Mindy arrived. They both knelt by the bloodstain, applying a cleaning solution Mindy had brought.

"If this doesn't do it, we could sand down the wood and revarnish it." Mindy rubbed at the spot with a cloth. "I think this will work, though."

Jillian crawled along the aisle, carefully examining the shelving and the books. "Oops. More spatter." She sprayed her cloth with cleaner to avoid getting it on the books and then dabbed at the shelf support. "There may be a few books he has to throw away." She pulled out two with small spots on the spines and took them to the counter.

"He could discount them," Mindy said.

"I don't know . . . Even if we can get the blood off, it would look funny. And really, would you want to buy a book that had blood on it?"

"True."

"I'll make a box of the ones that definitely need to be destroyed and another of ones that could be salvaged but not sold. I mean, if people like us, who knew about the blood, wanted to read them, they'd be fine. Like this one." She held up a copy of *Penobscot Bay Islands*. "This would be fine on my shelf for a reference."

"But would you put it in the inn's library for guests to use?"

After a moment's thought, Jillian shook her head. "I think my conscience would make me warn them first."

"Why? Once we've disinfected them . . ."

"I know. I just . . . Well, let's set them aside and see what Carl thinks."

"Did you find any with bullet holes in them?" Mindy asked.

"I think the police removed a couple yesterday. I didn't see any."

Mindy stood and gazed critically down at the floor. "That's probably about as good as I can get it. There's one patch that still looks discolored, but most of it came off. I'd hate for Carl to have to rip out the flooring and redo it. But, like I said, he could sand it down and refinish it."

Jillian walked around the end of the row and looked at it. "Wow, that is so much better. Let's let it dry and see how it looks."

"Sure. Do you want me to vacuum?"

"That would be great. And go after any spots with a cloth. I'll keep looking for spatter. I don't want Carl to find a blotch of blood unexpectedly while he's restocking or talking to a customer."

"Absolutely not." Mindy went to the back room for Carl's vacuum cleaner.

When Jillian had removed all the damaged books she could find in the aisle where Stan was killed and wiped a few more spots from the floor and shelves, she looked around. Things didn't look too bad now. Obviously there were gaps in the stock on that one aisle. Carl would have to replenish the books. She wished she knew his system.

Mindy unplugged the vacuum cleaner and moved it into the carpeted children's section. "I should be done in ten or fifteen minutes," she called.

Jillian waved in acknowledgment. The hum of the vacuum started again. She turned toward the counter and was surprised to see Carl outside the front door, using his key. She rushed over and met him as he stepped inside.

"Carl! Is anything wrong?"

"No. I just couldn't settle down. I thought I'd come back and at least check over the till. I didn't count down the drawer last night, and I always do that. Not that we took in much before . . ."

"Come on in." Jillian couldn't send him away again. His forlorn face in itself was heartbreaking. She wondered what his son was up to today. Eric ought to know that his father needed him. "Do you want to see what we've done with the floor? It doesn't look too bad now."

Carl swallowed hard and walked slowly toward the travel book aisle. He stood there for several seconds, staring down at the floor where his friend had lain the day before. Finally he looked at her.

"People won't even notice that, will they?"

"I don't think so." Jillian waved toward the depleted shelves. "We removed some of the books. A few were really bad, and I think you'll have to destroy them. But there are others that only had little spots. I've cleaned them off as best I could. You might want to keep them or give them away."

Carl's mouth worked, but nothing came out.

"Actually, there are a few I'd like to buy." She took his arm gently and led him toward the counter. "That's the box of badly damaged ones. But this box . . ." She lifted out the island book and one called *Historic Villages on Maine's Mid-Coast.* "I'd really like these for my personal library. Now, I can't even tell where the spots were."

"You take them, Jillian."

"Oh, no. I want to pay you."

He waved a hand and turned away. "Take the whole box. Both boxes. Please. I don't want to even look."

"I understand. Do you need to make a note for your inventory purposes? I'll make a list for you. And I'd like to at least pay you your cost for these ones with hardly any damage."

He pulled in a deep breath. "If you wouldn't mind, I'd like it if you helped me with the inventory part. The insurance company will want to know what was lost." He blinked at the boxes and turned away. "I can bring it up on the computer, and you tell me the titles. Can we do that?"

"Certainly. You know the system best, but I'll do whatever you need."

"And then, if you and your sister—" He looked

toward the children's section, where Mindy was still vacuuming.

"Oh, that's not Kate," Jillian said. "It's our maid from the inn, Mindy Nelson. Do you know her?"

"I think I do." He frowned uncertainly. "Seems to me she comes in here now and then with her two little ones."

Jillian smiled. "Annabeth and Dillon."

"Yes, Dillon. He likes heavy equipment."

She arched her eyebrows, and Carl gave a faint smile.

"I try to always keep picture books with trucks and tractors in stock. I believe excavators are a favorite with him."

"That's wonderful, Carl. I'm always amazed at the personal service I get here."

"Well, if you and your friend could just take those away when we've finished, I'd appreciate it. I don't care what you do with them." He pecked at the keyboard a few times then looked up at her.

"All set?" Jillian asked, wishing she could do it for him. "I'll read off the titles for you. Or do you want the ISBN numbers?"

"Start with the title and author. If there's a question of editions, we can go to the identification numbers."

They were just finishing up his amendments to the inventory when Mindy shut off the vacuum.

She trundled it into the stockroom and came back to join them at the counter.

"Mr. Roofner, it's good to see you. I'm so sorry this happened."

"Thank you, my dear, for helping Jillian make the space . . . usable again."

"No problem," Mindy said with a smile.

"Well, I've asked her if the two of you can take away these books that were, uh, damaged in the—you know."

Mindy nodded, her face all sympathy. "Of course."

"If you can use any of them, keep them. It's my gift in return for your kindness. And please take a picture book for Dillon too, and one for . . . for your little girl."

"Annabeth," Jillian whispered.

"Of course. Annabeth."

"That's so sweet of you," Mindy said. "You don't have to do that, Mr. Roofner."

"Please. I want to. And call me Carl. You've done a wonderful job. I won't be embarrassed to open the store tomorrow."

Mindy's face softened and she patted his arm. "Thank you. The kids will be so excited."

He nodded. "Just tell us what titles you choose, so I can tick them off the inventory as removed for personal use."

"I'll do that." She started to turn away then looked back at him and Jillian, pulling something from her pocket. "Oh, I almost forgot. I found this under one of the shelves in the young adult section. Way back there in the corner, under the overhang on a shelf of anime books." She pointed. "I wouldn't have seen it, but there were several books on the floor, and I picked them up to reshelve them and noticed it. Some kid must have dropped it."

She opened her hand, revealing a folded piece of paper. Jillian took it and opened it into a half sheet of standard copy paper.

"A permission slip." As a teacher, Jillian had seen many over the years. "The parent is supposed to sign this, giving the child permission to go on a field trip next week."

"Is the student's name on it?" Carl leaned in so he could see it.

"No, it's all blank."

"It could have been there for weeks," Mindy said.

"Maybe." Jillian reread what little information was on the slip. "It's from this school district. The student is supposed to return it by Wednesday."

Mindy shrugged. "Maybe we should call the superintendent's office, although the kid will probably just tell the teacher he lost it and needs a new one."

"I was thinking maybe I should give it to Rick. It might not be significant, but I know they were looking for anything odd here in the store." Jillian looked questioningly at Carl.

"Do whatever you think is best." He pushed his glasses up on his nose and looked back at the computer screen.

"That's what I'll do." Jillian folded the paper and stuck it in her purse.

Mindy went to the children's area and came back with two picture books. Carl checked them off in his inventory program, and Jillian put them in a bag.

"I guess that's it, Mindy. Thanks for coming in. I'll see you tomorrow morning."

"Sure thing." Mindy chose a couple of books from the box of ones Jillian had salvaged. With a smile, she headed for the door.

After checking the lock, Jillian went back to the counter. Carl sat on the stool, his shoulders drooping. He looked up as she approached and gave her a grim smile.

"I keep thinking the same thing, over and over. Who would do this?"

"You don't think it was a random holdup, do you?"

Carl shook his head. "How could it be? Nothing was taken. The cash drawer wasn't opened, and poor Stan still had his wallet on him."

Jillian leaned on the counter, clasping her hands and studying his face. "Have you thought about his family? I don't know much, other than he was married. Do you know how things were between them?"

"They got along all right. Anita's retired. She used to work in an insurance company's office, but she got done three or four years ago. She wanted Stan to retire."

"But he didn't want to?"

Drawing in a slow breath, Carl looked around the store. "Not really. I think this was his second home. He liked coming here, even though I couldn't pay him a lot."

"You were close friends."

He nodded. "Stan and I go way back."

"What about kids?"

"They have a son and two daughters, Jennifer and Amelia. They're all grown up, of course. They're a few years older than my Eric. Amelia lives in Skowhegan. Anita called her while I was there yesterday."

"Does Amelia have children?"

"Yeah. Two girls. I talked to her for a minute, because Anita got pretty broken up while they were on the phone."

Jillian nodded. "What about Jennifer?"

"She's divorced. Moved away. Anita tried to call her while I was there, but no answer." Carl let out a heavy sigh. "The boy, now—not a boy, really. Sean's in his early thirties. But he's out of state too. Somewhere out west."

"You mean, Anita and Stanley's boy?"

"Yes, but Jennifer has a boy too. She—he was an early baby, if you know what I mean. He's in his twenties now. I think Jennifer was still a teenager when she married the father and had Justin."

"Oh." Jillian was a little confused, but she thought she had the kids and grandkids straight. "Do you know if anyone in the family was angry with Stan?"

"No, I don't think so. I never heard about it if they were. And he had friends in town, but I can't think of anyone who'd do something like this. I mean—he was shot, Jillian. Doesn't that say it was premeditated?"

"Maybe. I don't know." Maybe someone was enraged and didn't care who took the brunt of their fury, she mused, but she didn't want to say that out loud. "What about customers? Did anyone come in the store upset lately?"

He shook his head. "Your brother asked me that. This store is about the quietest place in town, other than the library. He said he was going to look at the camera footage, though, and see who came in yesterday afternoon. Maybe he'll see who it was."

"Maybe." Jillian hoped so. "Look, Carl, you don't have to open tomorrow."

Tears glistened in his eyes. "What else would I do?"

His words cut deep. Carl's wife had been dead

many years. His son didn't seem to be much comfort, from what little she'd seen of him and the few things Carl had said about Eric. His best friend had just been murdered. If she were in his position, she'd want to work too. Staying busy was sometimes the best medicine for grief.

"Will Eric come in tomorrow?" she asked gently. She didn't want to think of Carl being here alone at what would surely be an emotional time for him.

"He said he'll be here, at least until noon."

"I'm glad. I'll try to stop by later in the day and see how things are going."

Carl stood and stepped toward the boxes of discards. "Did we get these all checked off?"

"I think so."

Carl's gaze sharpened. "Oh. Did you get your Jules Verne book?"

"Not yet. It went out of my mind yesterday."

"Well, let's take care of that right now." He turned to a shelf behind the counter, where several bags with the store's logo awaited pickup. "Here you go." He told Jillian the price, and she got out her debit card.

"Thanks so much for ordering this for me. I've done some more thinking about the decorations for the room. I think I'll do the bedclothes and curtains up in patterns that remind me of India. And I found some throw pillows online with elephants. It's going to be adorable."

Carl smiled. "I'd like to see it when it's finished."

"Of course." She could see that her chatter about the inn had distracted him from thoughts of Stan's death, and she prolonged the conversation as long as she could. When he turned back to the box of books that still bore blood spatters, he sobered.

"Well. Thank you again, Jillian. You're a true friend."

Chapter 5

The screen blurred, so Rick sighed and sat back, rubbing his eyes. He'd spent two hours viewing videos of the inside of the Book Rack without much to show for it. Several customers could be seen back-to, entering the store, and some of them later went to the checkout counter, where Stan Chappell rang up their purchases. Then they left the store, passing beneath the camera and out of range.

He'd watched the shooting segment over and over—at least twenty times. The shooter stood just inside, probably right underneath the camera. Rick never saw him—or her.

A tiny blur appeared at the edge of the screen, and when he froze the image, Rick realized he was viewing the tip of a pistol's barrel. He was also able to make out a glint, which he assumed was the shell casing flying off toward the nearest shelf unit. That was it. No muzzle flash. Glare from the bright lighting overhead and sunlight coming in from the doorway must have shielded it.

Rick decided the shooter hadn't policed his brass because that would necessitate going into camera range. Smart guy. He hoped ballistics could help him. If only Roofner had placed his camera so that it covered the door, not the counter, he'd have a much better chance of identifying the gunman.

Of course, Stanley was clearly visible in the frame. He'd been between two rows of books near the front of the store, beyond the end of the counter. At the moment Rick figured the shooter entered, Stan swung toward the door. His face in a hesitant welcome, he took two steps. Did he recognize the newcomer?

His expression changed to disbelief, and then he was hit. He jerked backward, and his fall shook the shelving. Finally, only his feet were visible at the end of the aisle, and he lay still.

That was all. If Rick focused on Stanley, he didn't see the muzzle or the flying shell. If he focused on those, he didn't notice Stan's transformation from helpful clerk to terrified victim.

He ran a hand through his hair and took a swig from his coffee mug. *Ugh. Cold.* He started to rise and head for the coffee station but checked himself. He wasn't going to find anything new on this stretch of video.

A couple of other store owners had helpfully given the police access to their outdoor cameras' video feeds. The gift shop across the street gave a good view of the parking spots directly in front of the Book Rack. Watching that one, he could see people entering and leaving the store, though the distant view was sometimes blocked by vehicles.

Fourteen people entered the store between the time when Carl Roofner said he'd left by the back door, leaving Stanley in charge, until Jillian entered shortly after one thirty and discovered the body.

He recognized several people from around town. Kate had told him a couple staying at the Novel Inn had been there in the morning, and he'd found them on earlier footage, when Carl was still at the store. He wondered if any of the other bookstore browsers were tourists from out of town. At least two license plates on cars parked outside the store weren't from Maine.

He loaded two videos onto his phone and went out to the lobby of the police station. Sergeant Craig Watkins was on the front desk.

"You've got Sunday duty now?" Rick asked.

Craig smiled at him. "There's still a lot of carnival activity, so we called in a couple of extra officers. The chief let me choose—the desk or out on the beat. I guess you're here because of the homicide yesterday."

"Yeah. Detective Seaver, with the state police, is in charge of the investigation now, but as a local, I can't let it get cold. I'm heading over to the inn. Thought I'd show my sisters the camera footage in the hour before the shooting. They might be able to help me identify some people."

"Good luck. And say hi to Jillian for me."

Craig's face tinged red before he added, "Oh, Kate too, of course."

Rick laughed. "I'll do that." He'd thought a spark had struck between Craig and Jillian last summer, but not much had seemed to come of it. That had been the busiest time of year for both the inn and the police force. And then Craig had gone for several weeks of extra training in the fall. Rick was sure Jillian would be glad to know the sergeant hadn't forgotten about her.

Walking through the inn's front door, he found Kate at the desk in the small lobby.

"Well, hi," she said. "What's up?"

"I'm working on the Chappell case, and I thought maybe you and Jill could help me identify some customers going into the store yesterday."

"Jillian's not here," Kate said. "She's over there now."

"How come?"

Kate sighed. "I was downtown earlier, and I walked past the store. It was closed, but I could see Carl inside. Blubbering. I tried the door, and it was open, so I went in. Carl said he'd gone over to clean up so he could reopen tomorrow, and Rick, he just couldn't handle it. I called Jillian. She's closer to him, you know. She and Mindy are over there now, cleaning the floor."

"That's too bad. That he's so shook up, I mean. He and Stanley were apparently best friends."

"Yeah. I think he feels a bit of survivor guilt for going off and leaving Stan alone at the store yesterday."

Rick pulled his phone from his pocket. "Do you mind taking a look at this? I've got video from that gift shop across the street. It's mostly to show who's in front of their store, but you can see the Book Rack's door—barely—and it has a pretty good view of four or five parking spots in front of the bookstore."

"Okay. What am I looking at?" Kate took his phone and studied the screen.

"I started it after Carl left the store. It will run up until you see Jillian arrive."

"Can you fast-forward it?"

"Yeah, but . . ."

"Oh, that's Penny Hastings." Kate paused the video. "You know her, don't you?"

"Uh . . . is she the elementary school secretary?" Kate nodded.

"I thought she looked familiar." Rick took out his notebook and wrote Mrs. Hastings's name in it. "Keep going."

A few minutes later, Kate stopped the flow and frowned at the screen. "I can't say for sure, but that could be Mr. and Mrs. Bulmer."

"From church?" Rick grabbed the phone and squinted at it. "I guess it could be. He's got a hat on, and he's blocking her."

"Well, you can ask them if they were there."

Kate checked the time stamp. "That was just after one o'clock."

Rick scribbled *Bulmers?*

Kate fast-forwarded the video and then backed up a little each time people moved near the bookstore on foot. "And there are the Bulmers leaving. I'm almost sure it's them. Hey, wait a sec! That's a kid."

"Yeah, I thought so too, but I have no clue who he is."

"Could even be a girl in that hood." Kate shook her head. "I don't know."

In the video, a woman got into one of the cars in front of the bookstore and drove off. From the right, a man approached on foot. He glanced around as he ambled down the sidewalk.

"Pay attention to this guy," Rick said. "I think that's the shooter."

"Really?"

"Yeah, but the SUV pulling in cuts off your view."

"Right." She frowned over the screen for a long moment. "There! He wasn't inside more than ten seconds." She pointed to a figure moving quickly down the sidewalk away from the Book Rack's entrance. "Too bad that big SUV parked right there. You might have been able to see his face when he came out."

"Story of my life," Rick muttered.

Kate watched the screen for a few more seconds

and paused the video. "There were, what, six or eight people I didn't know?"

"About that. I made a list and checked them off as they came back out of the store."

"Okay." Kate held his gaze and inhaled sharply. "There's one who didn't come out, though."

Rick nodded. "The kid."

She looked down at the phone. "Did you keep watching it?"

"I did. All the way until Jillian went into the store about sixteen minutes later. That kid never came out."

Chapter 6

Jillian parked beside Rick's police department SUV at the inn instead of driving down to the carriage house when she arrived home. Her brother sat behind the front desk, scowling at his phone.

"Hi! Glad you're here." She pulled off her gloves, noticing a mouthwatering smell of cooking lingering in the air.

"I was hoping I'd see you," Rick said. "I've got something I'd like you to look at."

"Sure. And I have something for you." Jillian ducked behind him and through the door to the office, where she tossed her jacket on a chair. As soon as she emerged into the lobby, she held out the paper she'd brought along. "Mindy found this in the bookstore while she was vacuuming. It was hidden under the bottom of a shelf unit in the comic book section—not easy to see."

He unfolded the permission slip. His features sharpened as he studied it. "You think this has to do with the murder?"

"Not directly. Maybe not at all. But the field trip hasn't happened yet. We thought someone might have dropped it yesterday."

Rick pulled in a deep breath. "Yeah. Could be. Can you look at this? It's video of everyone who went in the store yesterday, from the time Carl left until you went in."

She stared at him. "Does it show the shooter?"

"I think so, but not clearly. And some other people I could use help identifying."

Jillian glanced at the clock over the desk. "Won't that take a long time?"

"Not as long as you'd think. We can fast-forward. There are several periods where nobody's on camera."

"Okay. Let's go in the office."

Kate breezed in through the dining room. "Oh, there you are. I just took a casserole out of the oven—two, actually. One's for us, and I thought you might like to take one over to Carl and Eric later."

"That's a great idea."

"Carl?" Rick frowned at Kate. "Why not Stanley's family?"

"Well, Carl and Eric live alone, and they don't really have anyone to hover over them and bring meals when they're upset. I'm sure Mrs. Chappell has someone."

"We were just going to look at some security camera video," Jillian said.

"I've seen it. I'll stay out here while you look." Kate plopped down on the stool Rick had vacated. "Oh, and I took a reservation for Tuesday night."

"Good." Jillian led the way into the office and flipped the light switch. She went to the desk

78

chair, and Rick pulled over a spare Windsor chair.

For twenty minutes, he started and paused the video for her, asking if she recognized anyone. Jillian confirmed the Bulmers' identity and gave him the name of one other local woman Kate hadn't been able to put a name to.

"Okay, now this next one is kind of important," Rick said. "He goes in, but I never see him exit. Even after the shooting."

"Is it the killer?" Jillian brushed back a strand of her short hair.

"I don't think so. I just want you to look at this kid."

"Kid?" She frowned and turned her attention to the small screen. As she watched the slight, hooded figure enter the store and walk toward the back, she drew in a slow breath.

"Boy or girl?" Rick asked.

"I'd say a boy."

"That's what Kate and I thought."

Jillian swiveled to look him full in the face. "That permission slip—it could be . . ."

"Yeah. Maybe someone on the school's faculty can tell us who it is."

"It's really hard to see, and that parka is like a thousand others."

"I know. What else can I do?"

Jillian sat back and thought about it for a few seconds. "I'm not sure you'd want to, but if I were you, I'd ask Ashley and Joel."

He froze. "Ask my kids?"

"Why not? Just show them that little clip. There's no violence in it. They might be able to save you a lot of time and headaches."

He clenched his teeth then nodded. "You may be right. It's not a bad idea. Let me show you the view from across the street."

After watching the section where the young person strolled down the sidewalk and went in, she was no closer to making an identification.

Rick leaned in close. "And you're positive he wasn't in the store when you got there?"

"Well, I didn't exactly check every corner, but as far as I could tell, nobody else was in there, and no one came in before Dave Hall arrived. I'm sure of that."

"Okay, now take a look at this guy," Rick said. "This could be the shooter. You can't see his vehicle—he comes into view on foot. See him there? His face is covered, but you can tell he opens the door and goes in. A minute later . . . Well, less than a minute, actually. A few seconds later . . ." He advanced the video. "There. That's the best view I have. But now a big SUV pulls in and blocks him."

Jillian studied the frozen shot and shook her head. "It's not very good. What about the inside camera? He must be on that."

"No. Just the tip of the gun. I don't think you want to see that. It's a little disturbing."

80

"It shows . . . Stanley?"

Rick nodded. "I watched it hundreds of times, and trust me, it's no help in identifying the killer. If I look sharp, I can see the shell casing we found fly off. I think he left it because he didn't want to go where the camera would record him."

Kate spoke up. "Yeah, that's odd. He must have known about the camera, don't you think?"

Jillian stared at her brother. "Maybe he'd been in the store before."

Rick gave a little groan. "You could be right, but I don't like the idea of watching hundreds of hours' worth of video."

"Let me watch it again." Jillian backed up the footage and focused intently as she watched the man approach the store entrance. "He looks back."

"Yeah, but he turns his head the wrong way for our purposes." Rick shook his head.

"Is he limping?"

"What?" He grabbed the phone and watched the sequence again. "Hmm. Maybe, just a little. But when he comes out . . . Nope, can't tell."

"What will you do now?" Jillian asked.

He let out a heavy sigh. "I have to figure out who would step inside a small, independent bookstore, shoot the clerk, and walk out again, just like that. It's not our case anymore, but I can't do nothing."

"Aren't the state police letting you work with them?" Kate asked.

"Sort of, but Detective Seaver is definitely in charge now."

"The kid," Jillian said with an abstract air.

Rick frowned at her. "What about him?"

"Do you think he saw it?"

"I don't know. It happened so fast. Only one shot was fired."

"So the shooter had a good aim."

"I'd say so."

"And when the kid entered, he made straight for the back, where the children's and young adult books are."

"Yeah, he wasn't in camera range for long."

Jillian frowned. "Mindy and I cleaned the entire floor. We didn't find blood anywhere except in Stan's immediate surroundings." She rested her hand on her chin. "You've got the video all the way until I go in?"

"Yes. Nobody else entered for the next twenty minutes, then you showed up."

"Isn't that a little odd that no one else came?"

"I don't think so. It's not a high-traffic store in winter, and there was stuff going on in the town square."

"True. Carl was disappointed there weren't more customers."

Rick shrugged. "I figure it was just a lull."

Jillian took the phone from him and watched

herself walk between two parked vehicles to the Book Rack's door. "I guess if they were handing out awards down near the library, not many people would be browsing the shops a few blocks away."

"You were one of the few people to walk that piece of sidewalk during that time period. A few others strolled past, but if they didn't go in, they wouldn't see the body."

"I guess I'm on that indoor camera too?"

"Yeah. You walk in, pause, and go running to where Stan was. Once you're between the shelves, you hunker down, and I can't see much, just a little movement, and that's about it until Dave got there."

She handed the phone back. "I'm sorry, Rick. But if that kid was in there when it happened . . ." She thought about it for a moment. "There's a back door off the storeroom, where Carl has his desk and stows extra stock. You saw it."

"Carl says he went out that way himself," Rick said slowly. "He parks his car out back so he doesn't take up a parking spot on the street."

"So, the teen could have gone out the back."

"I'd think so. I'll have to check the door, but if you can open it from the inside, and it locks on closing, that would be a definite possibility." He stood.

"He must have been terrified." Jillian placed a hand on his sleeve. "Ask your kids, Rick."

"Yeah, I think I will." He shook his head. "If only Carl had a camera on the back door, and over the counter facing the front door. No such luck."

"I'm sure his budget is limited, and he's probably never had a serious problem before."

"Right. Talk to you later." Rick shoved his phone in his pocket and left the room.

Jillian found Kate in the kitchen. "Rick's gone. I was thinking I'd make some cookies to take to Carl and Eric with your casserole."

"Sounds good," Kate said. "Hey, about the guy in Room 9."

Jillian knew at once the guest she meant. "He has a name. Mr. Schuman."

"Well, yeah."

Was Kate blushing?

"What about him?"

"I called his room while you were gone and—"

"Why?" Jillian gave her a hard stare. "You know he wants to be left alone."

"I just asked if we could do anything for him— you know, fresh towels, or take away his trash."

"And?"

"He said he'll leave his trash outside his door later."

Jillian thought about that. "I guess it's okay."

Leaning toward her, Kate whispered, "Do you think we could open it? See what's in his garbage?"

"No. Absolutely not."

"But he's on our property, so . . . once he throws something away, it's not his anymore."

"Kate—"

"Aren't you curious? What if he's doing drugs in there?"

Jillian pulled in a slow breath. "Did he sound high when you talked to him?"

"Well, no."

"And do you think that if he was doing something illegal, he'd put the evidence in the trash?"

Kate's face skewed. "Probably not. But aren't you curious?"

"Evidently not as curious as you are."

Chapter 7

Jillian rang the doorbell at the Roofner house, balancing a plastic box of gingersnaps on top of her padded casserole carrier. From inside, she heard voices—or one voice. She turned her head and listened intently.

"—better call me, you hear? Right now!" This was followed by an expletive, and she winced.

She puzzled over what she'd heard. Footsteps approached and she pulled back. When the door was opened by a man about her age, she smiled.

"Hi, Eric. I don't know if you remember me— I'm Jillian Tunney, and we've met at the store. I called earlier and told your dad I'd bring over some supper for the two of you."

"That's really nice of you, Ms. Tunney." He caught the cookie box as it slid sideways and nearly fell to the ground. "Let me take that."

"Oops, thanks. And it's Jillian."

"Come on in." He led the way through the living room into the kitchen beyond. Setting down the plastic container, he turned to face her. "Dad's lying down upstairs. I can tell him you're here . . ."

"Oh, no, don't do that," Jillian said quickly. "If he's resting, I don't want to disturb him. I know this whole thing has upset him terribly."

"It has." Eric looked around. "Why don't you set that down right over here."

"Thanks." She stepped to the counter and lowered the casserole. "It's still warm, but if you want, you can put it in the fridge—it's not that hot. When you're ready to eat, just stick it in the microwave."

"Okay." Eric eyed her with speculation. "You're over at the inn now, right? The one the Gages used to own."

"That's right. My sister and brother and I inherited it when our folks died."

"Sorry." He looked a little embarrassed, as if he'd made a huge social gaffe.

"It's okay. We miss them terribly, but we're going ahead with the inn. Kate and I run it together."

Eric nodded. "They say you found Stan yesterday."

"That's right. I left before you got back. Where was it you'd gone?"

"Clifton. They had a big snowmobile rally over there." He frowned. "I never should have gone. Dad asked me to work with Stan."

"It's not your fault. No one would have thought something like that would happen. Stan was such a nice man. Who on earth would want to hurt him?"

"That's what Dad keeps saying." Eric swallowed hard. "Personally, I think it was random."

"You think someone just wanted to—what? Kill someone?"

Eric shook his head. "I don't know. But sometimes a kid will just go off his nut, you know? Nothing else makes sense."

"Maybe you can tell me who Stan's friends were, besides your dad," Jillian said.

"Can't think of many. Bill Rutter maybe. And maybe he's friends with his neighbors. I just don't know."

"Who's—" She stopped as Eric's phone rang with a catchy tune.

He pulled it from his pocket and looked at the screen then tapped it a couple of times. The music stopped, and he put it back in his pocket.

Jillian hesitated but didn't want to waste this chance to talk to Eric. "You said Bill Rutter? Who is he?"

"Just some old geezer Stan goes fishing with now and then. Oh, and there's Zeb—"

Her ears perked up, but Eric's phone blasted his ringtone again.

"You'd better take that," she said.

He scowled down at the screen and muttered, "Yeah, I probably should. Is there anything else?"

The phone continued to ring, and she said quickly, "You mentioned Zeb. Did you mean Zeb Wilding?" It was such an uncommon name that, in this small town, she thought there was a good chance.

"Retired navy guy?" Eric asked.

"Yes."

Eric nodded. "I know Stan plays chess with him sometimes."

"Thanks."

She edged out the door. As it closed, she heard Eric shout, "Where the—?"

She walked cautiously down the steps and to her car, avoiding an icy patch. She had two names, Bill Rutter and Zeb Wilding. Interviewing Zeb, her next-door neighbor, would be a piece of cake. She'd played chess with Zeb herself several times. He was a very good player.

She'd have to look up Rutter. Or maybe Zeb knew him. She headed the car toward home with a shot of optimism.

Twilight had descended by the time she got back to the inn. She stood on the porch for a moment and looked toward Zeb's house. She could see his roofline and the top of his flagstaff. It seemed he'd taken down his signals for the night.

She took it as a good indication that her eighty-year-old friend was all right. That morning he'd flown his usual pennants that sent her the message "All is well." If he hadn't removed them at sunset, she'd have worried about him.

When she went inside, Kate was coming down the curving stairs.

"Hi. Did you see Carl?"

"No, just Eric. He didn't tell me much, but he did say Zeb was a friend of Stanley's. I thought I'd pop over to Zeb's house. Are there any cookies left?"

"Yeah, quite a few. I put some on a plate by the coffeemaker, but there's at least a dozen in the kitchen."

"I think I'll take a few to Zeb." Jillian didn't bother to take off her coat and hat. She shoved her gloves into her pockets and went through to the kitchen. Kate followed, and Jillian asked, "So, what's going on here?"

"Nothing much. Most of the guests are out eating supper."

"How about Mr. Schuman?"

"Haven't seen or heard from him." Kate watched as she put half a dozen gingersnaps in a zipper bag. "What can I do while you're gone?"

Jillian was about to suggest she fix supper for the two of them, but Kate's wistful expression told her that her sister meant she wanted to help with the mystery surrounding Stan's death.

"Maybe you could do a little research on Stan Chappell's family? I don't think I've ever met his wife, Anita. And Carl mentioned they had two daughters and a son, but none of them lives in Skirmish Cove."

Kate's face brightened. "I can do a little poking around. I'm good at that."

"Yes, you are. Keep in mind, you may be

covering ground Rick's already been over."

"Yeah, but it's nice to take a look for ourselves, right?"

"Right." Jillian picked up the bag of cookies. "I'll be back in a little while, and I'll see what I can scrounge up for supper."

"Oh, I made us a casserole when I did Carl's. Do you want to eat over here, or at the carriage house?"

"Here's fine. That way, we can discuss what we find out."

Kate grinned. They both took seriously the responsibility for one of them to stay in the inn at all times unless an emergency came up, as it had earlier with Carl.

"Great. I'll be here."

Jillian hurried out through the storeroom and off the side porch to the path that led through the woods and over a small stream to Zeb's property. Her boots thudded on the bridge her father had built several years earlier. Lights glowed in Zeb's snug living room and his kitchen. She dashed up the front steps and knocked.

"Ahoy, Zeb," she called. "It's Jillian."

The door opened on her dear friend. His face was one big smile, and she couldn't help returning it. She held up the bag of cookies.

"Brought you something, chum."

"Oh, wonderful! You know my sweet tooth, don't you?"

"I think we've made an acquaintance." She walked in and set the bag on the counter in his neat little kitchen—or galley, as he called it. "Got a minute, Zeb?"

"Of course. You know I don't go out at night anymore. Root beer?" He never drank caffeine in the evening.

"I'd love one."

After pouring two glasses full, he handed her one and picked up the bag of cookies.

"Want one?" he asked as they settled in comfortable armchairs in the next room.

"No, those gingersnaps are for you," Jillian said. "We have more at home."

He smiled as he unzipped the bag and took one out. Holding it to his nose, he sniffed it. "Ah. Nothing like home-baked cookies." He took a bite and closed his eyes as he chewed.

Jillian loved watching the old man. He'd become like a grandfather to her since she and Kate had moved back to Skirmish Cove. The eccentric old sailor had a million stories, and he didn't hesitate to share them.

"I've been to see the Roofners." She took a sip of her root beer.

Zeb's eyes popped open. "How's Carl doing? I heard about poor Stanley's murder. Terrible thing."

"Yes, it was. I didn't actually see Carl tonight. He was resting, but I talked to Eric for a few minutes."

Zeb's mouth quirked, and Jillian picked up an attitude.

"You don't think much of Eric?"

Zeb shrugged. "I didn't say that."

"You didn't have to."

He took a drink from his glass. "Well, you know, boys aren't always as respectful as they should be. Eric's not a boy anymore. He ought to grow up."

Jillian nodded slowly. "You feel he doesn't show his father the respect he should?"

"Oh, he doesn't insult Carl to his face, at least not that I've seen, but he ought to be more responsible. More dependable."

"Yesterday, he was off at a snowmobile rally when Carl seemed to think he should have been at the store with Stanley."

Zeb's disdain was more obvious now. "Snowmobiles." He snorted. "What are they good for?"

"Recreation, I guess."

"Exactly. Nothing useful."

"Mr. Tanner uses a sled behind his to haul out his firewood."

He waved a hand through the air. "All right, so they're somewhat useful. But a thirty-five-year-old man should be helping his father when he needs him. Carl wanted to hand the store over to him one day, but I don't see it happening soon."

"I guess Carl's near retirement age." Jillian sipped her soda.

"He's sixty-seven, but he can't even think about retiring. Eric's not dependable. And he hates the store."

"What do you mean? I've seen him working in there before."

"Only when he has to. I think Carl has to make him feel guilty before he'll do it. Carl and Stan are too old to be unloading cartons of books and—" Zeb stopped and blinked rapidly.

"It's all right," Jillian said softly. "I know you and Stan were good friends."

"We were." Zeb's voice cracked.

She smiled. "I heard you two played chess together."

He nodded. "Stan was a good guy." He wiped his cuff across his eyes. "Have you heard anything about funeral arrangements?"

"Not yet. I expect it will be in tomorrow's paper."

Zeb took a second cookie from the bag and ate the whole thing before speaking again. "Anita must be upset. I should call her."

"What can you tell me about their family?"

He lifted one shoulder. "It was just Stan and Anita the last fifteen or twenty years. Both the girls got married. The younger one, Amelia, lives in Skowhegan, I think. Stan showed me some pictures of the grandchildren not long ago. And Jennifer . . ."

"Carl told me she's divorced."

"Yeah. Sad case, that one. She doesn't come home much. I think she felt like Stan and Anita didn't approve of her."

"Why not? The divorce?"

"Well, yes, and . . . they say she had a boyfriend. That's why her husband left her. She used to live in Bar Harbor, but she moved out of state. Pennsylvania, I think."

"And isn't there a brother, too?"

Zeb nodded. "Sean. Haven't seen him in years. He moved to Texas, maybe. Or California?"

"Hmm. And Jennifer has a grown-up son," Jillian prompted.

"That'd be Justin. He's not with his mother anymore. Haven't seen him in years."

"What about Amelia's kids? Are they adults too?"

"No, they're still at home. But the oldest one's got to be a teenager. Seems like Stan said one of them was starting college next fall. That was one reason he kept working, to help out with the grandchildren's tuition. He was real eager to see at least one of them go to college. None of his own kids did."

"I see. Do you know Bill Rutter, by any chance? Eric said he was also a friend of Stan's."

"Sure, I know Bill. He goes out fishing a lot. I think he was a school bus driver. Retired now. I don't think I've seen him this winter, but as far as I know, he's still around."

"Maybe I'll look him up." Jillian drank the last of her root beer. "I told Kate I wouldn't be gone long, so I should go, but I have one more question."

Zeb met her gaze expectantly.

"Do you know if anyone—in the family or otherwise—was angry with Stan?"

"You mean, angry enough to shoot him?"

She nodded.

Pressing his lips together, Zeb shook his head slowly. "Not that I can think of. Stan won the chess tournament in Bar Harbor last year, and one guy was pretty mad, but there was no question that Stan won the trophy fair and square." Zeb held up both hands. "Sorry, that's all I can think of."

"Okay, well . . ." Jillian stood, wondering if it would be worth visiting Mrs. Chappell and asking to see Stan's chess trophy. "I'd better get going. Don't get up." She stooped and brushed his cheek with a kiss. "I'll see you soon."

"Thanks for coming by. It's always good to have you aboard." Despite her words, he lumbered to his feet and walked her to the front porch. The captain couldn't let a visitor disembark without at least being on deck to watch.

Chapter 8

"Do you really think it would hurt to ask them?" Rick frowned at his image in the mirror as he adjusted his uniform.

"I don't know . . ." Diana quickly straightened the comforter on their bed and went to the closet. "I mean, they're kids. If they do recognize someone on that video, what then? Will they have to testify in court?"

"No, nothing like that." Rick turned to face her. "Look, I'm planning to go over to the middle school today and ask some of the staff there. If need be, I'll go to the high school too. It would just be a shortcut if we can find out who that kid is without spending hours interviewing teachers."

Diana let out a sigh. "Okay. They'll probably think it's cool to help on a murder investigation. But please show Ashley first. She's older. And whatever you do, tell them not to go bragging to their friends about it."

That made sense to Rick. Teenagers could twist things that were innocent on the surface into weapons.

"Okay, I'll see if Ashley's ready for school, and I'll take her in the family room. If Joel comes downstairs while I'm talking to her, try to steer him to the kitchen, okay?"

"That shouldn't be a problem." Joel always wanted breakfast first thing when he got up.

On the other hand, Ashley was nearly three years older than her brother. At fifteen, she considered herself quite grown up. She might even refuse to look at the video if she had picked up some offbeat idea about students' rights.

Rick hurried across the hall to his daughter's bedroom and tapped on the door.

"Yeah?" Ashley sounded a little groggy.

"You up?" Rick asked. "I wondered if you could help me with something."

"Not shoveling snow, I hope."

"No, nothing like that. This has to do with the case I'm working on."

Her door opened a few inches. Ashley had on flannel pj's covered in kittens. Maybe she wasn't as sophisticated as she thought she was.

"What is it?"

"A video from a store's security cameras. I was hoping you could help me identify one of the customers."

Her eyes scrunched up. "Not that bookstore where the murder happened?"

"Yeah, that's the one." Rick glanced down the hall to make sure Joel wasn't within earshot.

Ashley's forehead crinkled. He thought at first she'd flat-out refuse, but after a moment she cocked her head to one side.

"Is it someone you think I know?"

"I'm not sure, but I think it's a kid about your age."

"A kid shot the store clerk?"

"No, no, no." *I'm doing this all wrong.* Rick put out a hand as if he could stop horrible images from flooding her mind. "Sorry, it's nothing like that. All you'll see are videos of people going in and out of the store. Not the . . . the body or anything like that."

"Aunt Jillian saw it, didn't she? I heard Mom talking to her on the phone."

"Yeah, she did. Not the shooting, just the aftermath. I was really sorry about that."

Ashley pulled in a deep breath. "Give me a couple minutes. I've got to get dressed."

"Okay, meet me in the family room. And thanks."

He went down to the kitchen and poured himself a mug of the coffee Diana had programmed the machine to make. Taking a sip, he closed his eyes for a moment. Coffee was a blessing. On mornings like this, it really helped him get going. Some days he doubted he'd make it to the end of his shift without the pick-me-up. The invention of automatic coffeemakers beat sliced bread any day in his book.

"There are worse addictions," he muttered.

"Huh?"

He spun around to find Joel, clad in jeans and

a gray sweatshirt, coming through the kitchen doorway.

"Nothing. How you doing, bud?"

"Okay. I wish the bus didn't come so early."

"Well, it's only a mile and a half to school. You could walk it."

"I'd have to get up even earlier to do that. Besides, it's January."

"True. We had a nice weekend for the carnival, but I heard it's supposed to be colder today."

Joel opened the cupboard and studied the cereal boxes critically.

"Good morning," Diana said cheerfully as she walked in. She threw Rick a glance then said, "Joel, how about some scrambled eggs?"

Joel grinned. "Yeah. Thanks, Mom. And bacon?"

"I don't think we have any bacon."

"Aunt Jillian and Aunt Kate serve it every morning at the inn."

"And people are paying them for that."

Rick carried his coffee mug out the door and past the dining room. Ashley was just coming down the stairs. He smiled at her and jerked his head toward the family room. By the time she got there, he had the video up on his phone and accelerated it forward to where the teen arrived.

Ashley came in looking a bit distracted. "Okay, now what is it?" She plopped down on the couch.

Rick eased down beside her. "It's just a few

seconds of video. Here, tell me if you recognize the kid going into the store." He started it and handed her his phone.

She frowned at it then looked up. "That's it?"

"Yeah. Let me replay it for you."

"I can do it." She managed the phone's settings quicker than he could. She watched it again.

"Well? Any thoughts?"

"Not really. Is this all you've got?"

"Pretty much. Boy or girl?"

Her frowned deepened. "Boy. Definitely."

"How can you tell?"

"By the way he walks."

Rick eyed her closely. "So, you know someone who walks like that?"

"Do you have a shot of him coming out of the store?"

"No, I don't. There's a short clip of him inside the store. Hold on." He took the phone and brought up the video from the inside camera. "Okay, I don't know if this will help. It's a little closer, but you still can't see his face."

After a moment, she nodded, studying the screen. Finally she looked up. "It kind of looks like a kid in Joel's class, but I'm not sure. I don't think he's from the high school."

"I thought he might be junior high age."

"Then why did you ask me?" Ashley stood. "I've got to get moving, Dad."

"Sure. Thanks a lot." He took the phone and sat

back with a sigh. He'd hoped to avoid bringing Joel into this.

He cranked himself off the sofa and ambled toward the kitchen. Joel ran past him toward the front door, his backpack dangling from one hand.

"Wait, Joel. I need to ask you something."

"Can't. I'll miss the bus."

Ashley was putting on her jacket, juggling a Pop-Tart and a geometry book. "Sorry, Dad. Gotta go." She followed her brother out and slammed the door.

Rick winced and went into the kitchen. Diana sat calmly at the table with a plate of scrambled eggs and toast in front of her.

"Any luck?" she asked.

"Not really."

"Sorry." Diana stood. "Want juice? I made plenty of eggs."

His coffee. Rick realized he'd left the mug in the family room. It was going to be one of those days.

Twenty minutes later, as he was walking out the door, his cell rang. *Ashley?*

"Yeah, kiddo. Whatcha got?"

"Well, there's a boy on our bus that I didn't think of before. His coat looks like the one in the video." She and Joel rode the same bus every morning. It stopped to let out the middle school kids before taking the older students to the high school.

"Are you at school?"

"Yes," Ashley said. "I haven't gone in yet, but I need to."

"Who's the boy you mentioned?"

"Clint something. I snapped a picture as he was getting off the bus, right behind Joel. I'll send it to you."

"Good. And thanks."

"Well, he wasn't the one I was thinking of when we talked. I asked Joel, and that boy's name is Jeremy McLeod. I don't have a last name on this Clint guy."

"That's very helpful," Rick said. "Send me your picture, and then get inside."

"I will."

She clicked off without saying goodbye, but he figured she wouldn't want any kids walking past her to know she was talking to her dad.

His phone pinged, and he opened Ashley's photo. He stared at it in silence for a long moment then scrambled to bring up the security video that showed the boy going into the bookstore.

Yes. The jackets were similar, the build was the same. He'd have to bring them up side by side when he got to work, but that looked like a very strong possibility to him.

"What's the matter?" Diana asked, coming out of the kitchen. "I thought you left."

"I'm leaving now." Rick pulled her in for an

103

extra goodbye kiss. Maybe today would be a good day after all.

"Look at it carefully," Rick said to Eric Roofner an hour later. So far, Eric had claimed to recognize only one customer from the video, a middle-aged woman who visited the store at least once a week.

"I did."

"Eric." His father's voice held a testy edge.

"What? I've looked at it twice. Mrs. Kelly is the only one I know for sure."

Rick took this time to observe the father and son. Eric was definitely at the end of his attention span. Was there something more going on? Was he intentionally being vague? Rick leaned back a little and continued to listen to the duo.

"What about Susan Howell?" Carl asked.

"If you say so. I don't really know her."

"But you've waited on her."

"I suppose."

"I know that boy's been in here several times, but I don't know his name," Carl said.

Eric's eyebrows drew together. "I don't know how you can tell. You can never see his face."

Quickly, Rick switched to the outdoor camera, near the end of the time he was interested in.

"Take one more look at this guy for me. I know you can't see his face very well either, but think about it."

Eric gazed at the screen for several seconds as the man pushed inside the Book Rack, paused, and came back out. The vehicles parked out front blocked the image, but Rick was sure the man had his hand in his pocket. He had to be concealing a weapon. Rick was nearly positive that pedestrian was the shooter.

"Nah." Eric stood, shaking his head. "I told you, he doesn't look familiar."

Was his tension simply impatience? Rick studied his face carefully.

"Not even a little bit?"

"No. I said no. I wasn't even here when this happened."

"Okay. Well, thanks for trying."

Carl looked up at the clock on the wall behind the counter. "It's time to open the store. Is that all right, Officer Gage?"

"Yeah, it's fine. I'm heading out. Let me know if anything turns up, or if any of your customers says anything suspicious."

Carl grimaced and headed for the front door, where he turned the sign so the OPEN side showed to pedestrians outside and unlocked the door.

"You'll be here with your father all morning?" Rick asked Eric.

"Why?"

"Because he's on edge today. He probably shouldn't be here alone. A lot of people may come in out of curiosity. Some will want to extend their condolences, but some will just want to get some details on the murder. It may be rough on your father."

Eric huffed out an impatient breath. "I told him I'd stay until noon, but he'll have to hire someone else part-time. I can't be here every day."

"Well, I'm sure you can work it out," Rick said. "Until we find out who did this, he should have someone with him all the time."

"Whatever."

"Eric, did you get those new magazines out?" Carl asked as he turned away from the door.

"Not yet."

"I wanted them out before we opened."

Eric scowled. "I had to stop and help the policeman."

Carl waved a hand at him. "I'll do it myself."

"Dad." Eric's voice rose as he followed his father toward the back of the store. "I'll do it. I told you I'd do it. You stay near the till."

Rick let out a sigh and stepped toward the door as a group of three women entered, chattering brightly.

"Good morning," Rick said and slipped outside.

Jillian looked up from her computer screen at about half past eleven to see Mindy in the office doorway.

"Hi, Mindy. I just printed your check." Jillian

stood and went to the printer, where she removed the weekly paychecks for Mindy and the two night clerks.

"Thanks, I can really use it." Mindy took hers and looked at it with a big smile.

"That includes your time at the bookstore yesterday. Thanks so much for helping me with that."

"No problem." Mindy tucked it in her purse. "Say, I've got a small bag of trash from the hallway. It was outside Room 9. What do you want me to do with it?"

"Put it right in the dumpster with the rest of the trash."

"Okay. I wasn't sure, because it's the DND guy—you know."

Jillian knew. The Do Not Disturb guy—Schuman. "Yeah, Kate and I had a discussion about it. I don't think we want to poke into his trash. It doesn't seem like the right thing to do."

"He's so mysterious." Mindy shivered.

"I'd say he's quiet. But he hasn't done anything suspicious. Our guests deserve their privacy." They had appropriately put him in the Rip Van Winkle Room.

"Okay. I'll drop it in the dumpster before I leave. Do you want me to come in tomorrow?"

"We could probably use you for a couple of hours."

Mindy smiled. "Great. I'm glad your business is going so well, and I'm glad to get the work."

Jillian went back to her desk and slid Don and Wayne's checks into envelopes. Rick walked in just before noon.

"Well, hello." Jillian stood and stretched. "I've been sitting too long. Find out anything about Stanley?"

"Not a lot. I did locate that kid on the video, though."

"Really?" She stepped eagerly toward him. "Who is it?"

"Clint Hunley. He goes to the same school as Joel. In fact, they ride on the same bus every day. Ashley recognized him, and the school confirmed it."

"Wow."

"I called his parents to ask if I could interview him. They had no idea he was in the bookstore so close to the time of the murder. They said I can go over there at three thirty, when Clint comes home."

Jillian thought about that. "So either he wasn't there when the shooting happened, or he just clammed up and didn't tell anyone."

"Yeah. I'm pretty sure he went out the back door. Carl didn't know his name, though he thought he recognized Clint after I showed him a school picture."

She nodded. "He was probably terrified, poor

kid. I hope the interview goes well. Oh, and you might want to add Bill Rutter to your list of interviewees."

"What? Why?" Rick asked.

"It's probably nothing, but Eric told me he was friends with Stan. I went over to Zeb's last night because Eric mentioned him, too, when I asked him about family and friends."

Rick frowned. Did she and Kate overstep again? Or was her brother just kicking himself for not getting this information himself?

"I wrote down some bits he said about Stan's family, but you probably know all that." Jillian opened her top desk drawer and took out a small memo book. "Stan used to go fishing with this Bill person, and he liked to play chess with Zeb. Oh, and Zeb thinks Bill Rutter was a retired school bus driver."

"I thought the name rang a bell. He drove Ashley's bus when she was little." Rick took the slip of paper Jillian held out. "Thanks, sis. I'll speak to Mr. Rutter if we don't tie things up quickly."

"You're hoping Clint can tell you something."

He nodded. "I'm sorry there's a kid involved in this, but he may know something important."

"Rick, if he was in the store when Stanley was shot, he may need to talk to somebody. A counselor, I mean." Jillian thought of all the young people she'd taught over the years. Some of them reached out when they experienced trauma. Others clammed up.

He nodded soberly. "I'll mention it to his parents. The school probably has someone available. Listen, you and Kate be careful, you hear me?"

"Yeah. Thanks for caring."

Chapter 9

Kate stopped at the post office for stamps then took the ad copy she'd prepared with Jillian's approval to the newspaper office. Personally, Kate favored online promotion, but Jillian insisted a lot of people still read the local paper. They wanted to keep the bookings going as spring approached and had budgeted a small amount monthly for advertising.

When she came out, she glanced down the street. She wasn't far from the Book Rack, and a quick visit there wouldn't take more than five minutes. She had plenty of time left for the grocery shopping.

She stepped into the store and looked toward the counter. A heavyset man too young to be Carl sat there studying his cell. Though she didn't know Eric Roofner personally, she recognized him from earlier visits to the store.

He looked up, and she called, "Hi. Just hoping you've got the new *Country Living*." She wasn't an avid fan of the magazine, but Jillian was, and they'd found a few creative decorating ideas in it for the inn.

"I just put them out this morning," Eric said.

"Thanks." Kate strode to the magazine section, which stretched along the side wall from the checkout to the back of the store.

She quickly located the magazine she'd mentioned and then noticed a puzzle monthly for kids. Joel might like that. He had a sharp, rather mathematically inclined mind. His birthday was coming up. Kate picked up the magazine and leafed through it. The logic problems and code puzzles looked interesting. Lots of geometric graphics and word problems on topics modern preteens would like.

"I told you, quit calling me."

Kate stiffened, staring down at the pages of the magazine. Eric Roofner might think his low, intense voice wouldn't carry, but he was wrong. The kids' periodical section was on the end of the long magazine row nearest the counter. He must not have realized she was so close.

"No, that's not—"

Kate sneaked a look at him. Did he recognize her as Jillian's sister—or worse, as Officer Rick Gage's sister?

"No, I won't," he said sharply into his phone. "Now leave me alone." Eric stabbed at the phone and then lifted his gaze.

Kate looked down at the magazine, wishing she hadn't stopped to examine it. She was sure he was staring at her. She put the puzzle book back on the shelf and edged a couple of steps away, where adult crosswords, word search, cryptogram, and coloring books faced her. She pretended intense interest in one and didn't look toward the counter for at least two minutes. Could she leave without buying anything? She didn't want to check out under Eric's scrutiny.

Someone moved into the row behind her. She turned to her left, away from the checkout. Carl was walking briskly up the center aisle with two books in his hands. He must have been in the back room.

He went straight to the counter and spoke to his son. Kate let out a slow breath and walked to the front, clutching her copy of *Country Living*.

"Hello," Mr. Roofner said with a smile. He looked tired.

"Hi." Kate held out her magazine. "Just this today."

Carl took it and laid it on the counter. He ran a hand-held scanner over the bar code and rang it up on the cash register. "That'll be four-ninety-nine."

Kate stuck her debit card in the slot and soon had the bagged magazine in her hand.

"Thanks, Mr. Roofner."

"You're welcome, Kate."

Eric had moved away from the checkout while she completed the transaction and was straightening books on the discount table. Kate was glad she didn't have to acknowledge him. She made straight for the door.

Outside, she pulled in a deep breath and almost ran to her Jeep. She pulled her keys and grocery list from her coat pocket. "Hannaford, here I come."

"So, you were in the bookstore when a man came in," Rick said, watching the thirteen-year-old boy carefully. "Was anyone else in the store?"

"Just the store clerk, I think." Clint's lips quivered as he spoke.

"Did you see the man who came in from outside?"

The boy shook his head. "I didn't see anything. I just . . ." He glanced at his father.

"It's okay," his dad said. "Just tell Officer Gage exactly what happened. You're not in any trouble."

Clint drew in a shaky breath. "I was looking at a manga book, and all of a sudden . . ." He started trembling all over. "Somebody shot off a gun."

"How did you know it was a gun?" Rick asked.

Clint shrugged.

"Did you look?"

He shook his head. "It was really loud. I jumped, and then I laid down on the rug in the corner. I didn't want anyone to see me."

"Then what?"

"Then I . . . I waited." Clint licked his lips. "It was real quiet, but my ears were ringing." He glanced up at Rick. "I've heard people say that, but it really happened. I wasn't sure if I could hear anything. I wanted to get out of there, but I was scared."

"Of course you were," Mrs. Hunley said. Her husband put his hand on her arm, and she pressed her lips together.

"So what did you do?" Rick asked as gently as he could. "We didn't see you leave the store on the security camera."

"I . . . I waited there a few minutes, by the mangas. I was afraid the guy with the gun would come back there, but he didn't." He looked up at Rick then down at the floor. "I started to go toward the door, but when I got about halfway, up near the front of the store, I saw . . ."

Rick waited a few seconds then said, "It's okay, Clint. You can tell us."

"I saw feet. On the floor. The guy was . . . he was lying down in one of the rows of books."

"Did you go look at him?" Rick asked.

Clint shook his head. "I was too scared. I . . . I ran back toward the kids' books, and I saw a door. It said 'employees only,' or something like that. I pushed on it, and it opened, so I went in there and shut the door."

"Then what?"

"Well, I looked around. There were lots of boxes, and a desk, I think. But I saw another door with one of those lit-up exit signs over it. I ran out and found out I was in a little parking place behind the store. I took off for home. When I got here, I ran up to my room." He glanced at his mother.

"I was here," Mrs. Hunley said. "I called out to Clint, but he didn't answer me. He stayed in his room most of the afternoon, I think."

"I was really scared." It was barely a whisper.

"You did fine, buddy." Rick patted his shoulder. "You said 'the guy with the gun.' How did you know it was a guy?"

Clint's face wrinkled in utter confusion. "I—I don't know. Maybe I glanced toward the noise."

"Did you see a man?"

"I—no. I just remember hitting the floor. I don't know if I looked. I thought I didn't."

"Okay. Is there anything else you want to tell me?"

Clint shook his head.

"Anything you'd like to ask me?"

"He was dead, right? The old guy."

"Yes, Mr. Chappell died. I'm sorry you were so close to it when it happened."

"Do you know who did it?"

"We're working on it." Rick looked at the parents. "You folks can be very proud of Clint. He did exactly right, to hide and then get out the safest way he could find."

Mr. Hunley took his cue and stood. "Thanks, Officer Gage."

"You're welcome." Rick rose and handed the man a card. "You can call me if anything else comes up." He glanced at Clint. "Any of you."

Mrs. Hunley stood and moved toward the door. "Thank you for bringing us the permission slip."

Rick looked down at Clint, who was still huddled in an armchair. "Clint, I hope you have a good time on the field trip."

The boy nodded but didn't speak or make eye contact. Rick walked with both parents to their front door and turned.

"Look, my sister is a retired teacher, and she told me most schools have counseling available to the students. Clint may need some therapy, or at least someone to talk with. He's obviously shaken by this experience."

"Why didn't he tell us?" Mrs. Hunley whispered. "We never would have known."

"I'm glad you found out he was there." Mr. Hunley extended his hand to Rick. "I'll talk to him after things settle down, about the importance of cluing in the adults when something happens. And we will make sure he gets the opportunity to talk to a professional."

Kate practically flung the groceries from the canvas tote bags. She shoved them into groups on the counter while Jillian scooped up handfuls of similar items and put them away.

"Easy." Jillian grabbed an egg carton from her sister's hand. "What's your hurry?"

Kate huffed out a breath. "I don't know. I didn't mean to take so long at the store."

"Well, there's no rush, and we don't want these scrambled before morning." Jillian opened the refrigerator and slid the eggs inside.

"Did I tell you I stopped at the bookstore?" Kate asked.

"You did. Was Eric there, helping his father?"

Kate paused with a basket of mushrooms in her hand. "I'm not sure how much he was helping. While I was there, he was messing with his phone. And he took a phone call that . . . I don't know, it made me nervous."

"In what way?"

"He told whoever it was to quit calling him. To leave him alone."

Jillian paused with a mesh bag of onions in her hands. "When I went to the house, he was trying to get hold of someone. I was standing on the steps and I heard him say something like, 'You better call me now' in a really angry voice. I thought at the time he was leaving a message. So, what else did he say in the store?"

"I don't know. Not much."

"Well, after he let me in the house last night, his phone rang, and he rejected the call. When it started in again, I told him he'd better take it, and I left."

Kate frowned. "You think that's significant?"

"I don't know. It could have been the same

person calling back, and he didn't want to talk to them in front of me. Did you see Carl today?"

"Yeah, he came out from the back and cashed me out. I was glad because Eric was creeping me out, and I didn't want to go to the counter and have him wait on me."

Kate's body language, more than her words, made Jillian uneasy. Ever since she drove up with the back of her Jeep full of groceries, Kate had moved too fast, as though she needed to outrun somebody.

"Is this it for groceries?" Jillian scooped up the empty shopping totes.

"Yeah, except for our personal stuff."

"Go ahead and take that to the carriage house. I'm going to give Rick a call."

"What for?"

"I don't like the way Eric's been acting."

Kate stood still for once and eyed her thoughtfully. "You think he has something to do with the murder?"

"I don't know. I'm sure they've checked his alibi and made sure he was in Clifton that morning. But we don't know him. We've only seen him for a few minutes at a time, and yet both of us thought he was acting weird with his phone." Jillian took an armful of tote bags to the pantry closet.

"Okay," Kate said. "I'll be back in a little while. I can stay on the desk until Don gets here."

"That's six hours from now. I'll take a turn later, but a couple hours off would be nice."

"Sure. You need to relax for a while."

"Oh, and let's not put anyone in the Virginian Room unless we're maxed out. I want to be able to go in there and ponder the redo."

"Okay." Kate hurried into the storage room that held the side door. She'd parked out there to make it easier for them to unload the supplies.

Jillian called Rick, but she got his voice mail. She sighed while the recording played. "Hi, Rick. It's Jill. Please call me when you can."

Everything was shipshape in the kitchen, so she went out to the front desk to await Kate's return. They still had two incoming guests who hadn't yet checked in. She grabbed her Kindle from the desk in the office and settled down in the lobby to read.

A few minutes later, a couple arrived, and Jillian jumped up to greet them. They expected to stay only one night, and the check-in went smoothly.

"Would you like a view of the bay?" she asked with a big smile. "Our David Copperfield Room is open, on the second floor. Or we have a couple of rooms available on the third floor."

"Ocean view, definitely," the woman said.

"Great." Jillian entered their names in the computer just as Kate peeked in from the hallway. "Oh, this is my sister. Kate, would you mind showing the Brookses to David Copperfield?"

"I'd be happy to." Kate stepped forward with a dazzling smile. "Do you have more luggage?"

As the three of them headed for the elevator, Jillian's cell rang, and she snatched it up.

"Rick! Thanks for calling."

"Sorry for the delay. I was interviewing a witness."

The boy, Jillian thought. "Oh, good. Anything you can tell me?"

"Not over the phone. So, what's up?"

"Kate was at the bookstore earlier this afternoon. There was something that concerned her, but it may be nothing. Anyway, if you have a moment . . ."

"I'll drop by there," Rick said. "After I see you, it'll be time to knock off for supper."

"Great. We'll both be here."

Twenty minutes later, hot coffee in hand, Rick sat down with his sisters in the inn's office. They left the door to the lobby open so they could see if anyone came to the front desk wanting assistance.

"Okay," Rick said in low tones, "what was it that raised a red flag for you, Kate?"

"It was Eric Roofner. I was at the store, and he took a phone call I found a bit disturbing." She outlined for Rick everything she remembered about Eric's manner and what he'd said over the phone.

Rick pursed his lips. "Could it have been a woman he broke up with?"

"I don't think so. Well . . ."

"You said he told the person to leave him alone, and to quit calling him."

"True. He sounded . . ."

"Angry?" Jillian asked.

Kate shook her head. "More panicky."

Rick wagged a finger at her. "See now, that's important. What made you think he was panicking?"

"I guess his tone, like he was stage whispering. And then he glanced around like he wanted to make sure no one could hear him."

"Maybe he just didn't want his father to hear him taking a personal call on store time," Rick said.

"I don't think Carl is that strict."

"Did he see you when he looked around?"

"Yes. I was looking at the puzzle magazines for kids, thinking of Joel. I looked away, but he had this expression, like he'd been caught red-handed."

"Did he speak to you?"

Kate shook her head. "I waited until his dad came from the back room because I didn't want to face Eric at the counter. Carl rang me up, and Eric left the checkout area."

"Okay. Well, that sounds fairly innocuous to me." Rick raised his eyebrows in question at Jillian.

122

"It's not just that," Jillian said earnestly. "When I took food over for him and Carl Saturday evening, I went to their house—I told you what I heard through the door."

"Yes, you did."

"He was yelling. And once I was inside, Eric acted funny with his phone then too. Someone tried to call him, and he cut it off. He was really antsy. It happened again, and it made me think I should get out of there so he could take the call."

"Like maybe the woman he just broke up with?" Rick's face was a bit smug, a bit admit-I'm-right.

Jillian sighed. "Okay, I admit, Eric gives me an odd vibe. Maybe men don't feel it."

"Well, he definitely bickers with his father." Rick frowned. "It's certainly not enough to get a warrant for his phone."

"I want to see the store video again," Kate said.

Rick jerked his head. "Why?"

"I want to look at the shooter. Are you absolutely certain that guy isn't Eric Roofner?"

Shaking his head slowly, Rick said, "We've checked every aspect of his alibi. He definitely went to Clifton. Officers have talked to several people who can place him at the rally within twenty minutes of the shooting. It would have taken him longer than that to get to Clifton from the store."

Kate's shoulders sank, and she deflated with a huge sigh.

The front door opened, and she jumped up and headed toward the lobby. Before she reached the doorway between the rooms, she swung around and said, "I bet if you sat down with him for fifteen minutes, his phone would ring."

She shut the door behind her as she greeted a guest coming in from outside.

Jillian looked at her brother. "She may be right. Unless the caller finally took him seriously and decided to leave him alone."

Rick took a sip from his mug and sat there for a moment, his brow furrowed like a cornfield. "I'll talk to Eric again, but I'm going to let it sit a while, at least until tomorrow."

"Was the boy any help at all?" Jillian asked, prepared to be told to butt out.

Rick huffed out a breath. "Not really. I advised his parents to get him some counseling. He saw Stanley's feet after the shooting. I don't think he took a closer look at the body. Just ran out the back."

"Good for him. Still, it's traumatic for anyone, let alone a boy that age."

"Yeah. He hadn't told his folks anything, can you believe it?"

"Yes." Her long experience with teenagers made it very plausible to Jillian.

Rick drained his mug and stood. "Okay, I'm going home and spend the evening with my family."

"I'm glad. Give them all a big hug and tell them you love them. And remind the kids they can come to you with anything."

"Always." Rick's phone rang, and he pulled it out. "Excuse me. It's work."

"Sure." Jillian stepped out the door into the hallway. The guest was on the elevator, and the door closed on him.

"Hey," Kate called softly from the lobby door. "You guys done?"

"I think so, but Rick took a call." Jillian walked toward her. Just as she reached the corner where the lobby met the hall, Rick opened the office door and charged toward the exit.

"Gotta go. Carl Roofner had an accident. I'm headed for the hospital in Bucksport."

Chapter 10

As Rick dashed out the door, Kate turned to Jillian. "What can we do?"

"I don't know. Probably nothing."

Kate frowned. "He said Bucksport, right? If it was really serious, they'd have taken Carl to the medical center in Bangor."

"We can hope. But maybe they'd take him to Bucksport first, to stabilize him." Jillian turned toward the dining room door. "I hope it's not bad enough to make them tranfser him. I'm going down to the carriage house, and I'll fix us some supper. Maybe we should make more food for Eric."

Kate scowled at her sister. "He'll be at the hospital with his father."

"Right."

The front door opened and a man came in pulling a wheeled suitcase. "Hello." Kate moved into place behind the lobby desk.

Jillian made good her escape, going out through the dining room.

When she'd registered the walk-in guest and given him his key, the landline phone purled. Kate picked it up.

"Novel Inn."

"Kate? It's Rick. I'm at the hospital, and it

looks like Carl will be okay. I figured you two would want to know. They're keeping him overnight for observation."

"What happened?"

"He said when he locked up the store tonight and went out back to his car, another vehicle came tearing down the alley and knocked him down."

Kate caught her breath. "But he's all right?"

"Well, no, he's got a slight concussion and a lot of bruises. He managed to jump out of the way and only caught the fender. It threw him a few yards, and he hit his head on the dumpster."

"Ouch."

"Yeah. He's lucky nothing's broken."

"Is Eric there?" Kate asked.

"He followed the ambulance. Carl was alert enough to call him, and Eric called the ambulance and went right to the store. He was there when I got there."

"Did you catch whoever did it?"

Rick sighed. "Unfortunately, he was long gone when I arrived. Since it's dark and there's only a low-wattage bulb over their back door, Carl wasn't sure what color the truck was. But it was a Chevy pickup, so definitely not Eric's. He drives a Dodge."

"That's a relief."

"Yeah. Carl said he saw a Chevy logo bearing down on him as he jumped. Eric tried to tell

127

me it was an accident, but I'm not buying it."

"Why would he say that, when it was obviously a hit and run? Nobody goes zooming through an alley like that by accident."

"Beats me."

Kate twisted the phone cord. "This is awful, Rick. It can't be a coincidence."

"I know. Two people attacked at that store within a week. The state police are already working on Stanley's case."

"You didn't tell me that."

"It's standard procedure. I've got to call the detective in charge and tell him about this. Should have called him first, actually, but I figured you and Diana would be worried."

"All right, let's get off the phone. I'll fill Jillian in on this."

A few minutes later, Jillian appeared at the dining room door. "Supper's ready."

"I have an update from Rick," Kate said.

"Oh, I heard the phone ring on the extension in the carriage house. That was Rick?"

"Yes. Carl's going to be okay."

They sat down to eat together.

"I can give you a break when we're done," Jillian offered.

"I don't need one," Kate said. "You were on the desk all afternoon. I told you, I can stay until ten."

"Tell me everything Rick said."

Kate repeated the conversation as best as she could. "Now you tell me something—have you heard a peep out of Mr. Schuman?"

"Nope. Nothing all day. Well, Mindy picked up his trash."

"This is really weird." Kate stared at Jillian until she met her gaze. "I think we should check on him."

Jillian sighed. "I don't like to disturb someone with a sign on their door. He might be sleeping."

"You don't think he's sick, do you?"

"No, I don't."

Kate's lips stuck out like a pouting toddler's.

Jillian held up both hands. "Fine. I'll call his room. Or you can go up and tap on his door."

"I'll run up."

"All right, go." Jillian plopped down on the stool behind the desk.

Kate dashed to the elevator and rode it up to the third floor. *I could have made it faster by the stairs.* But then she'd be out of breath when she knocked on his door.

"Mr. Schuman?" She rapped softly on the door of the Rip Van Winkle Room. "Mr. Schuman, are you all right?"

A moment later, she heard movement inside. *At least he's alive.* To her surprise, after a few seconds, the door opened as far as the security chain would allow.

"Kate, right?"

"Yes. I'm sorry to disturb you. We wondered if you need anything."

"Nope, I'm all set."

"Can we bring you anything to eat, or—"

"I'm fine. I may come down for breakfast early. What time does it open?"

"We're usually in the kitchen by six, and we serve from then until ten."

"Okay, is it crowded early on?"

"No, it's usually pretty quiet until seven or so."

What she could see of his face, which included one eye, was quite handsome. He hadn't shaved for a few days, and she thought he might look good with a beard.

"Great. I'll plan to come haunt the dining room early."

She smiled. "Terrific. See you then."

The door closed and the lock clicked. Even so, Kate couldn't quit smiling all the way down the two flights of stairs.

As the sisters stocked the warming table for breakfast the next morning, Kate cast a baleful glance at two couples who entered the dining room. She'd been watching the door like a hawk, and now she seemed disappointed.

Jillian greeted the guests cheerfully and assured them there were plenty of fresh blueberry muffins. She followed Kate into the kitchen.

"What's the matter, Kate?"

"Nothing."

"Oh, come on. Something's bothering you."

Kate sighed and turned to face her. "Mr. Schuman said last night he'd be down early for breakfast, but I haven't seen a sign of him. And now other people are coming down." She leaned a little and peered into the dining room.

"Maybe he started to come down, and there were already people in there, so he decided to wait."

"Maybe." Kate scowled and opened the refrigerator. "Maybe I should check on him."

"And maybe you should leave that man alone."

Her sister didn't look happy, but Jillian left her to sulk and went to check on the coffee and hot water carafes. Their guests had given them stellar reviews for their breakfast service, and she didn't want that to change.

An hour later, the dining room had emptied and most of the guests had either checked out or left for the day. Jillian caught Kate while she was mopping up a minor spill where a family with toddlers had sat.

"Can you watch the desk for a while? I thought I'd run to Bucksport and visit Carl at the hospital."

"Are you sure he's still there?" Kate straightened with a dustpan full of muffin crumbs in one hand and the broom in the other.

"Yeah. I called Rick, and he says they're keeping him one more night."

"Okay. I'll work on the ads for next month."

"Good." Jillian smiled. "Thought I'd take him a few cookies."

"And pump him for information about the hit-and-run?"

"Well, our brother isn't exactly a fount of information."

Jillian made sure the dining room and kitchen were in order before setting out and arrived at the hospital carrying a plastic bag of cookies. On her way to see Carl, she spotted Eric pacing the far end of the hallway beyond the door to his father's room. He seemed immersed in a conversation, his cell pressed to his ear. Maybe he'd come into the room when he was done.

She was nearly to the door of Carl's room when Eric raised his voice.

"No! No, I will not meet you. My father's in the hospital, as if you didn't know. Why do you want to know that?"

He threw a glance over his shoulder. Jillian pretended she hadn't noticed him and hurried into the double occupancy room. A young man was drowsing in the bed nearest the door. The curtain between him and his roommate was pulled halfway, and Jillian walked past it to find Carl sitting nearly upright, browsing a *Time* magazine.

"Well, hi, Jillian." Despite the purple bruising

spreading over his right eye socket and cheek, his face brightened and he laid aside the magazine.

"Hello, Carl. I called the nurses' desk, and they told me you weren't going home today, so I brought you some cheer." She held up the bag of half a dozen homemade oatmeal-raisin cookies.

"Oh, you girls will spoil me."

"Well, if you don't want them," she said with mock affront, holding the bag back and over her shoulder.

"I do, I do!" Carl laughed.

She drew up a chair and sat down beside him, placing the bag of cookies on his tray table.

"I saw Eric in the hallway."

"Yes, he popped in a few minutes ago, but he's going back and run the store today."

"Isn't it time to be open?" Jillian glanced up at the clock on the wall opposite the bed.

"He said he put a sign on the door saying he'd open an hour late today."

"I see. Do you have anyone else who can help you out?"

"Not really. But I'm going home tomorrow, and I plan to be back in there the next day."

"You might need some rest." She eyed him critically. "I heard you're concussed."

Carl waved his hand. "I feel fine. A little woozy when I stand up, but really, I'll be fine."

"No headache?"

"Well, they're giving me something for it."

She nodded. "Some of those bruises look painful."

"They look worse than they feel."

Probably due to the medication, Jillian thought. He might be in for a surprise when he left the hospital and tried to resume his regular routine.

He squinted at her. "I really could have gone home this morning. I probably should have."

"Oh, I think you *should* do what the doctor tells you. Listen, I'm thinking that I could come in and help you for a few hours a day, your first few days back. Or Kate. I'm sure she'd be happy to help out too."

"Eric and I can handle it."

"Are you sure? Eric seems pretty busy."

"Well, I told him he's got to give up snow-mobiling and skiing for a week or two and do his part at the store."

As Jillian nodded, Eric strode in from the hallway.

"Gotta go, Dad. I have to make a stop before I go to the store."

Carl flicked a worried glance at the clock. "You will open by ten, won't you?"

"I'll be there. Just . . . take it easy." As he spoke, Eric looked at Jillian, and she had a feeling he appraised her the way he might a rather old and worn out Arctic Cat. "I'll come in tonight after I close, Pop. See you later." He walked to the door and peered out into the hall for a moment then left the room.

Carl closed his eyes. His face was gray and slack. He looked old.

Lord, help this family. Jillian hesitated then reached to touch his hand. "Carl, let us help you. We can fill in for the next couple of days. I mean it."

He let out a long breath and opened dull eyes. "Something's going on with him, Jillian."

"What do you mean?"

"He came in earlier, while I was asleep. But I woke up. He was sitting where you are, checking his phone messages." Carl pressed his lips tight together.

"You heard something that bothered you," Jillian said gently.

"Someone demanded a meeting. And just now, Eric said he had to make a stop. What if he's going to meet this person?"

Jillian thought about how that fit with what she'd heard in the hall. "Who was it? Do you know?"

"I didn't recognize the voice, but it's a man. He didn't give a name. Eric seemed to know who it was. And his face . . ."

"How did he look?" Jillian asked. "Was he angry?"

"No. He looked . . . scared."

Jillian didn't know what to say.

Carl shifted on the bed. "Maybe I'm imagining things, but I don't think so. When he saw that I was awake, Eric went out into the hall. And then you came in."

Jillian tried to remember the exact words she'd heard Eric say. "He told someone he *wouldn't* meet them." She eyed his face, hoping he'd take some relief from that.

Carl said nothing, staring toward the opposite wall.

"Maybe the stop he's making is something else entirely." She tried to make her voice sound normal. But if the errand was innocent, why didn't Eric tell his father what it was?

"Or he changed his mind and is going to meet him after all." Carl looked over at her. "Will you do me a favor?"

"Of course."

"Go by the store after you leave here— say, ten thirty or so? If it's not open, give me a call." He waved toward the phone on his bedside table. "I have my cell phone. Call that number."

A wave of dread swept over her. She wouldn't mind putting Carl's mind at ease. But what if Eric hadn't opened the store as he'd promised?

She gave Carl a forced smile. "I will. Now get some rest."

Leaving the hospital, she mulled over the odd

visit. Rick would say it was nothing. *None of your business, sis.*

With some misgiving, she got into her car and took out her phone.

Chapter 11

"I really like the poster. Can we frame it?" Kate said as they unloaded Jillian's haul from the import store.

"Yeah, I'm thinking in a gold frame. Maybe we can find something in the antique shop."

"Or the attic."

"Right you are." Jillian gazed down at the large picture she'd unrolled on the front desk. "It can be the focal point of the room."

"And this fabric will be beautiful for accents." Stroking the white cloth with red geometrics and shot with gold threads, Kate gave her sister a big smile. "I'm starting to warm to the idea of Phileas Fogg."

"I'm so glad. Do we want to do the whole room in an India theme, or—"

"No, I think there should be a suggestion at least of the Reform Club. The ominous ticking clock. You know."

Jillian nodded and rolled up the poster. "I'm glad I went to the import place. I almost didn't, but Rick assured me he would have somebody watch the Book Rack and let me know if Eric followed through."

Kate folded the fabric, along with some tasseled gold cords Jillian had bought. "I can help you with the throw pillows."

"Thanks. I didn't find exactly the right thing for the curtains. I might have to go to Bangor, to the big fabric outlet."

Jillian's cell rang and she answered it. Kate glanced at her own. It was a quarter to eleven. Jillian had been watching the time constantly while she related her visit to Carl, her concerns about Eric, her arrangement with Rick, and finally her shopping finds.

"Well, that's not perfect, but it's better than nothing. Thanks, Rick. I'll give Carl a buzz and let him know." Jillian closed her call and made a face. "Eric opened the store at ten twenty."

"Not ten o'clock," Kate said.

"No, but he's there now. I'd better tell Carl."

"And I've got a box lunch for two to make."

"Everything under control there?"

"Yes, but I told them it would be ready at eleven, so I'd better get moving."

"Wait, you didn't bother Mr. Schuman, did you?"

Kate scowled at her. "I most certainly did not."

"Okay, good." Jillian scooped up her purchases and hustled into the office, and Kate headed for the kitchen.

On Wednesday morning, Kate moseyed along Main Street and paused at Anne's Apparel to study the clothing in the front window. Jillian had insisted she take the morning off once the breakfast rush was over. The sun was out, and the snowbanks were settling and shrinking. Kate was glad to have some free time, especially on a pleasant day.

After a foray into Anne's, she came out with a new blouse and a pair of stud earrings. She checked her phone. It was still early, but a text from Jillian prodded her.

Did you check BR yet?

Kate sighed. Her sister's one stipulation was that she stop by the Book Rack. Carl Roofner had cut short his hospital stay, discharging himself last night, and planned to be back in the store today. Jillian wanted to check up on him. Kate had suggested she simply call the store, but no, Jillian didn't want to smother him. She insisted Kate could check by walking by and glancing inside to see who was at the counter.

She meandered toward the bookstore and slowed her steps as she approached the entrance. A display of cookbooks filled the window on the side. *Breakfast Delights.* Maybe she'd find some new muffin recipes in there, although she and Jillian had garnered enough to last a lifetime from their mom's recipe files and the internet.

Was that Carl's gray hair bobbing behind the window display? A few more steps put her in front of the glass doors. The Open sign faced out, and everything inside looked normal. A couple of customers were browsing the fiction section.

Resigned to completing her assignment to Jillian's satisfaction, Kate pushed the door open.

After straightening a pile of hardcover books, Carl looked up and smiled at her.

"Hello, Kate. Can I do anything for you today?"

"Just came in to browse, Mr. Roofner."

"It's Carl."

She nodded. "I guess my sister told you she wants to decorate one of the rooms at the inn with a Jules Verne theme."

His face brightened. "Yes, she did. She ordered a special copy of *Around the World in Eighty Days*."

"That's right." Kate's mind was spinning. Words spewed out before she had a chance to stop them. "I thought I'd surprise her and buy a few of Verne's other books to place in our little library at the inn."

"That's a great idea. We have a few in the classics section. Come, I'll show you."

She followed him midway down the center aisle and off to the left.

"There you go. *Twenty Thousand Leagues under the Sea*, and *Journey to the Center of the Earth*, besides *Around the World*. I've ordered a couple of copies of *Five Weeks in a Balloon*, since your sister mentioned it."

"Wonderful." Kate picked up one each of the first two paperbacks he'd mentioned. "I love the children's book Jillian brought home. It's going

141

to be a favorite with our young guests, I'm sure."

"That's good to hear. How's the redecorating going?"

"We're just getting started—still collecting things."

Carl glanced around the store. He looked worried, or maybe he just wanted to be sure no one was waiting for him at the counter.

Kate dropped her voice. "Carl, how are you? Is everything going okay?"

"As well as it could, I guess." He looked down at the floor and shook his head slightly. "I'm worried about Eric. I can't say too much . . ." Again he glanced around.

"Is he here today?"

"Oh, yes. He won't leave me alone in here, after what happened to Stanley. And he wanted to—" He broke off, looking at her with apprehension, his mouth slightly open.

"What is it?" Kate asked.

He let out a sigh so mournful Kate wanted to give him a hug, but she settled on just waiting with what she hoped was a sympathetic expression.

Carl darted a quick look over his shoulder. "He's out back, unpacking a shipment that came in yesterday afternoon. I don't know if I should . . ."

"If you should tell me something? Because my brother's a cop?"

142

"No, no. Rick's been wonderful. Such a helpful young man. I really appreciate our police department here in Skirmish Cove."

"They're good guys."

"Yes, they are." Carl straightened his shoulders. "All right, I heard Eric talking to someone on the phone. And when Jillian was at the hospital yesterday . . ." He recapped the scene from the hospital that Jillian had described the night before, stressing his concern about the mysterious caller.

"And you think the same person called him again?"

Carl winced. "I do, but that's not the worst of it. This morning . . ."

Kate sensed a change in his voice and she thought she saw a glint of fear in his eyes. She laid her hand on his arm. "What is it?" she whispered.

"He wanted to bring his gun to the store."

Kate peered toward the magazine section, where she'd stood Monday and overheard Eric's end of another disturbing phone exchange.

"Maybe he's worried the shooter will come back."

"Maybe. I don't know, but—" Carl broke off. "Excuse me, I have a customer."

He hurried toward the counter, where a woman was waiting with a book and a magazine in her hands and looking around expectantly.

Kate let out a long, slow breath. Apparently the woman needed further assistance. Carl left the counter and led her to the opposite side of the store. Kate tiptoed to the EMPLOYEES ONLY door at the back of the room. She pushed it open just a crack and heard talking. Eric was on the phone again, it seemed. He had quite a crush on that phone of his.

". . . All right, all right. I'll be there. But you're not going to change my mind. And if you follow through with it, you'll be sorry."

Kate held her breath and cast a glance around. Carl was taking the woman back toward the counter. The only other customers in the store were a woman with two toddlers in the children's nook and a man browsing the periodicals.

"Don't you *dare* come here," Eric said. "Yeah, I got it. Higgins Park, three o'clock."

Kate let the door close gently and moved hastily away, still clutching her two paperbacks. On impulse, she snatched another book off the nearest end cap and strode toward the counter.

"I think I'm all set, Carl."

He'd started to step from behind the counter but jerked his head up and resumed his place when she spoke.

"Did you find everything you wanted, Kate?"

"I think so." She looked down at her two Jules Verne books and a hardcover copy of *Getting Out from under Guilt*. Was that why she'd grabbed another book? Guilt? She raised her gaze to meet Carl's. "It's a gift," she said quickly.

"He has a good reputation."

It took her a second to realize he was talking about the author, a renowned psychologist.

"Right. That's what I hear too."

She forced herself not to cringe when the total showed on the cash register.

"You're out of your mind!" Jillian glared at her sister in disbelief. "I'm calling Rick."

"Fine." Kate turned away with a scowl and stomped out of the office.

". . . is unavailable. Leave a message after the tone."

Jillian sighed. At the tone, she blurted, "Rick, call me as soon as you can. It's urgent."

She sank down into her desk chair and closed her eyes. *Breathe, Jillian.* Kate wasn't really insane, but . . . She had to be crazy to want to go to this clandestine meeting Eric Roofner had set up. Foolhardy at the very least. What thirty-three-year-old woman in her right mind would even consider such a thing? And who would set up a meeting in an oceanside park in winter?

Lord, show me how to handle this. Kate can be impulsive, but she's not usually this reckless. Just . . . I don't know. Let Rick call me back, I guess. Thank You.

Half an hour later, she hadn't heard a word

from Rick. She couldn't concentrate on her plan for overhauling the Virginian Room. The desk phone rang, and she took a weekend reservation.

Finally, she reached for her cell once more. "Rick, it's Jillian. I know you're busy, and I'm sorry. *Please* call me."

She tossed the phone on the desk and sat back. Hearing footsteps, she rose and went to the hall door. Kate was coming in from the dining room, wearing a completely different outfit than the one she'd worn into town that morning—jeans and a dark sweatshirt.

When she saw Jillian in the doorway, she stopped walking. "Did you get lunch?"

"Not yet."

"It's almost one o'clock."

"I'll get a sandwich. You want something?" Jillian asked.

"I ate at the carriage house." No smile, no chit-chat. "What did Rick say?"

"He hasn't called."

They gazed at each other for a long moment.

"I thought I might call Diana," Jillian said at last. "Rick might have taken a day off. You know he put in a lot of hours last weekend."

"I could call her while you make yourself a sandwich."

"Okay." Jillian walked past her and into the inn's kitchen. For once, there was bacon left over from breakfast. She'd left a half-used packet of

146

premade salad in this fridge, too, so she fixed herself a BLT without the T.

As she carried it out to the dining room, her plate in one hand and a can of Diet Pepsi in the other, Kate came in.

"Diana says Rick had to go to Augusta today. She doesn't think he'll be back until suppertime."

"What for?"

"Business. Some training or other, and he was going to try to stop at the morgue and see if they'd finished the autopsy on Stanley."

Jillian scrunched up her face, less hungry than before. She plunked her plate and drink down on the nearest table. Kate came over and sat down across from her. She put both hands on the table and leaned toward Jillian.

"Look, if Rick won't be here in time . . ."

She wanted to go spy on Eric. Jillian took a big bite of her sandwich and gazed at Kate while she chewed.

Kate jerked restlessly but didn't back off. "Aren't you even curious?"

"Why would I be? What Eric does has nothing to do with Stanley's death."

A frown marred Kate's face. "How do we know?"

"Because Eric was in Clifton that day. The police have spoken to his witnesses."

"An iron-clad alibi." Kate sat back and heaved out a big breath.

"Why are you trying to make Eric guilty?" Jillian asked.

"Who else could it be?"

"Have the cops checked up on Stan's family?" She took another bite.

"What, his widow and two daughters? You're kidding, right?"

Jillian swallowed. "There's a brother too, and Jennifer has a grown-up son."

"Their brother's in California. You think he came here, shot his grandpa, and flew home?"

"Somebody did."

Kate drummed her fingers on the tabletop while Jillian continued eating her sandwich and washed it down with Pepsi.

"Okay." Kate sat forward. "You have a point. They should check out other people, and they probably are doing that. Stan's family and friends."

Jillian's heart sank. If they started looking closely at Stan's friends, that would include Zeb. That sweet octogenarian shouldn't be bothered with this. But, yes, they should at least talk to Bill Rutter, the fishing buddy.

"In the meantime," Kate said, "I think Eric is up to something. Could be drugs, could be girl trouble, could be some kind of crime. But it's not nothing. It's something he's trying to hide from his father."

Jillian couldn't dispute that. She tipped up

her soda can to give her a moment to think.

"All right." She set the can down with a plink. "Here's what we do in a situation like this. We call Craig Watkins."

Kate opened her mouth and closed it.

"You know we shouldn't go there without informing someone at the police station." The more she talked, the better Jillian liked what she was saying. Not to mention it might mean the chance to see Craig again. She and the sergeant had gone out a couple of times last summer, but then they'd both gotten busy. Craig had been away for several weeks, and the inn had experienced a big rush in the foliage season.

"We can't both go, anyway," Kate said.

"Well, I'm not letting you go alone. That would be crazy! I'll call the station." Craig would probably be on the desk today. Jillian stood and picked up her paper plate and can.

The front door opened.

"Maybe that's Rick," Kate said, but Jillian knew it wasn't.

"Probably one of the guests."

She headed for the lobby, tossing her lunch trash in the large garbage can as she passed it. A man in a parka, jeans, and work boots stood in front of the check-in desk with his hand poised to ring the bell. Taking quick stock, Jillian knew he wasn't one of their current guests.

"Hi. I'm Jillian. How may I help you?"

He turned toward her and ran an appraising gaze over her from head to toe then met her eyes.

"Hi. I'm looking for somebody. I hoped maybe you could help me find him."

Jillian steeled herself but kept the pleasant smile on her lips as she moved behind the desk. "Could you be more specific?"

"Yeah, I need to know if a certain person is staying here."

"I'm sorry. I can't give out information about our guests."

"I just need to know if he's here."

"And I can't tell you that."

"But I haven't even told you his name."

Here it comes. She tried to prepare herself, determined not to give away anything with her expression or her body language.

"His name's Michael Schuman."

Why wasn't she surprised? She applauded herself mentally for not batting an eyelash. "I still can't tell you."

His eyes narrowed. "You'd tell me if he wasn't here."

"No. I can't tell you either way."

He studied her for a moment then leaned on the desk. "Look, I need to tell him something. It's urgent."

"Maybe the police could assist you."

They stood staring at each other for a moment.

"Would you like me to call them?" Jillian

asked. "To help you find the person you need to see so urgently, I mean."

He straightened, pulling in a deep breath. "No, thank you." Without another word he left, shutting the door none too softly.

Chapter 12

Jillian stood still, her heart hammering.

"What was that all about?" Kate emerged from the kitchen, her hands on her hips.

"Tell you in a minute." Jillian raced to the window just in time to see the man get into the back seat of a four-door sedan. She ducked sideways and gazed across the room at Kate. "Look out that window and tell me if the green car is still out there. To the left of the steps."

Kate went cautiously to the farther sidelight by the door and peered out. "It's sitting there. Hey, isn't that Chet Putnam's car?"

"Yeah. He drives for Uber. Get away from the window."

Walking backward, Kate asked, "What did that man want?"

Jillian faced her. "He said he needs to find Michael Schuman on an urgent matter."

Kate's jaw dropped. "And you said you couldn't tell him if Mr. Schuman's staying here, right?"

"Absolutely. We have a strict policy. You know that."

"Good for you. I'm not sure I could have held him off without giving things away." Kate crept to the door and took another peek out the sidelight. "Chet's backing up."

152

Jillian darted a glance around the fold of curtain at the other window. "Okay, he's going."

"Heading toward town." Kate faced her. "We need to tell Mr. Schuman."

"Yes, but I couldn't rush right up to his room with that guy sitting a few feet away. Schuman's room is on the front. If he went to his window, they might see him."

"Well, they're gone now." Kate stepped toward her. "We need to tell Mr. Schuman right away. Or do you want to call his room?"

"I think I should tell him in person."

"We can both go."

Jillian shook her head. "I don't want to leave the desk unattended. You stay here in case that man comes back."

Kate's expression clouded. "We've got the camera out front. We could show the video to . . . to the guest."

"Hmm. Only if we have to. I mean, it's probably nothing to worry about, right?" Jillian sought Kate's face for reassurance, but clearly her sister wasn't buying it.

"You could be right," Kate said. "Or not. Did he give a name?"

"No. I should have asked."

"Well, go ahead. If he comes back and gets pushy, I'm calling 911."

"Right." Jillian started out the door and turned back. "Kate, do you realize what this means?

Schuman isn't quarantining himself or working on his blockbuster novel. He's hiding from someone."

Kate stared at her, apparently speechless for once.

Jillian hurried to the elevator and rode it to the third floor, fumbling for words. The main thing was not to upset a guest. Well, no, the main thing was his safety. That was what she'd lead with.

The Do Not Disturb sign still hung on the door handle. She knocked gingerly.

After a moment of silence, she knocked again, louder. "Mr. Schuman? It's Jillian Tunney. I need to speak to you."

Footsteps sounded, and then the latch on the door was thrown. A six-inch gap opened.

"Hi," Jillian said. "I'm sorry to bother you, but someone came here looking for you."

His face froze. "Looking for *me?*"

"He asked for you by name. We have a strict privacy policy, and I told him we couldn't give out any information about our guests." She glanced around, but the third-floor hall was empty at the moment. "He tried to infer something from that—he said you must be here, or I'd tell him you weren't."

"What did you say?"

"I said that wasn't so, that we don't reveal personal information and suggested the police could assist him."

A slow smile crossed his face, and he opened the door a little wider. "Thank you. I guess that's all you could do, short of lying."

"We won't lie about it."

"So, if he comes back with a cop, you'll tell him?"

She frowned, thinking that over. "I think I'd ask the officer to step into my office and repeat our policy. If the police insisted on knowing, I'd tell them you were here, but I'd also request that they not tell that man. Do you think it's someone you know?"

"Probably."

Her mind whirred, suggesting wild theories on why he would hide out here. "Is there anything we should know, Mr. Schuman? For your safety, I mean. And that of our other guests."

"No. I assure you, I'm not doing anything illegal. I just don't want to talk to him right now."

"He said it was urgent."

"I'm sure he did."

She nodded slowly. "Is there anything we can do for you?"

He sighed and glanced over his shoulder. "I was planning on going out to find a laundromat this afternoon, but if he's cruising around town looking for me . . ."

"Kate and I can do your laundry."

He hesitated. "Would ten dollars cover it?"

"Sure." She'd nearly said five was enough but

caught herself. With their time, the electricity, soap, and water . . . Maybe she should have said twenty.

"Uh, can I give you my laundry bag?"

"Of course. I'll take it now if it's ready."

He walked to the closet and returned with one of the plastic bags they left in each room. "I didn't realize you could do laundry here."

"We don't usually, but I'll take it down to our private quarters at the carriage house."

"Thanks." He reached for his wallet.

"I can just add it to your bill if you want."

"Great."

"Anything else you'd like?"

"I admit, I'm running a little short on protein bars."

"We can get you some. Hey, why don't you let us bring you up a dinner tray tonight?"

"Room service?"

Jillian shrugged. "It's not our usual service, but we do make exceptions."

"That would be nice. Thank you."

"Any allergies or other restrictions?"

"No, I'll eat just about anything."

She smiled. "We'll bring you something around six. And if that man turns up again, either Kate or I will call your room phone."

"Sounds good, Ju—was it Judy?"

"Jillian. And my sister is Kate." She gave him a bright smile.

"And I'm Mike, but that's not for publication."

She nodded, still smiling. It was much better than calling him the DND guy or the mystery guest. "Talk to you later." She hefted the laundry bag and walked briskly to the elevator, resisting the impulse to look back. She could see why Kate was attracted to him.

When she got to the lobby, Kate jumped up.

"What'd he say?"

"He said it's probably someone he knows. In fact, I think he knows exactly who it was, but he doesn't want to talk to him. We keep on refusing to give any information unless that guy brings a cop. With a warrant."

"A warrant?" Kate's eyebrows drew together.

"He didn't say that. I did. If anyone asks—anyone—we won't deny or confirm that Mr. Schuman is staying here." She held up the plastic bag. "But we will do his laundry, and we'll take him dinner tonight—for both of which we'll be paid."

Kate grinned. "All right! What do you think is the deal?"

"No idea. But if that man shows his face here again, be cagey. If we make the tiniest slip, he'll assume we've been talking to Mike."

"Mike?"

Jillian gulped and took a quick look into the hallway to be sure they couldn't be overheard. "Mum's the word. Now, do you want to do the laundry, or should I?"

157

"That depends." Kate glanced at the clock. "Did you call Craig about the meeting in the park?"

Jillian caught her breath. "I forgot."

"It's almost time," Kate whispered. "We'd better go. If we leave right now, we can still make it."

"No. We need to call Craig."

"You do it. I'll put you-know-who's laundry in the washer."

"Put it in the storage room for now. I was going to wash it at the carriage house, in case anyone came in. We wouldn't want Mr. Arrogant to see us folding our guest's clothes, would we?"

"Good thinking."

"But we can't both leave at once," Jillian insisted. "What if he comes back?"

Kate smiled. "Relax. Don's on his way. I told him it was an emergency and that under no circumstances is he to reveal whether any person is or is not a guest here."

"You called Don while I was upstairs?"

"Yes." Kate's gaze slid away. "But I assumed you'd called Craig."

"I'll do it now. You go stash the laundry."

As Kate hurried off, Jillian pulled out her cell and hit the nonemergency number for the police station. To her relief, a warm, familiar voice said, "Skirmish Cove Police Department, Sergeant Watkins speaking."

"Craig! It's Jillian. We have a bizarre situation. You're aware of what's been going on at Carl Roofner's store."

"I am."

"Well, Kate and I believe his son Eric is going to meet an unsavory character at three o'clock in Higgins Park. Kate overheard him setting up the meeting. We're heading there now."

"What? Jillian—why are you going there?"

"Because it's two forty, we're closer than you are, and we didn't have a chance to call you earlier. Someone needs to find out who Eric is meeting."

"No, wait. Jill, don't go. I'll send a man—"

"Rick's in Augusta, and you're tied to the desk. We're going now. If one of your other officers gets there in time, we'll stand down."

Kate entered the lobby and dangled her keys in Jillian's face.

" 'Bye, Craig." Jillian hit *end* before he could say anything else.

"My Jeep's out front." Kate was already half-way out the door.

Jillian grabbed her down parka and ran after her.

Don drove in as Kate backed out of her parking space. Jillian ran her window down, and Don stopped his pickup beside the Jeep.

"Hey," Jillian said. "We should be back in an hour."

"What's up?"

"No time to explain," she said. "Just do not, repeat, do *not* give out any guest information, either over the phone or in person."

"Got it. Is your brother aware?"

"No, but Sgt. Watkins is." She hesitated. Craig knew where she and Kate were going, but not about the Schuman situation. Further explanations would put their timely arrival in jeopardy. She smiled. " 'Bye, Don."

She rolled up the window and scowled as Kate drove out onto the street and headed toward the park. If they got to the meeting place with time left over, she'd give Don a buzz. Or not.

"What's the matter?" Kate asked.

"Nothing. Well, not nothing. You know."

"Yeah, everything." Kate's face quirked. "I don't know what else we could do."

"I told Craig that if one of his men shows up, we'll keep out of it."

"What did you do that for?"

"Because this person Eric's meeting could be dangerous. Remember, you said Carl mentioned a gun."

Kate sighed and flipped her turn signal. The park ran down to the shore and offered a boat landing and space for beachcombing at low tide. The view of the bay from here always took Jillian's breath away.

"Where do you think they'll meet?" Kate asked.

"I don't know. Someplace where they won't be noticed right away."

No one was using the boat ramp today. It was too cold, Jillian surmised. Who would want to go out on the bay in this frigid weather?

"Not here." Jillian looked around. "Maybe over there, near the picnic tables." Tall pines towered over the area, where half a dozen tables with firepits nestled in the shade.

Kate pulled into a row of parking spaces where four other cars sat. "Shall we get a table and pretend we're having a late lunch?"

"A very late lunch." Jillian got out of the Jeep and scanned the other vehicles. Two had out-of-state license plates. "I'm surprised anyone would come here now. It's freezing."

"Maybe they're a few Winter Carnival hold-overs? Come on." Kate strode toward the picnic tables.

Jillian followed, swiveling her head to search beneath trees and beside rocks. The snow had mostly melted on warmer days, and no storms had blown through for at least a week. The ridges left by the truck plowing the parking area had shrunk, and under the big trees, hardly any snow remained.

When she reached the nearest table, Kate slid onto one end of the bench and sat facing the parking lot. Jillian sat on the opposite side without lifting her legs over the plank bench, so she could get out quickly if she wanted to.

"Do you think we're too conspicuous?" Kate asked.

"Probably. Oh, and I told Mr. Schuman we'd bring him dinner at six. Shouldn't be too much trouble, but we need to get home in time." Jillian took out her phone.

"Who are you calling?"

"Craig."

"You already told him we were coming here."

"Okay, but what about Don? It might be good for someone else to know where we are."

"We need to just stay quiet and watch who comes to the park."

Jillian sighed and put the phone in her pocket. "We can't see the whole park, you know."

"True, but that's all Eric said, was Higgins Park. If they'd had some more specific place—"

"Then Eric might not have repeated it."

"Give them time." Kate looked toward the parking lot, where an SUV was pulling in. Two young women got out and ran laughing toward the beach.

Jillian took her phone out again and looked at the time. "It's two after three." She put it away and hugged herself. "I didn't wear a hat. My ears will freeze."

"There's an extra one in the back seat of the Jeep."

Jillian thought about that for a minute. Kate,

with a forest green knit hat pulled down over her ears, was obviously not going to budge.

"Who would choose this for a secret meeting at the end of January?"

Kate rolled her eyes. "It's perfect. Hardly anyone would come here, so hardly anyone would see them. Public, but sparsely populated."

"Oh, brother. I'm getting the hat."

Kate held out her key ring, and Jillian took it. She got up and trudged toward the parking lot. The two vehicles with Maine plates that had been there when they arrived sat undisturbed. She was pretty sure Eric drove a pickup. He must, since he hauled his snowmobile trailer all over the place. She couldn't remember seeing it at Carl's house, though. But it could have been in the garage.

And their meeting might not even be today. What if the man had said tomorrow, or some other day, and Eric simply hadn't repeated that part?

As she pushed the button that unlocked the doors, a small maroon car pulled in. Jillian tried not to look at it too blatantly. It came to rest a few parking slots down from the Jeep. She turned her gaze into the dim interior, looking for Kate's extra hat.

"Great. That's inconspicuous." She pulled out a bright pink stocking cap and pulled it on with a sigh. At least her ears wouldn't fall off from frostbite. When she straightened and closed

163

the door, she flicked a glance along the row of vehicles. A man who was probably a bit younger than her had left the new car and was meandering toward the beach, looking around as he went.

She hurried her steps toward their picnic table, but she couldn't see Kate. Where had her sister gone?

As she rushed past the trunk of a car with a Pennsylvania plate, Kate popped up in front of her.

"Did you see him?" she stage whispered.

"Of course I did. What are you doing?"

"Getting ready to follow him."

Jillian hovered between falling in with her sister's reckless whims and flat-out refusing to cooperate. "Eric could see us if we follow this guy down to the beach."

"He may already be down there waiting."

Jillian sighed. "And I have a hot pink head now."

Eyeing the cap critically, Kate started to smile. "Sorry. If I'd known what we were going to do in advance, I'd have stocked camouflage for both of us."

A man came trudging up from the boat landing with a kayak on his shoulder.

"Can't believe he went out on the water in a kayak today," Kate muttered.

"Well, at least he came back safe." *Which is more than we can guarantee for ourselves.* Jillian suddenly wondered if Kayak Man could be Eric's contact. Maybe the kayak was his camouflage. She snapped a picture as he hefted the light craft into the back of an SUV.

"Hey," Kate whispered, "take pics of all the cars here."

Sometimes Kate had good ideas. Jillian whipped her phone out and took a picture of the car driven by the man who had just arrived. As the kayaker drove out, she snapped another shot of his vehicle, making sure it would show the license plate. Then she quickly clicked behind each car in the lot. She paused long enough to make sure the tag numbers were legible in the photos, then hurried to catch up with Kate.

They followed the path down toward the water. The muddy trail was frozen solid today.

When they reached the tide flat, Kate led her toward a jumble of boulders. Behind the biggest one, Kate pointed. "He's over there, near the slope."

"Okay. Tide's going out, so we should be all right here." Jillian's shoes sank half an inch or so in the wet sand. She wished she'd stopped for boots.

"Where's Eric?" Kate poked her head over the top of their boulder.

"We don't know he's the one Eric said he'd meet."

Kate scowled at her. "Be logical. That guy is obviously waiting for someone."

They stood there shivering for another five minutes.

"I'm cold," Jillian said.

Kate took another peek. "He's still there, but there's no sign of Eric. What if we go closer and pretend we're collecting shells or something? We could speak to him—you know, just a friendly 'Hi, how's it going?' We'd get a good look at him that way."

"Bad idea."

"Why?"

"He'd remember us, for one thing."

"So?" Kate scowled at her. "Come on, Jilly, we have to do *something*."

"What if he's not Eric's guy?"

"Then what's he waiting there for?"

Jillian huffed out a breath. "I have no idea, but I'm not going to stay out here and freeze to death waiting for—"

"He's moving." Kate scrunched down beside her. "He's heading for the path."

"Ha. He's giving up, and so should we."

"We can't just let him leave."

"Why not?"

"Come on, let's jog. We can pass him and say hi."

Jillian pulled her phone out in resignation. "You go. I'll take pictures. Maybe he'll turn around and I can get one of his face."

Kate was already off, trotting over the wet sand

in the stranger's wake. Jillian hurried to focus. The stranger was already too far away for a good shot. She clicked one of Kate's back and, beyond her, the stranger walking up the path to the parking lot. He reached the head of the path before Kate did, and she hung back.

Jillian hastened her steps and caught up with her sister at the top of the path.

"He's leaving," Kate said. "He was too quick for me."

"It's okay."

As their target drove out and headed up the coast road, Craig drove in from the opposite direction.

"Sorry it took me so long—I had to get Officer Hall in to cover the desk. What's up?"

"There was a man here, waiting down on the beach," Kate said. "We sort of hid and waited too, but Eric Roofner never showed, and now the other guy has left."

"We're not even positive he was the person Eric said he'd meet." Jillian gazed earnestly at Craig, hoping he'd decipher her unspoken plea for forgiveness.

"And now he's gone," Kate added mournfully, turning to look up the road where the car had disappeared.

"And you have no idea who he was." Craig looked at Jillian.

"No, but I . . ."

"What?"

"I sort of took a picture of his license plate. Of all the plates in the lot, actually, in case he wasn't the one meeting Eric. Is that okay?"

Craig smiled. "Of course. Can you send it to me now?"

"Sure." Within seconds, she'd sent it to his phone, along with the one of the stranger's tiny figure, seen over Jogging Kate's shoulder.

"All right, this should be helpful. I'll look into it. Meanwhile, you two look as if you should go home and get something hot to drink."

"Aren't you going to lecture us?" Kate asked.

Jillian couldn't tell whether he was grimacing or trying not to laugh.

"I have a feeling it wouldn't do any good, but okay. You ladies should not put yourselves in potentially dangerous situations."

"Wow, compared to Rick, you're Mr. Nice Guy," Kate said.

Jillian just gave him a sober nod.

He walked with them to Kate's Jeep and opened the passenger door for Jillian.

"I'm sorry we dragged you out for nothing," she said.

"It's okay. It was nice to see you," he murmured.

"Same here."

Oh, yeah. Craig's smile beat the DND guy's any day.

"How about if I call you later?"

"I'd like that." She climbed into the Jeep and waved to him through the window.

At the park's entry, Kate stopped to wait for a passing truck. Jillian gazed at it listlessly then stiffened.

"Hey! Isn't that Eric?"

Kate had started to pull forward but slammed on the brake. "Craig's behind us. Tell him."

Jillian jumped out and ran to the squad car behind them. Craig rolled down his window.

"That was Eric Roofner. He just drove by in a black pickup, headed toward town."

"Are you sure?"

"Ninety percent. No, ninety-five."

Craig gazed down the road, but the truck was long gone. "Okay, there is another entrance to the park farther up, but there's not much there. The path down to the beach is steeper, and there are only a couple of picnic tables. I can't think of anything else."

"Fewer people," Jillian said.

"That's probably why they chose it."

She met his gaze, her mind staggering. "Unless the guy we followed was our target, and he and Eric missed each other."

"I'll check the other parking area. But if he saw my car here, it might have spooked him. Whatever happens, I'll look into the pictures you gave me."

"I guess that's all you can do." She plodded back to the Jeep with the oppressive feeling she and Kate had somehow dropped the ball this time.

Chapter 13

At home, Kate dropped Jillian off in front of the inn and drove her Jeep around the building toward the carriage house. Don sat at the front desk, chatting with one of the guests.

"Oh, hi, Jillian," he said as she entered. "Ms. Carmichael was just saying she'd seen some colorful flags flying at the next house. I told her that's probably your neighbor."

"Yes, he's a retired naval officer. He flies signal flags to let us know he's all right." Jillian caught Don's eye, which took a few seconds, as he seemed more interested in eyeing Ms. Carmichael. "Everything calm here, Don?"

"Quiet as the town cemetery."

"Good. If you don't mind, I'll step out on the porch and take a quick look at Zeb's signal."

She went out the way she came in and followed the wrap-around porch to the best vantage point. Enough of Zeb's flagpole showed over the treetops for her to see his alphabet signals. Each day he posted an "all clear," a summons for Jillian, or some other message.

Today the flags read, from top to bottom, YZJ—his signal for her to visit him. How long had that message been flying? She was sure she'd seen his usual "all clear" that morning when she walked from the carriage house to the inn, but that was ten hours ago.

Kate came out of their garage below, and Jillian waved to her then started toward her. They met near the head of the path leading toward Zeb's little house.

"Zeb's signaling me. I need to run over there. Can you relieve Don?"

"Sure. I hope he's okay."

They both knew that if Zeb was seriously ill, he wouldn't be able to go outside and run the flags up the pole. He did have a phone, so this probably was not an emergency. Even so, her father's old friend didn't use the system just to get attention. Jillian took his signals seriously.

The footbridge over the stream was a little slippery. Jillian slipped on the ice but grabbed the handrail. Had her dad worried about Zeb as he grew older? Maybe that was why he built this bridge. Going around by the road to reach Zeb's house would have taken a lot longer.

Across the bay, the sun sank low, strewing bands of color across the sky. She should have paused long enough for those neglected boots and a flashlight.

Zeb opened the door to her knock with a big smile. "Well, thought maybe you didn't see it."

"Sorry, Zeb." Jillian kissed his cheek and walked inside so he could shut the door. "I was out this afternoon, and I didn't see it until we came back just now."

"We?"

"Kate and I."

His white eyebrows shot up. "You both left the inn together?"

"Don't worry. Don Reece covered for us."

"Must have been important." Zeb leaned toward her. "Anything to do with Stanley's murder?"

"No—well, I don't think so."

"Have a seat?"

She recognized longing in his eyes, so she smiled. "Sure, for a little while."

Zeb's small house on the bluff was as tidy as a ship captain's cabin, as it should be. She sat down in one of the two armchairs situated near the fieldstone fireplace, wishing she'd brought him a treat. A cheery fire crackled, and she held out her hands to it.

"I've been thinking a lot about Stan." Zeb's wrinkled face was sober now.

"Lots of memories?"

"Plenty. We had some good times."

Jillian nodded, sensing there was more to come.

Zeb pulled in a deep breath. "One thing that came to mind . . . Stan had a feud with Richard Hale."

The name wasn't familiar. "I don't think I know him."

"Oh, he's gone now. Died a decade or more

ago. But he and Stan used to fight. Every time they met up, they'd go at each other."

"Really? Fistfights?"

Zeb chuckled. "No, but with words, you know. Insults, jabs."

"What started it?" Jillian asked.

"I don't know, but they'd been at it for years." He sighed and met her gaze. "If Richard was still alive, I'd say he probably had it in for Stan. But Richard's beyond that now."

"Maybe someone else agreed with Richard. If you knew what the fight was about . . ."

"I had an inkling it might have been a lady."

Jillian sat a little straighter and eyed him closely. "A lady? Stan was married to Anita."

"Not always. He never told me so, but he always bristled when Richard looked at Anita."

"You mean . . ."

"I thought maybe, when they were younger, they might have, you know, fancied the same girl."

She thought about that for a moment. "I suppose I could ask Anita about it, but . . ."

He waved a hand. "Naw, don't stir it up. I was just thinking, and that's what came out."

"Was this Richard married?"

"Yes, he found someone later in life. He must have been forty when he tied the knot with Adele Penney. They were together until he died."

"But you don't think there's any connection between them and Stan's death?"

"No. Couldn't be, could there?"

"I wouldn't know."

"No, no. Of course you wouldn't. I'm sorry I brought it up."

"Don't be."

"Has anything else come out about it? Has your brother told you anything?"

"Not much. There was a young boy in the bookstore when it happened. He says he didn't see the man who fired the shot, but of course, he heard it. He was petrified, and he ran out through the back room, out the back door into the alley, and then home."

"Good for him."

"Yes. It would have been helpful if he'd seen something, though."

"Mmm." Zeb sat frowning at the fire. "They can't set the funeral yet, you know."

"I hadn't heard anything. I suppose the coroner hasn't released the body."

"Not yet."

Jillian hesitated. "Kate's and my outing today . . . We'd heard Eric Roofner say he was meeting someone this afternoon, and we went to see if we could find out anything. But Eric never came to talk to the man we were watching." She hesitated and decided not to spill everything.

"Did you recognize this other person?"

"No. He waited on the beach for a while and then left."

175

"What did he look like?"

"I'd say mid-thirties—about Eric's age or a little older. We didn't get close, and he was all bundled up in winter gear, but he looked average height. He was wearing a black cap, but I think his hair was brown. That's about all I could see."

"No beard or glasses, or anything like that?"

"Nope."

Zeb sighed. "Guess you can't do much."

"We told Sgt. Watkins."

Zeb cocked his head to one side. "Not Rick?"

"He went to Augusta today."

"I see. What did Watkins say?"

"He'll check it out."

"Guess that's all you could do then."

"I took a picture of his car," Jillian said.

"You took a camera with you?"

She smiled. "On my phone."

"Oh, that's right. Most of those new ones have cameras, I guess."

"Yeah, they do. Well, I guess I'd better get back to the inn." She rose, wondering if she was missing something.

"I have to go to the eye doc tomorrow," Zeb said.

"Oh? Regular checkup?"

"Yes, but . . . I think my eyes are worse. He said I might have to have surgery sometime, and that time may be coming."

So this was what really was on Zeb's mind. She sat down again. "Your cataracts."

He'd complained since she and Kate moved in last spring that he couldn't focus his brass spyglass as well as he used to, and that he didn't trust himself to drive anymore.

"I can take you to the doctor appointment," she said.

"It's in Bangor."

She did some quick calculations. "What time?"

"One in the afternoon. I always ask for the first afternoon appointment, for two reasons."

"What are they?" she asked with a smile.

"One, I don't have to get up early and rush around to get there in the morning, and two, since it's right after the doctor's lunch, you don't have to wait so long to be seen."

"Hmm. Sounds like good reasoning to me. Kate or I will pick you up . . . is noon early enough?" She could tell by his expression that he thought it wasn't. "Eleven forty-five."

He nodded then. "Guess I should have mentioned it sooner. I'm sorry."

"No, it's all right."

"Well, I was hoping Stan would take me when I first scheduled it. Then, with him gone, I asked Lonnie Pruitt, but he's busy tomorrow."

Jillian laid a hand over his. "It's all right, Zeb. Don't ever hesitate to call on us when you need help."

"I hope, if I get the surgery, I'll be able to drive again."

"I hope so too, but you have friends. Let us help you when you need it."

Jillian was just stepping onto the inn's side porch when her phone rang.

"Hey, it's Rick. Everything okay?"

"Yes, Sgt. Watkins handled things."

"You called me twice. What happened?"

"Nothing much, as it turned out. Craig can fill you in."

"Okay, I'm going to stop in at the station before I go home."

"Talk to you later," Jillian said. She hit *end,* but the phone rang again before she could put it back in her pocket. She gazed down at the screen. *Craig W.* "Hello?"

"Hi, Jillian. Just thought I'd update you."

"Thanks. By the way, you'll have to update Rick too. He just called me, and he'll be at the station soon."

"Good. I didn't find Roofner or anyone else at the other entrance to Higgins Park, but I, uh, found out who owned the car you saw in the parking lot."

"Am I allowed to know who?"

"Probably not." She caught a chuckle in his voice. "But he's not a resident of Skirmish Cove. I think we'll contact the State Police on this one. They can talk to him and ask what he was doing

178

at the park today. It may not be related to the murder, but then again, it might be."

"Sure. I understand."

"You and Kate be careful, okay?"

"I guess that was foolish of us, to go there on our own like that."

"Yeah. It could have ended badly. And it could be you were spotted. Eric may have driven by and stayed away from his contact because of it."

"I didn't think of that."

"More likely he noticed the squad car. Best to let us handle it, though."

She swallowed hard. "Right. Say, could you compare the picture I sent you with the video Rick has of the shooter at the Book Rack?"

"Yes, we'll look at them."

"I know neither one is clear, but if the body type is totally different, or something like that . . ."

"Right. On another note, are you busy Friday night?"

Jillian's pulse ramped up. "What did you have in mind?"

"Nothing too strenuous. Dinner and some down time together?"

"I'd like that. The inn's pretty well booked this weekend, or I'd invite you for an evening of peace and quiet in our library."

"There's a puzzle night at Patti's Pizza."

"Oh, I've heard of that, but I haven't ever been. Is it a trivia contest?"

"No, it's not that loud. When you order, you get some puzzle sheets to solve and you can work on it while you eat. There's no prize or anything, just some minor glory—every Friday they post last week's winners."

"Sounds like fun, and about my speed competitively."

"We could ask some friends along to help us if you want."

Jillian had a mental flash of Kate yelling and whooping as she revealed an answer. "Maybe another time. I'm with you about the quiet time for now."

"Great. I think I need that. And it will give us a chance to talk. We haven't done much of that lately."

"Do you want to meet there?"

"No," Craig said. "I'd like to pick you up."

"Okay. Strictly casual?"

"Very."

She had walked in through the side door and the storage room as she talked. When she and Craig signed off, she was in the kitchen. Kate stood at the counter, stocking a basket with items from the refrigerator.

"Hey. I'm going to take some of this stuff down to our kitchen so it doesn't go to waste. What do you want for supper?"

"Is there sandwich stuff?"

"Plenty," Kate said. "And we've got salad veggies at our place."

"Let's do that. Or I can go fix it and bring you a tray, if you want to stay on the desk."

"I'll do it. Don's gone until ten, so one of us needs to be here. How's Zeb?"

"He's all right. I promised to take him to the eye doctor tomorrow in Bangor."

Kate nodded and closed the refrigerator door. "That's doable. I'll sit tight while you're gone."

"Well, don't forget I told Mr. Schuman we'd bring him a dinner tray tonight."

"Oh, that's right." Kate looked up at the ceiling. "Okay, I got it. You stay here."

Jillian positioned herself in the office with the lobby door open while Kate went to fix their meal. A few guests went out for the evening, and a couple came in after a long day of shopping and sightseeing.

A few minutes before six o'clock the desk phone rang, and she picked it up. "Novel Inn. This is Jillian."

"Jillian, I'm so glad I got you. This is Val Pressey, from church."

"Hi, Mrs. Pressey."

"I'm head of the social committee this year, and I wondered if you and Kate would be able to do a meal for the Chappells. Anita's daughter is here, but we're trying to supply a meal a day until the funeral."

"Oh, of course."

"Great. Now, let me see, Sheila's taking them a chicken meal tonight, so if you could do something different tomorrow evening."

Jillian clenched her teeth. Kate would have to cook while she was in Bangor with Zeb. Or she could fix something tonight. She looked at the clock.

". . . and Anita's diabetic, so they don't want sweets. Although, if the other daughter and the grandchildren come in, that may change. Now, what do you think you'll fix, so I can add it to the list and we can avoid duplicating?"

"Has anyone done tacos?"

"Hmm, let's see . . . You know, Jillian, your mother used to make the most fabulous cabbage rolls."

"Oh, well, I think we have her recipe." Jillian had never made the dish herself, but how hard could it be? "Let me check with Kate. If we can't do those, we'll come up with another beef dish."

"All right, dear. Thank you."

Jillian hung up wondering how much time the cabbage roll recipe would require. Maybe she could cook the ground beef tonight and start some yeast roll dough, and then Kate could put it all together tomorrow afternoon.

She began a list of ingredients to check on and

hoped this commitment didn't involve a grocery store run.

Kate came in through the dining room carrying a tray with a bowl of salad, a sandwich of deli cuts, and a big glass of iced tea.

Jillian gave her a tentative smile. "Thanks. We're now on the list to take a meal to Mrs. Chappell tomorrow."

"Okay."

"Remember, I have to take Zeb to Bangor."

"Oh, right." Kate frowned a little as she set down the tray. "Do you want this here or in the dining room?"

"Might as well eat here." Jillian pulled the dishes off the tray onto the desktop. "We need to do a beef dish, and no sweets. Anita's diabetic."

"Is it just for her?" Kate asked.

"No, one of the daughters is there. I'm not sure which one, or if she brought any grandchildren along. Although Mrs. Pressey said the other daughter might arrive . . ."

"So, dinner for at least four, then?"

"Probably a good idea."

"Let's call her and find out for sure."

Jillian started to reach for the phone and paused. "Hey, do we have Mom's cabbage roll recipe?"

"I think so, yeah."

"Val mentioned it, and how good it was. I sort of felt like she hoped we'd make that."

"I've never made it before."

"Me either. We'd need a cabbage for sure. I don't know what else."

"I'll snoop around for the recipe after I take Mr. You-Know-Who his supper."

"Okay. And I thought I'd start some yeast roll dough tonight." Jillian picked up the phone.

A few minutes later, she heard the elevator open as she hung up. Kate walked in.

"Everything okay with him?" Jillian asked.

"Yes, he was very grateful. I think he's been living on protein bars."

"Doesn't surprise me. Anita said her other daughter Amelia's coming tomorrow afternoon from Skowhegan and bringing her three kids. She says it would be great to have a meal all prepared, but not to fuss. Something simple that the kids will like."

"So, nix the cabbage rolls?"

"I think so. She mentioned macaroni and cheese."

"How about American chop suey?"

"Sure. Mrs. Pressey will be happy if we give them something with beef in it."

"And maybe we should make cookies instead of yeast rolls. Anita might not want dessert, but I'll bet the kids will."

Jillian rocked her head back and forth. "Okay, and finger vegetables?"

"Sounds like a good kid meal to me. Now, eat." Kate gave her a squeeze and disappeared with two empty trays.

Chapter 14

When Jillian arrived home Thursday afternoon at four, Kate was again in the kitchen. She looked up from the carrots she was slicing into sticks.

"Hey! How'd it go?"

"Okay." Jillian shrugged out of her parka. "The doctor says Zeb's not ready for cataract surgery yet, but honestly, I think his vision's getting so bad he's discouraged."

"That's too bad."

"Yeah, the doctor said maybe six months from now."

Kate gave a low whistle. "He won't like waiting that long."

"No, he won't. And he'll probably need more chauffeuring. He doesn't feel comfortable getting behind the wheel."

"Do you think he's all right living there by himself?"

"I'd feel easier if he had someone with him," Jillian admitted.

"We could offer him a room over here until the surgery."

Jillian considered that. "He wouldn't like it, at least not for long. But yeah, it's a possibility. Let's see how it goes. He's going back in June. Meanwhile, we just need to keep an eye on him."

"Does Zeb have any family?"

"Not much, I don't think. He was never married. He's got a nephew named Lee who comes around once in a blue moon. He tried to set me up with him last fall."

Kate grinned. "I remember. Maybe the church could help out?"

"Good idea. Whichever of us goes to church Sunday can mention it to the pastor. Maybe he could assign somebody to just drop in once a week and check on Zeb. Have a little visit."

Kate nodded. "I'm sure he'd love that, and it would give us a day when we knew somebody was looking in on him."

"Okay, what do you want me to do to help you?" Jillian was impressed by what Kate had accomplished already.

"Want to do the celery sticks? I've got oatmeal cookies and brownies."

"Wow, you're ambitious."

"Kinda." Kate grinned. "You must be tired. I can take this stuff over if you want."

Jillian took a paring knife from a drawer and sank onto a stool. "Would you? I'd appreciate that."

A woman about her age opened the door to Kate.

"Hi. You must be Jennifer. I'm Kate."

She laughed. "No, I'm Amelia."

"Sorry. I brought you supper."

"Come on in."

"I have more in the car."

"Oh. Then let me take this." Amelia carefully took the still warm pan from Kate.

A different woman opened the door as Kate plodded onto the porch with the cookies and vegetable tray.

"Hi, I'm Jennifer. Come on in. It's really cold out tonight."

"Yes, it is." Kate went in quickly and was grateful when Jennifer shut the door behind her.

The sisters looked a lot alike, with dark hair and brown eyes, but Kate couldn't see much of a resemblance to Stan. When she entered the kitchen and was greeted by Anita, she understood. Both girls looked like their mother.

"Thank you so much." Mrs. Chappell reached for the veggies. "This is so kind of you and Jillian to do this."

"It was no trouble," Kate said, though she'd spent at least two hours preparing the dishes.

Amelia set the pan of chop suey on the stove and gave it a stir. "The kids will love this. We really appreciate it."

"I always loved it as a kid."

All three women, especially Anita, had bloodshot eyes and sober faces. Kate felt slightly awkward, but she decided to say what was in her heart. She pulled her gloves off and shoved them in her pockets then pulled in a breath. "I'm really sorry about Stanley. He was such a nice man. I only knew him from the bookstore, but he was always courteous and helpful."

"Stan loved working in the store." A wistful smile touched Mrs. Chappell's lips.

From another room, shrieks that sounded like a sibling squabble erupted.

"Oops, that's my boys. I'd better go settle their hash." Amelia hurried out of the room.

"It must be nice to have your family here, Mrs. Chappell," Kate said.

"It is, but I wish it was for a different reason."

"Of course." Kate swallowed hard. When she'd worked in a medical office, she'd learned to deal with patients who'd received bad news, but she'd never found it easy to talk to those who'd lost a loved one.

Jennifer put the bags of cookies on the counter near the toaster. "My son, Justin, is driving up from Pennsylvania as soon as we have a date for the funeral, and our brother plans to fly in from California, but we don't know yet when we can have it."

"That must be hard," Kate said.

"Very." Mrs. Chappell sat down with a sigh at the small table in one corner. "Sean was here at Christmas, and he can't really afford to fly out again, but what can we do?"

"We're all going to pitch in to help pay for his ticket," Jennifer said. "But since the service is on hold, we are stuck in limbo. He can't stay away from his job for more than a few days."

Anita shook her head. "I'm not sure what's taking so long."

"The autopsy, Mom."

"But they know what killed him. He was shot."

"Well, they'll tell us when they're done." Jennifer gave Kate a weak smile. "Would you like some tea?"

"No, thanks. I should get back to the inn."

"Do you serve dinner for your guests?"

"No, but sometimes we have new people checking in during the evening." Kate glanced toward the door.

"At least we have Stanley's will," Anita said.

Jennifer's eyebrows rose. "Of course, Mom. You made your wills together. But everything goes to you, right?"

"Almost. Your father wanted a few special things to go to you kids and the grandchildren."

"But not until you're gone, right?"

"No, he wants it to happen now."

Jennifer eyed her with a frown. "Well, it must be something of sentimental value, because I know you guys never had anything expensive."

Nope, I don't belong here. Before Kate could make her excuses and leave, Mrs. Chappell spoke again.

"He wanted me to make sure Sean has a keepsake. All of you, but Sean especially."

189

"That was nice of him," Jennifer murmured. She turned to the cupboards and began taking down plates and glasses.

"I guess I'll head out," Kate said quickly. "It was nice meeting you all."

"Same here," Jennifer said.

Her mother nodded. "Thank you again. One of the girls will bring the dishes to you at the inn."

"Thanks."

She met Amelia near the front door. The kids had settled down and were watching TV.

"Oh, you're leaving?" Amelia asked.

"Yeah. Nice meeting you."

"You too." Amelia gave a little shrug. "Mom's worried about the funeral."

"I hope they let you have it soon."

"Me too. It's troublesome. And she wants my brother here, and Jennifer's boy. Jenn and I can only do so much to comfort her." Amelia gave a little laugh. "Listen to me. I'm sure you don't want to hear about *Justin,* the favorite grandchild."

Kate smiled. "I have a brother. I think I know what you mean."

"Not unless your mother doted on him."

"Oh. Well . . ."

Amelia waved a hand. "Forget I said anything. It's always a little tense when we're all together. Dad disapproved of some things Jennifer did, but he loved Justin. His oldest grandchild, you know?

190

He and Mom always spoiled that boy. Then my kids came along, and . . . well, without Dad to smooth things over, sometimes the resentment comes out. Well, anyway, good night."

" 'Night." Kate pulled her hood up and stepped out into the crisp air. February was nearly here. What was left of the snow crunched under her feet as she strode to her Jeep. She shivered and adjusted the controls of the heater before backing out of the driveway.

"All right, I know he's here."

Jillian stared at the man who had just charged through the front door. "I beg your pardon."

"Mike Schuman. Someone told me they saw him come in here."

"Who?"

"It doesn't matter. Just tell me what room he's in."

Jillian stood and pulled back her shoulders. "We've been through this before. I cannot share guest information. Please leave."

"No. I want to see my cousin."

"Your cousin?"

"That's what I said."

"And I said *please leave.*"

"And if I refuse?" he glanced toward the hallway.

Jillian's lips quivered, and she clamped them together hard, thinking. "I will call the police."

"This is a public place."

"No, it's private property. We happen to lease rooms to guests."

He met her gaze with steely eyes. "Okay, I'll take a room."

"Unfortunately, we're all booked up."

"Sure you are." He raised his chin.

"It's true." She stood perfectly still and met his stare.

"I'll be back." He stormed out the door, letting in a blast of cold air.

Jillian hauled in a shaky breath. She strode to the front door and locked it, then she grabbed the phone. "Rick, that man was here again."

"What man?"

She put a hand to her forehead. Hadn't they told Rick about this? "The one who demanded to see one of our guests yesterday. I never admitted the man was staying here, but this guy says someone told him he's here, and he says he'll be back. Rick, I'm scared."

"Breathe, Jillian. Is Kate there?"

"No. She took dinner to the Chappell family."

"Okay, I'll be right over. Lock the doors."

"They are locked."

"All right. Hang up, Jill. I'll see you in five minutes."

He was gone. Jillian swallowed hard, stood, and went to the front door. She opened it a crack and peered out into the parking lot. Everything was peaceful, but her stomach roiled. She closed the door again and confirmed it was locked. She whirled back through the dining room and kitchen to the storeroom. Good. The side door was already locked, as she'd expected. They rarely left it unlocked, but her nerves had insisted she double check.

She walked through the rooms one by one to the hallway, leaving the lights on behind her. Usually she wasn't jumpy, but this situation was starting to get to her.

Gazing down the corridor to the elevator, she considered looping in Mr. Schuman. Or should she wait for Rick? Wait. A noise in the lobby drew her. Her heart racing, she walked to the doorway. Two women who were staying overnight on their way to Calais, on the eastern edge of Maine, were coming down the stairs. Evelyn and Amy, mother and daughter.

"Hi," Jillian called with a smile, relieved that she'd remembered their names. She hoped they wouldn't sense the strain she was under.

"We thought we'd run out for some takeout and bring it back to the room. Is that okay?" Amy was carrying her winter jacket, and Evelyn already had on her cream woolen coat.

"That's fine. Or you can eat in the dining room if you want. It's usually empty this time of night, and there'll be coffee and juice available."

"Thanks." Amy glanced at Evelyn. "Ready, Mom?"

"I think so."

Amy pulled on her coat, and Jillian walked with them to the entrance. "This door will be locked when you get back this evening. You can use your key card or the doorbell outside. Just push it, and my sister or I will let you in."

She stood on the porch while the two women left with cheerful goodbyes and walked to their car. As soon as Amy started the engine, Jillian stepped back inside and made sure the lock engaged.

Not two minutes later, Rick called her.

"I'm outside."

"Good." Jillian dashed to the door and opened it. "I'm so glad to see you."

"He's not back yet?"

"No. I'm not sure if he meant tonight or . . ."

"Okay, take me to the guest's room. The one he's looking for."

"Maybe I should wait here, in case someone else comes."

"The guests have keycards."

She nodded, feeling stupid, and checked the door once more to make sure it was secure. Schuman's room was on the third floor, so she and Rick walked to the elevator. If someone rang the doorbell, she'd run down the hall to the stairs, then down the two flights to the lobby. Surely that would be faster than the elevator. Or would it?

"Which room?" Rick asked.

"Oh, Rip Van Winkle." Jillian pushed the button for the third floor, and the elevator door closed. As they ascended, she fought back pangs of claustrophobia. She wasn't afraid of elevators. Or getting stuck in them. Or confronting a criminal when the door opened. She shuddered.

"You okay?" Rick eyed her critically.

"Yeah."

The sliding door revealed the third floor's hallway. She stepped out and turned left, toward the front corner room.

"He knows you, right?" Rick said. "You knock."

Jillian gulped and rapped on the door. "Mr. Schuman? It's Jillian. We need to speak to you."

After a few seconds, the door opened with the chain in place. Mike Schuman looked past her toward Rick, who wore his Skirmish Cove P.D. uniform.

"Who's this?"

"My brother, Rick Gage."

"Is there a problem?"

"Sort of," Jillian said. "You remember a man came here yesterday looking for you?"

He nodded.

"Well, he came back tonight. I made him leave, but he scared me, and I called Rick."

Schuman let out a huge sigh and unfastened the door chain.

"Look, I'm sorry about this. Can you describe the man for me?"

"Well, he was kind of tall—maybe as tall as you. And his hair was brown . . ." She gazed at Schuman's thick brown hair. "And about your age. More or less."

Rick laid a hand on her shoulder and edged closer to the doorway. "Do you think you know this man, Mr. Schuman?"

He frowned then gave a little shrug. "It's probably my cousin."

"And you don't want to see your cousin?"

Schuman hesitated a fraction of a second. "Look, Officer Gage, I don't want to cause trouble for your sisters, but no, I don't want to see my cousin right now."

"Is there something I should know?"

"He said it was urgent," Jillian put in.

"I promise you, there's nothing illegal going on, and there's no family member in critical condition wanting to see me before they die. Nothing like that."

Rick eyed him keenly.

"How can you know that?" Jillian asked.

Schuman shifted his gaze to her. "Because Peter is my only living family member. My mother died five years ago, and my dad passed away last month. His parents and our mutual grandparents are all deceased, and neither of us had siblings."

"No other cousins?" Rick asked. "Aunts, uncles?"

"No. Nobody that he'd try to chase me down for if they were sick. This is . . . it's about something else."

"And you know what that is."

"Yes, Officer. I know what it is, and it's like I said, nothing illegal. But I can't see Peter—and he can't see me—for another week."

"Another week?"

"That's right."

"Well, I'm concerned about my sisters' safety and that of their guests. Your cousin came here and intimidated Jillian."

"I'm sorry. But I really don't think they're in any danger, especially if they don't admit I'm here."

"Well, it sure sounds to me like he's positive you're staying here." Rick looked at Jillian. "Can you and Kate keep this up for another week?"

"I suppose so. Now that we know Mr. Schuman's getting enough to eat, and not in danger. But we'd really like to clean his room, and—"

"They brought me a supper tray tonight," Schuman said. "Don't worry, I'm paying for room service. And the laundry."

"Oh, yeah," Jillian said. "We'll get your laundry to you in the morning. Today was kind of hectic."

"That's fine."

"You're doing laundry now?" Rick's tone and raised eyebrows shouted skepticism.

"It's just a courtesy service," Jillian said. "Mr. Schuman insisted he couldn't leave the inn right now to go into town."

"Oh, brother." Rick scowled at the guest. "Let the maid clean your room, you hear me?"

"Sure, but I can't sit in a public area while she does it."

Rick rolled his eyes and shook his head.

"There's another thing," Jillian said.

Rick focused his frown on her. "What's that?"

"We are booked up right now—that much is true. Except for the Scout Finch Room. It shares a bathroom with this one. So far, we've been able to accommodate all our guests without putting anyone in there."

A look of panic froze Schuman's face. "I can't share a bathroom with someone. What if he—"

"He did ask that we give him a room. I told him we were maxed out." Heat flooded Jillian's face. "That wasn't the strict truth, and I don't like lying to people. I rationalized it because we usually save the adjoining rooms on this floor and the one below for families. But if someone else came asking for a room, I really couldn't turn them away. We can't afford to turn down business."

"I'll pay for both rooms," Schuman blurted.

"And as soon as another room opens up, you can move me."

Jillian looked to Rick for wisdom.

He shrugged. "There's always the secret room."

"What?"

Jillian couldn't believe the way Schuman pounced on that. "That's supposed to be a secret," she hissed at Rick, hoping her glare scorched him. "It's for family only. Not guests."

Rick clapped his hands to the top of his head. "Look, Jill, I'm sorry, but this whole scene is a farce. If you're going to start hiding people, maybe you should talk to the Federal Marshal's Service about taking in people for witness protection."

"Not funny."

Schuman reached out a hand. "No, really. I'm serious. I'll take this secret room, and I'll even pay extra."

Jillian shook her head slowly. "There's no windows in there, and no bathroom."

"Oh."

"That's right," Rick said. "You couldn't stay in there for more than a few hours. But maybe . . ." He looked at Jillian. "Maybe you could show him where it is, and if his cousin comes back, he could dive in there until he's gone."

She stood stock still. "I can't believe you're suggesting . . ."

"It sounds good to me," the guest said.

Jillian lifted a hand. "Mr. Schuman—"

"Mike."

"Mike. I just don't know if . . ." She trailed off as she caught the sound of the elevator moving and stared toward it.

Schuman ducked inside his room and closed the door all but a crack. The elevator opened, revealing a wild-eyed Kate.

"Hey." She hurried toward her siblings. "What's going on? The front door was locked."

"Yes. Did you lock it again when you came in?"

"I . . . no. I saw Rick's vehicle, and I—"

"Go lock it," Rick said.

Kate's jaw dropped.

"I'll go." Jillian gave Kate a pat on the shoulder. "Rick and Mike can explain everything, and you can decide whether or not to let Mike in on a family secret."

Since the elevator was still on the third floor, she opted for that over the stairs and was soon in the lobby. She was about to secure the front door when one of their guests drove in. She waited until he was inside then activated the automatic lock.

"Hello, Mr. Ralston. I hope you had a nice dinner."

"I did, thank you. I've wrapped up my business here, so I'd like to check out tonight and get home."

"Of course."

Another empty room, Jillian noted as she went behind the desk. "We have your credit card. Would you like a receipt now?"

"Sure. I'll just go up and get my things. You can give it to me when I come down."

A few minutes later, Ralston returned with his suitcase, and she handed him the printed receipt.

"Oh, aren't you charging me for tonight?" He glanced at the clock. "It's way past your checkout time."

"No, no one needed a room for the night, so we'll err on the side of leniency." She smiled at him, thinking the only potential customer she'd refused to admit was Peter Schuman, but she was glad she'd done that.

"Well, thank you. I called my wife and told her I'd be home by midnight, and she's happy about that."

"Great. Drive safely." After he left, she again made sure the door was locked and neutralized his room key card.

Kate and Rick came down the stairs.

"All set with Room 9?" Jillian found she didn't even want to say Mike Schuman's name aloud where someone else might overhear.

"Yeah," Kate said.

"Did you show him . . . ?"

"We did," Rick said. "He's promised not to tell anyone else."

Kate leaned close and dropped her voice. "If

201

we tip him off that his cousin's here, he's going to slip into the library and open the secret door."

"And how do we tip him off?"

Kate grinned. "We worked out a plan. If we're both here, one of us will stall the cousin while the other goes into the kitchen and calls Mike's room from there. If only one of us is on hand, we'll call each other, and the one who's not in the lobby will call Mike."

Jillian frowned. The plan sounded far from foolproof.

Rick nudged Kate. "Don't forget the password."

"Oh, yeah. In case someone else is hanging around, we say, 'The extra pillow you requested will be right up.' And he knows he should hide."

"The extra pillow." Jillian stared at her and sighed.

"Yeah, sounds pretty innocent, right?"

"Sounds like a mouthful to me. I mean, if that man comes back and starts yelling at me, I can't see myself saying, 'Excuse me, I have to call a guest and tell him his pillow's ready.'"

Kate's mouth skewed. "When you put it that way . . ."

"Whatever," Rick said. "Just call me or the station if he makes trouble."

"Okay." Jillian decided not to fight the two of them. "Thanks for coming, Rick. Did he tell you why he doesn't want to see Peter?"

"Nope, and don't you pester him about it."

As Rick answered Jillian's question, he stared pointedly at Kate.

"I won't. But I'd better run down to the carriage house and get his laundry going." Kate dashed out through the dining room.

"Can I get a coffee to go?" Rick rubbed a hand over his eyes.

"Sure, anytime. You know that." Jillian walked with him into the next room and got him a to-go cup. "This batch isn't too old."

Rick poured himself a small amount and tasted it. "Sold." He filled the cup and emptied two creamers into the brew.

"I thought you drank it black," Jillian said.

"I usually do, but partly because I'm always in a hurry."

"Huh. Well, Diana's probably wishing you were home. Otherwise, I'd invite you to sit down and chat."

He downed another swallow of coffee and put a lid on the cup. "Hey, you girls know you can call me anytime, right?"

"Yes, we do. But we don't want Diana and the kids to forget what you look like."

Rick gave her a weary smile. "I told your guest he had to let Mindy clean in there tomorrow morning."

"Good. And Mr. Ralston checked out a minute ago. We can give Mike the option of moving into the Liz Bennett room tomorrow."

"That's on the second floor, right?"

Jillian nodded.

"So, would you show him the secret room on that floor?"

"I didn't think of that. He doesn't need to know *all* our secrets."

"Give it some thought."

She frowned. "Well, I think the people in Scarlett O'Hara are leaving tomorrow. That's on three, and it's right off the lounge. And it's at the back of the house."

"Sounds like that might be an ideal room for this guy."

"Okay. But if we get a couple—" She waved a hand. "We'll figure it out."

"Good. I'll check in with you tomorrow, if I haven't heard from you first."

He went out, and she sank down on the stool behind the front desk. She was pondering the expected new arrivals for Friday when guests who'd been out for the evening began trickling in.

She checked the locks after the last stray was in for the night and realized Don would arrive any minute. She ought to do a quick survey in the kitchen and dining room to see what they'd need for breakfast, but she was too tired.

What progress had they made in this crazy day? Not much in the murder investigation, and they weren't done with Mike Schuman's cousin, she was sure. Jillian laid her head on her arms and dozed until the doorbell woke her. She sat up, blinking. Don was waving at her through the glass. She shoved up from the stool and plodded toward the door, trying to recall all the updates she needed to give him before she could head home to bed.

Chapter 15

On Friday evening, Jillian's nerves flared up as she prepared for her date. The inn had remained calm all day. Ordinarily, that would be a good thing, but in the middle of all the crazy things going on lately, it made her uneasy. What was going to happen next—and why hadn't it already happened?

As she bent toward the bathroom mirror, applying mascara, her cell phone rang. The screen showed *Novel Inn*. She stuck the wand back into the mascara tube.

"Yeah?"

"Craig's here," Kate said. "Do you want him to come down there?"

"Sure, if he doesn't mind."

That gave her approximately sixty seconds to finish her prep. She scowled at her reflection. Oh, well. Craig often saw her when she wore no makeup at all. This would do. A quick slide of lip gloss finished things off, and she headed for the door of the carriage house.

Slipping on her coat, she heard his truck tires crunch on the driveway. She hung her favorite scarf around her neck and opened the door smiling.

"Wow. Flowers in February."

He shrugged and held out the bouquet with a sheepish grin. "I'm trying to make up for lost time."

"Thank you. They're beautiful, and I know you've been busy."

"Too busy. I hoped things would slow down after the Winter Carnival."

"And now you've got a murder on your hands. Come on in." She turned to the small kitchen to put the yellow, orange, and white blooms in a vase.

"Well, Rick and the state police are doing most of the work on that, but yeah. It messes up our schedule and adds a ton of paperwork, not to mention dealing with the press and the terrified public."

"And the just plain curious, I'm sure." She ran water into a vase that had been her mom's as long as she could remember and reached for the cellophane-wrapped bouquet.

"There is that. We sent an officer to check on the store a couple of times today. Eric seems to be stepping up, but Carl said he could use some help." Craig leaned against the counter and watched as she arranged the flowers.

"Mmm. Carl did mention hiring someone else part-time, but I don't think he's had a chance. I told him Kate and I could fill in, but he hasn't called."

"He probably won't. Listen, I wish we had more

on that fellow you saw at the park Wednesday."

Jillian tried to feign indifference. "Kate and I made an assumption."

"Yes. Well, the man you saw lives in Waterville."

"That must be forty or fifty miles away. It's quite a drive."

"Not too far. But for a casual visit to a coastal park in wintertime, yes."

"I suppose he could have been visiting someone, or doing some business in Skirmish Cove that day."

Craig hesitated.

"What is it?" she asked.

"The State Police don't think it has anything to do with Stan Chappell's death."

"Surprise, surprise."

"Right."

"But you do?" She gazed into his soft brown eyes.

"Well, I think we should do some more probing." He shifted his stance. "I did find out he's married and the car he drove to the park is actually the one his wife uses most of the time. I'm not letting it go so easily."

"Thank you. Kate and I truly don't want to waste your time."

"I know. I think there's enough there to make it interesting. I'm trying to find a link between this guy and Eric Roofner. If you don't mind me asking, what do you know about Eric?"

"Just that he works part-time for his father at the bookstore, but he doesn't seem crazy about it. In fact, Zeb Wilding told me that Eric hates the store and doesn't like working there. I got the idea Eric would rather have a snowmobile shop or something like that."

"That makes sense. He was off at a rally the day Stan was killed."

Jillian nodded. "I barely know Eric, but I generally trust Zeb's judgment. He says Eric's not dependable and disrespects his father."

Craig nodded. "He's been at the store every day since his father was injured. Still . . . I'll check into this fellow in Waterville and see if he's a snowmobiler. Or a motorcyclist. We learned Eric's vehicle of choice in summer is a Harley."

"Guess I'm ready." Jillian dropped the wrapper from the flowers in the trash.

"Great. Let's go."

On the way, she thought over everything that had happened since the murder.

"I don't suppose you've had contact with the Chappell family?" she asked.

"Not personally. How about you?"

"No, but Kate took them a meal, and she met the two daughters."

"There's a son too, right?"

"Yes, Sean. I think he's in California. He's not

coming until they can hold the funeral. I guess he can't afford to come twice."

"Understandable. Did Kate get the impression the family was amicable?"

"You'd have to ask her. She did say it sounded as if Sean was the golden child. His sisters may be a little resentful."

"Huh. Rick's visited them. I'll see what he has to say about that."

Patti's Pizza was crowded, but Craig snagged a table as another couple was leaving. Jillian sat down to claim it while he went to get their puzzle sheets. A harried busboy came to clear away the previous patrons' dishes and wipe down the table.

"You have to place your order at the counter on puzzle night," the young man said.

"Thanks. We'll do that."

Craig dropped off the puzzles and discussed the menu with her. He went to put in their order, and a few minutes later their pizza and sodas arrived.

"So, I've been looking over these." Jillian waved at the print-outs. "Or would you rather talk about the case?"

"I think it's too noisy in here for that. What have we got here?"

"There's a modified cryptogram, a logic problem, and a math problem."

"Okay. Solve individually or together?"

Jillian gazed at him for a long moment. They might work faster on their own, but working with

Craig would be so much more fun. "Together, I think."

The next two hours were the most enjoyable she'd spent in a long time. They wouldn't win any laurels for solving speedily, she was sure, but she didn't care.

"Well, that does it." Craig penciled in the last answer. "That was fun."

"Yeah, it was. Do they do this every Friday?"

"Only once a month, I think." He gazed into her eyes. "We could make it a standing date."

"I'm game."

He grinned and gave her hand a squeeze. "Great."

On the way home, the quiet humming of the motor and semidarkness in the truck's cab lulled Jillian into complacency. When Craig spoke, she jerked out of her reverie.

"We're supposed to get some heavy snow this weekend."

"I hope Stan's son doesn't try to fly in the middle of that."

"Yeah." He looked over at her then back at the road. "Tell me more about your family. I know about your two sibs, but you have a daughter at least."

"Yes, Megan. She's a college sophomore and deep into her studies. She's only managed to get home once since Christmas." Jillian chuckled. "She swears the classes this year are twice as hard as they were freshman year. Of course, I pointed out that she's carrying eighteen credits this semester, which is a lot tougher than the fifteen she was doing earlier, no matter what the subject."

"Yeah, that's a lot. She's your only child?"

"Yes." Jillian exhaled slowly. "I, uh, I had some medical issues after she was born that took away the option of more kids."

"I'm sorry."

"I've made peace with it. And as things turned out, having just one gave me more energy for my teaching and let me focus on Jack and Megan." She glanced over at him, waiting for the next obvious question. "Aren't you going to ask about Jack?"

"I don't have to. Rick was in the department then. He told us his brother-in-law was the firefighter who was killed when the apartments in Bucksport burned."

Jillian nodded. "The building collapsed on him. Jack and another man were still inside, looking for one of the residents. Someone had told them the young man was still in there, but . . ." She drew in a deep breath. "It turned out he'd gotten out a window, and they didn't know it."

"I'm so sorry."

"I'm glad the young man got out. And Jack's coworker survived, although he was in pretty rough shape. It's hard, though."

"I imagine. How long now?"

She dashed away a tear. "Four years."

Craig came to a halt at a stop sign and reached over to squeeze her hand. "You seem to be handling it well."

"Without my faith and the rest of my family . . ." Jillian hauled in a deep breath. "I guess it made it a lot harder for me to lose Mom and Dad last year."

"Yeah, your family's had more than its share."

"I don't know. What's one person's share of sorrow?"

Craig was silent as he turned onto her street.

"What about you?" she asked, putting more enthusiasm into her voice. "How did you get to be forty and single? I hope your story's not as tragic as mine. If it is, I apologize."

He smiled. "Past forty. But the short answer is, I got married too young. No kids, which turned out to be a blessing. She left me after three years."

"Wow. I don't know what to say."

"Don't worry about it. I haven't kept up with her. I do hear snippets now and then. She bounced around for a while. The big shocker was when her name came up on a report out of Portland."

"You mean . . . a police report?"

"Yeah. She was arrested for embezzling from her employer."

"Wow."

He nodded. "The last I heard, she was in the Cumberland County Jail. She could be out now—I don't know. I make myself not find out."

That she could understand, but she wondered, in his position, if she'd have the self-discipline not to look.

Craig turned in at the inn's parking lot and pulled in between two cars. "Looks like you've still got a lot of guests."

"It's been great. We've actually had to turn some people away."

"That's amazing for this time of year in this location."

"God's blessed us. I think it's mostly the inn's theme and the reputation Mom and Dad built for it. Lots of the guests are repeat customers. We've heard some terrific stories about my folks and how they helped people."

"Sounds like a legacy to be proud of."

"We are, and we're trying not to do anything to besmirch the Novel Inn's good name."

Craig laughed and opened his door. Jillian wondered for about a nanosecond if she should get out too, but he was walking around to her side. She was comfortable waiting for him to open her door.

"Thanks," she said when he swung it wide and she got out. "Come in for a sec? We always have coffee."

"Do you have ice cream?"

She chuckled. They hadn't had dessert at Patti's. "We might have to go down to the carriage house for that, but we can check."

Don was on the front desk, and he gave her a lazy wave as they entered.

"I didn't realize it was this late," Jillian said. "Anything happening?"

"So little it would bore you to speak of."

Craig sniffed. "What's that tantalizing smell?"

"Kate's baking for tomorrow." Don nodded toward an empty plate beside the computer. "She brought me two muffins, and I must say they are excellent."

"Two," Craig said. "Wow. You must be special."

"Oh, believe me, I am."

Jillian grinned. "Come on, Craig, let's go see if she has any extras."

Five minutes later, Craig sat beside her at one of the dining room tables with a dish of cookies-and-cream ice cream, a blueberry muffin, and a glass of Coke. Jillian had opted for a muffin and a glass of water. Kate came from the kitchen and fixed herself a cup of hot tea.

"How can you drink that at this time of night and expect to sleep?" Jillian asked.

Kate shrugged. "I don't know. Coffee keeps me up, but this tea doesn't seem to." She pulled out a chair. "Last batch of banana-nut muffins is in the oven."

"Thanks for doing that."

"No probs. You can get up early and cook the bacon."

Craig laughed at them, and Kate arched her eyebrows in his direction. "What's funny?"

"Nothing. I just feel relaxed whenever I come here."

"Then you should come here more often," Kate said.

"Maybe I will."

Jillian sipped her water. "No more brouhaha from the Schuman family?"

"Haven't heard a peep out of either of them since this morning."

"I told Craig about it," Jillian said. "He agrees with Rick—if the cousin shows up, we call them immediately."

"Well, Mike did come down right at the end of the breakfast hours and got a rather hefty stash of breakfast foods. I gave him his clean laundry. That's the last I've seen of him."

"No need to open the secret room then." Jillian took a bite of her muffin.

"Nope, but I went in and dusted, just in case."

Craig shook his head. "You two are full of surprises. Rick's never told me about any secret room."

"Good," Kate said. "It should stay that way. It's a family-only secret. Unless, of course, one of our guests needs emergency protection."

"In that case, I feel privileged to be privy to the Gage Family Secret."

Rick marched into the inn's kitchen Monday morning, where his sisters were preparing more food to take to the buffet.

"Hi," Kate called. He looked more cheerful than he had all week. Maybe he had some news for them.

"Your parking lot is a mess. It needs plowing," he said.

Kate grimaced. Not what she'd hoped for.

"Yeah, Mickey Holt's coming over to plow at around ten," Jillian said. "We figured we'd better wait until most of the guests move their cars."

"If they can get out," Rick said.

"Has it stopped now? We had to wade up here from the house."

"Yeah, but there's a good eight inches on the ground. I didn't see your cars out front."

"We listened to the weatherman last night and put them down in the garage. Help yourself to some breakfast if you want."

"Thanks."

Kate picked up the steel bin she'd loaded with individual cheese omelets for an empty spot on the warming table. Rick followed her into the dining room, which was full of guests.

"Did you get some sleep this weekend?" Kate set the bin in place and then watched him load a plate. "Because apparently you didn't eat."

"Ha, ha. Diana was just getting up when I left, and I told her I'd eat here before I go to the station. And yes, I slept." He took the tongs and put one of the omelets on his plate.

Kate smiled. "Okay, so what's up?"

"Can I take this in the office?"

"Ooh, you want privacy. That means there's something important."

"Well, not for publication, anyway."

"Sure. I'll bring your coffee. Let's go."

"Let me snag a Danish first."

Rick grabbed one and followed her across the hall. By then, Jillian was in the lobby, processing checkout for a young couple who'd stayed the weekend. When she'd finished, she joined them in the office.

"Hey, what's up? We shouldn't leave the dining room unattended too long."

Rick swallowed a bite of omelet. "Just a quick update. The coroner is releasing Stanley Chappell's body. The family's been notified, and Anita said they'd like to plan the funeral for Saturday. That will give them time to make arrangements and for her son to get here from California and Jennifer's kid to drive up from P-A."

"Okay," Kate said. "Do you know where the funeral will be held?"

"Nope, but you can ask them. Or I expect it will be in the paper tomorrow."

Jillian looked at her sister. "Might be a good day to take Anita some more food."

"I can call Val Pressey and see what they have planned," Kate said.

"Great. I'll make some brownies, and you find out what else they need." Jillian turned to Rick. "It's been several days since I got in touch with Carl. Of course, the store was closed yesterday. I thought maybe I'd stop by the bookstore today."

"Sure. If you're going out anyway, you might as well stop in. Wait for Mickey to plow, though." He popped the last bite of Danish in his mouth and looked at the clock.

"What are *you* doing today?" Kate asked.

"Mostly verifying alibis. We're checking his friends and everyone in the family."

"Just for drill?" Jillian arched her eyebrows in her teacher look.

"Standard procedure."

"So you don't have a solid suspect," Kate said.

"No comment." Rick rose, placing his crumpled napkin on his plate.

"We'll take care of your dishes," Jillian said.

He left, and the sisters eyed each other. Jillian frowned.

"Do you think they're really looking hard at someone? I'm sure they've double-checked Eric's alibi. And Carl's, I suppose. Who else is there?"

"Well, there's the park guy."

"Yeah, Craig said they were checking him out."

"Who else would have motive?" Kate picked up Rick's dishes.

"I have no clue. I guess, like Rick said, maybe someone in the family, or one of Stan's acquaintances. But I can't see Anita having her husband killed. Or old Mr. Rutter, either."

"Face it, we know next to nothing about the Chappell family."

"True. We really only know what they've told us. Maybe the police are making sure Sean was really in California when it happened." Jillian took the dishes from Kate's hands. "I'll load the dishwasher and start the brownies if you want to check on the guests and call Mrs. Pressey."

Jillian left the inn in the middle of the afternoon. Their front parking area was finally plowed. Even Mike Schuman had slipped out to move his car for Mickey, a local man who ran a garage with his uncle. He'd plowed the long drive down to the carriage house too. The town's streets had been cleared by public works employees, but high ridges of snow edged every byway.

When she arrived at the Chappell house in midafternoon with brownies and shepherd's pie, Anita was alone.

"Thank you so much, Jillian," she said as she led the way to the kitchen. "My daughters and grandchildren went home yesterday, but Sean is flying in tomorrow, and the girls will be back. I think I'll save this casserole for tomorrow's supper. Jennifer's boy should be here by then too."

"How are you doing? We missed you at church yesterday." Jillian set the still hot dish down on the glass stovetop.

Anita sighed. "I'd have been there, but the girls were packing up and leaving. Everyone at church has been so kind—food for us, flowers, cards. Sonny Rittle from the Last Cup brought me a bag of gourmet coffee yesterday."

"Nice. Are you going to the airport tomorrow?"

"Amelia's picking Sean up in Portland at two thirty and bringing him here. I expect he'll be exhausted—his flight leaves really early out there. But I need him and the girls together, so we can plan the funeral service." Anita's forehead wrinkled. "I hope they don't fight."

"Do they not get along?"

"Not lately. Amelia got it into her head that Sean was our favorite child. It's not true. We loved them all. But when they hear Stan's will read, it probably won't help things."

"Why is that?"

"Well, of course the estate passes to me, but Stan wanted to make sure Sean got a few special things. Tools and guns, things like that. You know, boy things."

Jillian managed a smile and didn't voice her

thought that plenty of girls used those things too. "Did he leave anything for your daughters and the grandchildren?"

"Nothing specific, but I was thinking maybe I'd choose a few special things for them. But when I go, my girls will inherit all the dishes and jewelry and things like that." Anita shrugged. "We really don't have much of value. If there's anything left in our retirement funds, that will be split between Sean, Amelia, and Jennifer, and I expect the house will be sold and the proceeds divided."

"That's what my parents did." Jillian thought about it. "Of course, they both passed away at the same time. My sister and brother and I each got equal shares of the property."

"But you didn't sell their house—that inn."

"No, we decided to keep it."

"But no special bequests?"

"No, but we went through the little house down behind the inn—the old carriage house, where our folks lived—and we each chose some things we wanted to keep."

"Did your brother get all the tools?"

"No, most of those are still in the garage. Kate and I use them some when we're making repairs or gardening. If Rick wants something, he comes and borrows it."

"Hmm. Well, it's nice that you all get along so well."

"Yes." Her friendly bickering now and then

with Kate and Rick didn't seem worth mentioning. Apparently the grudges went deeper with the Chappell children.

"I know Sean's going to want his father's decoys too, but Amelia wouldn't stand for that."

"Were they mentioned in Stan's will?"

"No. But some of them are quite old, and Stan said they're worth something. Amelia told me yesterday that if I let Sean take any of them, she'll throw a royal fit."

"But they'll still be yours."

"Yes, but . . ."

Jillian pursed her lips. "Just a thought—you might want to have them appraised. Then you'd know what they're worth, and if Sean wanted to take one, you could let him buy it from the collection."

"Oh, I don't think that would go over. But it would probably be a good idea to know if Stan was right about them being special."

"I'm sure it would be."

Anita hesitated. "Stan was always short with Jennifer, after she got pregnant. But when Justin came along, he loved that boy."

Jillian was glad they hadn't ostracized Jennifer and her son. "What about Amelia's kids? They're all younger than Justin, right?"

"Yes, two boys and a girl. The youngest one is eleven."

"Well, I need to get going." Jillian wanted

plenty of time to talk to Carl. "Do you know what day the service will be?"

"I'm thinking Saturday. That's easier than a weekday for most people."

"I hope it comes together well for you." Jillian gave Anita's hand a squeeze. "I'll be praying for you and the kids."

Tears glistened in Anita's eyes, and she whispered, "Thank you."

Chapter 16

Several customers were browsing when Jillian entered the Book Rack, and Carl was at the checkout, waiting on a pair of women. Jillian was pleased to see he was moderately busy. Serving the customers' needs would help divert his thoughts from Stanley's death.

A twinge of guilt hit her. By talking to Carl, she would focus his thoughts on the murder again. Maybe she should leave him alone. He glanced up and spotted her, and his eyes lit up. He was definitely glad to see her. She let out her breath, glad she had come.

She strolled to a display of new arrivals and picked up a book with interesting cover art. The author was one she'd heard of, but she'd never read one of his books. After flipping it over, she was soon immersed in the back cover copy.

"Jillian. Thanks for coming by." Carl was at her elbow, and his lips curved upward, even if it was a subdued smile.

"How are you doing?"

"A little better. I'll have an ad in tomorrow's paper for a part-time worker."

She nodded, averting her eyes from the bruise on his wrist and the back of his hand. "I guess you need somebody."

"Yes, and not just because of Stan. I had a good talk with Eric last night. It seems I wasn't really listening to him."

"Oh?" Jillian cocked her head to one side.

Carl's cheeks scrunched up. "Eric doesn't care about the bookstore. He wants an outdoor business."

"Snowmobiles?"

"Something like that, yes. I've known where his interests lay, but I thought those were just hobbies. He's pretty good at tinkering with engines, though. He took auto shop in high school, and he loves motorcycles. He really wants to have his own shop for stuff like that. I think . . ." Carl's gaze drifted away, and he drew in a shaky breath. "I think I'm going to help him get started. At least I want to try."

"So you might need more than one new employee."

"Afraid so. But . . . if it will make him happy . . ."

What if it doesn't? Jillian swallowed the question and touched his sleeve. "Just leave yourself plenty of margin, Carl. If you're making new hires, you'll increase your expenses a little—at least temporarily."

"Yes. And I need to order new stock. If I neglect the routines of the business, it will go downhill fast. I . . . Maybe I should just sell the store and retire. But even if I decided to do that, the store would have to be in good shape. You know— financially healthy."

She nodded, but her heart ached a little for him. Without his beloved store, what would Carl do with himself? She hoped he didn't sell it without thinking it over thoroughly. The book in her hand gave her a way to change the tone. Holding it up, she asked brightly, "Is this guy any good?"

"Oh my, yes. I haven't read that one yet, but I plan to. I'm getting good feedback on it already."

"You sold me. Oops, someone wants to check out."

"Excuse me," Carl said quickly and hurried to the counter.

Jillian held on to the book and wandered to the periodical section. Had Eric come in today to help his dad, or was he leaving Carl pretty much alone? From what she'd witnessed, Eric was not the greatest book salesman. A thought flashed through her mind, but she'd have to consult Kate.

A few minutes later, she saw the younger Roofner come out of the back room with a stack of books in his arms. *Good. He didn't leave his dad here alone.* Was Eric trying to be helpful while his father recovered, or was he hoping to protect him from further violence?

When Carl was free, she went to the counter and paid for her book and a decorating magazine. She arrived home to find Rick and Kate gabbing in the office.

Jillian looked at the clock with deliberately widened eyes. "Wow! What are you doing here at three in the afternoon on a Monday?"

"Just making sure everything's okay here."

"We haven't heard anything from Peter Schuman since Thursday, unless he came by while I was out," Jillian said.

"He didn't," Kate assured her.

Rick nodded. "I spoke with Mike for a minute. He says if he can keep his head down until Friday, he'll be out of your hair."

"What happens Friday?" Jillian looked from him to Kate.

Kate spread her hands wide and shrugged. "He's not saying. But whatever Peter wants to find him for ends Friday."

"That's weird."

"The whole thing is weird." Rick shook his head. "Speaking of weird, Kate says you're going to change the Virginian Room to something else."

"That's right, Phileas Fogg."

Rick blinked. "Is that a person?"

Jillian wrinkled her face, making an effort at a horrified expression. "He's only the hero of *Around the World in Eighty Days*."

"Well, I kind of like the Virginian Room."

"Lots of people like the western theme," Kate said with a wistful note.

"Nobody will recognize that other guy's

name." Rick frowned. "What's wrong with the Virginian?"

"Nothing, I just . . ." Jillian let out her breath in a puff. "You don't even know the Virginian's name. The author never revealed it."

"So? I loved that show."

"Most people our age and younger don't even know about *The Virginian.*"

"They might not have read the book—only geezers do that. But they remember the TV series."

Rick's resistance surprised her.

Kate stepped closer to her. "We should do a room with a more modern theme. You know, something like Katniss Everdeen or Harry Potter."

"Oh, I don't know," Jillian said. "I'm afraid if we went too contemporary—for authors, I mean— we might run into some copyright issues."

"I'd better get out of here," Rick said.

Glad for the change of topic, Jillian turned to him. "Did you know Stan Chappell's son Sean is flying in tomorrow?"

"Nope. Have they scheduled the funeral?"

"Not for sure, but probably on Saturday."

Rick nodded. Was he going to be there, looking for suspects?

"Will you interview Sean?" she asked.

"Probably not. We checked. He was in California the day of the murder, so there's not much reason to do that."

"Okay. If I hear anything more, I'll let you know."

"Good." Rick nodded at Kate. "Thanks for the coffee."

Jillian had a feeling he'd taken a longer coffee break than he should have. As the front door closed behind him, she remembered Carl's problem.

"Oh, Kate, didn't Don say his daughter got laid off?"

"Yeah, Hannah lost her job at the dollar store. She knows she can get a summer job when the tourist traffic picks up, but she'd like something now. You know, it's hard to find an off-season job around here."

"Well, Carl Roofner needs a part-time helper—maybe two."

"That makes sense, with Stan out of the picture."

"Eric wants out as well. He wants to start his own business, and I don't mean a bookstore. Carl's going to let him try."

"Oh, wow. At least they're not fighting about it."

Jillian frowned. "It's more complicated than that, I think."

"But . . . you don't think Eric's disagreement with his father could be a motive for the shooting, do you?"

"I guess it could be, if he feels strongly enough about it . . ."

Kate's long tresses swayed as she vigorously shook her head. "No. If Eric went to the store all mad at his dad, he wouldn't have shot Stan. Why would he? That doesn't make sense."

"You're right. And Eric has a strong alibi. He was at that snowmobile event. But I don't think the shooting was random, either."

"Who else could have done it? You don't think Stan's wife or one of his daughters did it, do you? We know for sure that Sean was in California." Worry lines carved deeper on Kate's brow. "There's that grown-up grandson, Jennifer's boy, but still—I can't see any of them killing him— although any of them could be blaming Carl because of Stan's death and maybe tried to run him over."

"No. Do you really think so? Carl saw the vehicle that hit him. It wasn't one he recognized."

"A pickup truck." Kate's lips twitched. "I think we don't know enough about Stan's personal life."

Jillian scooped up her coat, scarf, and hat. "Hey, it's up to the police to dig into it and find a reason all of this happened. Anyway, Carl's putting an ad in the paper tomorrow for part-time help, but Hannah might be able to get a jump on things if you tell her today."

Kate's tight face relaxed. "I'll call her right now."

••••

"What's up, Sarge?" Rick looked up from his paperwork as Craig approached his desk the next afternoon. He'd been doing routine background checks and reports for hours, and it was nearly four o'clock. He hoped his superior's determined stride didn't mean they'd have to work late again.

Craig's lips formed a grim line. "Stanley Chappell's son, Sean, is here, and he wants to talk to you."

"Sure." Rick pushed back his chair and stood.

Craig lowered his voice. "Be forewarned. This guy isn't happy."

Rick raised his eyebrows. "With me?"

"With the whole investigation. You know the drill. Be polite, be discreet, but be firm."

"Got it."

Rick walked out into the lobby of the police station. He'd met Sean before. Stanley's son was approaching forty, and they'd had some run-ins before Sean moved to California a couple of years previously.

Though he had never thought about it before, Rick could now see a strong resemblance to Stan, both in Sean's light build and long face.

"Hello, Sean. Did you have a good trip?"

"No. But my mother told me people are harassing her since my father died. I want to make a complaint."

"Harassing her?"

"She said you've been to the house, and a state police detective, and your sisters have come around two or three times and—"

"Whoa!" Rick held up both hands. "First of all, I sent an officer to your mother's house the day Stanley was killed. He stayed with her until I could get there myself. Yes, I asked her a few questions, just going over your dad's movements that morning. I also asked her if she knew anyone who was angry with Stan."

"Of course not! I don't see why you need to upset her—"

"Your mother was quite calm when I spoke to her," Rick said. "I'm sure she was shaken by the shooting, but she seemed to understand that we needed to ask questions. When the state police came in on it, their people had to speak to her too. I believe they talked to your sisters as well. Look, Sean, this is a murder investigation. It's standard operating procedure."

"Oh, and your sisters are standard too?"

Rick pulled in a steadying breath. "As I understand it, the church social committee asked various members to take food to your mother, to help her out while she was grieving and hosting your sisters and their kids and anyone who came around to offer their sympathy. I'm sure they weren't there to snoop."

"Oh yeah? According to Jennifer, they asked plenty of unnecessary questions, and Ma was even telling one of them about Dad leaving his tools and stuff to me."

"I'm sure that conversation was voluntary on Anita's and your sister's part. I'm not sure what was said in the conversation, as I wasn't present. But I do know that Jillian and Kate have been trying to show some love, not only to your family, but to the Roofners as well. This has been hard on them too."

"Right." Sarcasm dripped from Sean's voice. "That's why Carl and Eric both went out of town and left my father alone in the store the day he was killed."

Rick struggled to keep his voice even. "I spoke to Mr. Roofner about that, and he made sure Stan didn't mind before he left the store. He said there weren't a lot of customers that morning, and Stan felt he could handle things alone for the afternoon."

"All I know is, if he hadn't been there alone, my father would be alive."

"You don't know that."

Sean glared at him. "And you don't know who killed him. You're looking for anything, because you don't have a single clue who that guy with the gun was. Well, I'm telling you right now, it wasn't anyone in my family, so you and your nosy sisters can just quit sniffing around, you hear me?"

"Oh, yeah, I hear you loud and clear. I can ask

Jillian and Kate to back off. But you need to realize that if the police—whether local or on the state level—need to speak to you or your family members again, they will do it. In fact, Detective Seaver may be contacting you soon and asking you for some information."

Sean's eyes narrowed. For a moment, Rick thought he would fling out another insult. Instead, he swung around and stomped out of the station.

Rick sighed and walked over to the desk, where Craig was on the phone. The sergeant hung up and looked expectantly at Rick.

"You did warn me," Rick said.

"Yeah. That was Seaver calling. I told him he could contact Mr. Chappell at his mother's house, and to expect some belligerence."

"I'm glad it's not me going there."

"Mmm. You don't think Jill and Kate were really snooping, do you?" Craig asked. "I know they've tried to stay on top of things."

"The way they told me, it was the other way around. They went to do a good deed, and the Chappell women just spewed stuff they didn't ask them, almost too much information. Anita told them her kids fight, and Amelia seemed to think Sean was Stanley's favorite kid, stuff like that."

"Well, you did fine with him, but it's probably a good idea if your sisters don't go over again for a while."

"I'll tell 'em. It's okay if they check on Carl Roofner, though, right? He and Jillian have gotten to be good friends, and I think he's pretty lonely right now."

"I don't see a problem with that, and I've still got a patrol officer checking in at the store several times a day." Craig picked up a stack of forms. "A call came in about a broken window at the Methodist church. Can you go by there? I've got Geordie on traffic this afternoon."

"I'll get my jacket and be on my way."

"Good, because otherwise I'd make a gift to you of this paperwork."

Rick hurried out with mixed feelings. He understood his sisters' frustration at not being able to jump into the thick of the investigation. The state police had seen to it that he was in that situation too. He wanted nothing more than to dig deeper on the Chappell case, but if he did, he could be interfering with Detective Seaver's activities, and he could make people like Sean Chappell angry because several people asked the same questions over and over.

Better to take care of something mundane like the broken window complaint and then go home for supper.

Kate couldn't suppress a slight resentment as she went over the checklist in Room 6. Jillian got out of the house a lot more than she did lately.

This time her sister was at a weekly Bible study.

She paused with her clipboard in her hand. *What's wrong with me? I love living here and working with Jillian. Forgive me, Lord. I really am thankful for all You've given us.* And she didn't really begrudge Jillian the Bible study group. Church services had been canceled Sunday because of the heavy snow. Maybe that was part of Kate's mood problem—she hadn't attended worship for a couple of weeks.

Poising her pen over the list on the clipboard, she looked around. Framed print of an illustration from the first American edition of *David Copperfield*—check. Tin with a scene on the lid of a Victorian stagecoach and the saying "Barkis is willin' "—check. Inkwell and quill pens—check. The Victorian curio cabinet beside the closet door was intact, with its display of seashells and a couple of antique snuffboxes. Nope, the guests who'd stayed in the room three nights hadn't stolen any of the theme decorations.

Kate gazed at the print of the Copperfields' housekeeper Peggotty's home on the shore in Yarmouth, England. She liked that picture better than one their father had found of young David and the smarmy Uriah Heep. She'd tried to persuade Jillian to hide that one in the attic. Her sister hadn't given in, but had agreed to hang it in a corner, where it didn't smack you in the face when you first entered the room.

In the distance, she heard a ding. *Oh, no, someone's down in the lobby waiting for help.* She dashed out into the game room and down the stairs that came out opposite the front desk. A man stood there with his back to her.

"Hello. May I—" She stopped as he turned toward her. Kate had only glimpsed Peter Schuman once, but she was sure he was the visitor staring stonily up at her. He had said he'd be back, but he'd left them alone for several days. Her stomach roiled.

"Where's my cousin?"

Kate swallowed hard. He was even more intimidating than Jillian had let on. "And—and who is your cousin?"

"Michael Schuman. I want to see him *now*."

Kate's knees shook as she went down the last two steps. "I'm sorry, is he a guest here?"

"You know very well he is."

"Sir, we can't confirm that."

"I say you can."

He took a step toward her.

Kate swallowed down her surge of panic. "No, I can't. I have to ask you to leave."

He held her gaze for several seconds then turned on his heel and strode into the hallway.

Oh, no! The elevator . . .

Kate dashed after him. He'd moved past the elevator to the end of the hall, where two guestrooms lay. Her pulse rocketed as he hammered on the door of the Anna Karenina Room.

"You in there, Mike?" He grabbed the door handle, but it wouldn't budge. He swung around toward the Jeeves Room and pounded on the door. "Mike? Open up!"

After a couple of seconds, the door opened a crack and white-haired Mr. Dunn peered out at him.

"I'm sorry—who did you want?"

Schuman turned away without a word and strode to the elevator. He stabbed the call button.

Kate's impulse was to hurry to Mr. Dunn's door and apologize profusely, but she had to act quickly if she was going to keep Peter Schuman away from his cousin. She caught Mr. Dunn's eye and mouthed "Sorry," then ran to the lobby desk and snatched up the phone and punched in the extension for Room 9. It rang twice, during which she heard the elevator doors open.

"Hello?" Mike said cautiously.

"Your pillow," Kate blurted. "Hurry. The new pillow—he's in the elevator. Get out of sight fast!"

She slammed down the receiver and pulled out her cell. Quicker to call Rick on that.

"What's up, Kate?" his reassuringly normal voice said in her ear.

"Hurry! It's the cousin! He's pounding on all the guestroom doors, looking for Mike."

Chapter 17

Kate shoved her phone back in her pocket and bolted for the stairs. When she reached the second-floor landing, she veered off toward the game room. *Whack, whack, whack!* Peter Schuman was assaulting the door of the Elizabeth Bennett Room.

"Open the door," he bellowed.

She ducked back around the corner and resumed her sprint up the stairs. At the top, she burst into the roomy lounge they called the library. Her gaze went at once to the bookshelves across the room. A man was disappearing behind the displaced shelf unit. She hauled in a breath and stood there for a moment, making sure it closed all the way.

Better not stay here. His cousin will guess he's on the third floor.

Turning, she made herself breathe more deeply and set a more relaxed pace as she descended two flights to the lobby. Mr. Dunn and three other guests were clustered around the front desk.

"What's going on?" one woman demanded. Ms. Knowles, Kate thought.

"Yeah," Mr. Dunn said. "What's that guy doing, knocking on all the doors?"

"I'm so sorry." Kate reached the lobby floor

and walked toward them, her hands outstretched. "That man is convinced his cousin is staying here, and he insisted on seeing him. I told him we can't reveal information about our guests, but—"

"Couldn't you just call the guy's room?" Ms. Knowles asked. "He scared me silly."

"The police are on the way." Kate reminded herself not to let on to anyone whether or not the man's cousin was a guest.

"Police?" asked a businessman staying in the Hercule Poirot Room.

"Yes—" At the sound of a siren approaching, Kate huffed out a breath and dredged up a smile. "In fact, I think they're here now."

She went to the front door and flung it open. Patrolman Dave Hall was mounting the porch steps.

"Hello, Kate. Rick says you have a problem guest?"

"Not a guest, someone looking for a guest. He's hammering on every door, demanding to be let in. He's bothering our other guests." She waved toward the group of complainers, which had grown to six.

Dave cocked his head and looked up at the ceiling. "Yup, I hear him. Where is he?"

"Last I knew he was on the second floor, but he may be up on three now. You can take those stairs or the elevator, down the hall."

As Dave disappeared up the curved stairway,

the front door opened and Rick pushed past a couple of the patrons.

"Library?"

"I'm not sure. Dave Hall just went up the stairs."

Rick turned to the stairway and took them two at a time. They could hear muffled voices, but the pounding seemed to have stopped.

Kate put a hand to her chest and sucked in a big breath. "Folks, I am so sorry. The Novel Inn will serve free snacks and non-alcoholic beverages in the game room and the library this evening, and if you wish to have a box lunch or a picnic basket tomorrow, we'll fix it for you gratis."

She and Jillian had discussed perks they could give inconvenienced guests, up to a free night's stay. But they couldn't offer that to the entire guest list—they'd go broke. Kate hoped the snacks and box lunches would meet with Jillian's approval.

Several guests murmured among themselves. Their eyes looked less panicky, and Mr. Dunn said, "I guess I could use a box lunch. I've got a long drive tomorrow."

"We'll have it ready for you when you check out." Kate gave him a grateful smile.

"Is it safe to go back upstairs?" Ms. Knowles asked.

"I think so. The police will probably bring that

man down the elevator, though, so you may want to use the stairs."

Several guests turned toward the steps.

"We're taking our kids to the lighthouse tomorrow," said Mrs. Stein, from the Scarlett O'Hara Room.

"Would you like a picnic basket?" Kate asked.

"That would be lovely."

"For four, right?" Kate picked up a pen from the desk. "Any allergies or special needs?"

By the time she'd taken the Steins' order and made a note of Mr. Dunn's box lunch, Rick and Dave were getting off the elevator with Peter Schuman in tow.

"But I *saw* my cousin's jacket in there. I *know* it's his room," Schuman insisted.

"Hush," Dave said. "You can put all that in your statement at the police station."

"This is ridiculous!"

"No, Mr. Schuman, this is the law," Dave said.

Rick gave Kate a tight smile. "Mr. Schuman will be leaving and not returning. Do you want to press charges?"

"Uh . . . for what?"

"Disturbing the peace comes to mind."

"Uh . . ." As she hesitated, Dave steered Schuman toward the door, and she saw that his wrists were handcuffed behind him.

The prisoner threw her a look of hate. "I know he's here, you—"

"That's enough," Dave said sternly. "Come on."

When they were out the door, Rick said, "We can keep him a few hours, even if you don't want to press charges, but it might be a good idea."

"What about terrorizing? Some of those women were scared. I—I was too."

"I don't blame you. Look, he's not from around here, right?"

"I don't think so. He came in an Uber the first time. I'm not sure about this time."

"There's a car with a New York plate right near the porch."

"That could be him. I can check it on our guest register and see if it belongs to one of the guests."

Rick nodded. "If he's from out of state, that means he doesn't have a local lawyer on tap. We can keep him tied up for a while, I'm sure. Where's Jill?"

"Out. She went to her Bible study, and then she was going to check on Carl, I think."

"Well, when she gets home, ask her if she wants to press charges."

"What would happen if we did?"

"We'd hold him over for arraignment. It would inconvenience him and probably embarrass him and cost him something for a fine and maybe legal help."

"And bail?"

"Well, disturbing the peace is usually a misdemeanor, so he probably won't have to post bail. He didn't actually touch anyone, did he?"

"Not that I know of. He didn't lay hands on me."

"Good. I don't know what this family feud is about, but he's taking it to the extreme. Talk to Jillian. Hauling him in may be enough to intimidate him into going home when we release him, but if he comes back here, he'll definitely be held on something more serious."

"Okay."

Rick put his hand on her shoulder. "You sure you're all right?"

She swallowed hard and nodded. "I may lock all the doors early tonight, though."

"You can do that. I need to get to the station and process his cousin."

"All right. Thanks, Rick. You and Dave were terrific."

"You did pretty well yourself, innkeeper lady." He gave her a quick hug. "Now . . . what about the, uh, extra pillow?"

Kate clapped a hand to her mouth. "I forgot! He's still in there. I'd better go tell him he can come out now."

When Jillian walked into the bookstore, it was empty. No one at the counter or in the aisles, but she heard muted voices coming from the back of the store. They did not sound happy.

She walked quickly toward the back room, and the agitated tones increased. Her heartbeat surged. That was Eric Roofner, she was sure.

"You said you'd give me money to set it up!"

She winced and pictured Carl cowering before his larger son.

The owner's voice was softer, and she leaned toward the closed door to catch his words.

". . . I said I'd consider selling the store. Eric, I don't have that kind of money right now. I wouldn't be able to help you with a down payment until this business is sold, and that takes time."

Jillian stomach clenched. Could Eric force his father to sell the bookstore?

"Well, I've found the perfect location," Eric all but screamed. "I won't find another place this good if I have to wait weeks."

"More like months," Carl said. "I can't sell the business overnight."

"Have you even started the process?"

"Not yet. I have to make some decisions. But I can make an appointment with Darren Purdue—"

"He's a lawyer, not a real estate agent."

"Yes, I know. There are several legal considerations—"

"Do whatever you have to."

Heavy footsteps warned Jillian, and she jumped away from the door toward the children's books.

The door opened inward, and Eric strode out into the aisle. He frowned at her.

"Hello, Eric." She clutched the picture book she'd grabbed from a shelf. "Is your father here?"

"He's out back." Eric hesitated a moment and then pushed the door open a few inches. "Dad, Jillian Tunney's here." He turned and walked toward the front of the store without further acknowledging her.

Carl came slowly out into the store and gave her a weak smile. "Hello, Jillian. May I help you?" He looked pale, and his hair was disheveled.

"Just thought I'd check in, since I was out and about this afternoon." She slid the book back into its place.

He glanced toward the counter, where Eric sat concentrating on the computer screen.

"Is everything okay?" she asked softly. "I heard . . ."

"I'm sorry. My son and I—He doesn't want to be here, but he refuses to leave me here alone."

"It's almost closing time." Jillian looked at the clock. "I could stay with you until five. That's when you close, right?"

"Yes, I usually close at five in the winter. I stay open later in the summertime."

"Why don't you ask Eric if he wants to head out?"

"We came in his truck."

"I'll take you home." She smiled. "It's only another forty-five minutes."

"Well, if you really think . . ."

"I do. I'm happy to stay, and it will give Eric a little break."

"All right."

Carl went to the counter and held a brief conversation with Eric. Their voices stayed low, and Jillian was glad, especially when a couple of customers entered. Eric went into the back room while Jillian perused a row of cozy mysteries, and Carl came to her side with an air of relief.

"He's going home and get some things done, I guess. Thank you, Jillian. I'm glad Eric wants to take care of me, but it was getting a little stressful."

"No problem."

Carl nodded toward the back room. "He's getting his coat, and he'll go out the back. He's parked in the alley."

"Why don't you give me a quick lesson on your cash register? I could come help you out now and then."

He seemed amenable, and Jillian chatted easily with him while he showed her the steps for cashing out a sale made with a credit card and then one with cash. One of the customers came to the counter, and Carl greeted the woman.

"Do you mind if my new helper checks you out?" Carl asked. "I'm training her."

Jillian carefully completed the transaction, and Carl nodded.

"You did that just right."

"You were great," the woman said. "Mr. Roofner, you're lucky to get her."

"I think so too."

At quarter to five, Carl began counting down the money in the register and put the cash and checks in a bank bag. He handed it to Jillian.

"I'll lock the front door and turn down the lights. Oh wait, you're parked out front?"

"Yes, just down a few spots from your door."

He went to check the back room and put the bank bag in the safe, then came out with his coat and gloves. Jillian retrieved hers from where she'd stashed them behind the counter.

"All set?" she asked.

"Ready if you are." They walked out of the dimly lit store, and Carl secured the door.

"Right over here." Jillian walked with him to her Taurus, garish red against the white snow-banks. "Don't get your feet wet." She wondered if she should help Carl, but he managed to step over the ridge of snow between the sidewalk and the parking space.

Soon they were on their way to his house. Sound was deadened by the thick layer of snow blanketing everything, and the surface glared in the sun's last rays. Carl lived outside the town proper, on a rural road where the houses were up to a quarter mile apart. A nice place to raise your kids, she thought.

"I feel like Eric expected too much of me," Carl said.

"You don't have to explain to me," Jillian said softly.

"No, but it would be nice to talk to *someone*."

"Then go ahead. We're friends, and whatever you say will stay between us."

He sighed. "After Stan was shot, I mentioned that maybe I should think about selling the store. Apparently, Eric took that to mean that I would, and soon. He hoped I could give him money to start his own business. But he doesn't understand. He wants to sell machinery, and that's expensive inventory."

"Maybe he could start out with a repair shop."

"Maybe. But that's not his dream. He wants a full-blown showroom with motorcycles and snowmobiles under one roof." Carl shook his head. "Not very realistic, I think, for a man who's not put aside much money over the years."

Jillian braked carefully, much earlier than she would normally at the stop sign. As expected, it took longer for the car to come to a halt than it did when the road was bare.

She looked over at her passenger. "I don't want to be nosy, but why does Eric expect that of you?"

"I tried to disabuse him of the notion. But to

tell the truth, I've probably spoiled him. He says I tied him to the bookstore and made him work part-time there for low wages since he was in high school. Says he didn't have a chance to get a better job and start the career he wanted."

"Do you think that's true?" Jillian waited for an SUV to pass and pulled out onto Carl's road.

"Not really. I never forced him to work for me. I started him in the store as more of a favor—giving him a summer job for pocket money, you know?"

She nodded.

"If he'd ever wanted to take another job, I wouldn't have stopped him. I think he likes being part-time, so he can take days off whenever he wants. It never seemed as though he resented working for me. Not until lately."

"How old is he?"

"Nearly forty."

Jillian tucked that away to mull over. She hadn't realized Eric was that old—she'd thought he was at least five years younger.

"Could be he's having a midlife crisis," she suggested as she approached the house. "He might be looking back and feeling as though he hasn't done anything significant. Everyone likes to think they're leaving a legacy with their life." A pickup parked on the shoulder narrowed the roadway to little more than one lane, and she steered cautiously around it.

"I suppose so." Carl craned his neck, gazing toward his driveway. "Looks like the plow didn't give us a lot of extra room."

Eric's truck, with a snowplow on the front end and a trailered snowmobile behind it, was parked in front of the garage.

"Should I park out here on the road?" Jillian asked.

"No, someone might come around the curve and not see you. Just pull in behind Eric. You won't be here long. But you'll have to be careful backing out."

Jillian parked and got out to take Carl's laptop from the back seat. As she leaned inside, Carl opened his door. She told herself to be quick, so she could get around the car and make sure he was steady on the snow-coated drive.

A couple of pops sounded from the direction of the house. She straightened with the laptop case in her hand. Carl peered at her fretfully over the top of the car. "Was that firecrackers?"

Something unseen squeezed Jillian's heart. "No. Gunfire. Get down."

Chapter 18

As soon as Rick was out the door, Kate locked it and hurried up the stairs. By the time she reached the third floor, she was puffing, but she didn't slow down as she crossed the library and pulled the lever beneath a shelf to open the secret door.

Mike Schuman jumped up from his chair in the little chamber and stared at her. His features relaxed as he recognized her.

"Thank heaven! I thought it was Peter."

"Nope, he's at the local police station as we speak, trying to talk his way out of a stay in jail for disturbing the peace."

"Wow. I feel kind of bad about that. I mean, he is my cousin. He'll probably never forgive me for this."

"Well, he terrified our guests." Kate stared into his eyes until Mike looked away.

"You're right. I could hear him down below, pounding and yelling. I'm sorry. I brought this on you."

"Yep, you did. Don't you think you should tell us what this is all about?"

Mike sighed and waved toward the chairs in the room beyond her. "Got a few minutes?"

"I should actually go down to the lobby. My sister's not here, and no one's down there at the moment. But you can come sit in the office with me."

He hesitated. "Do you think he'll come back?"

"It's possible. Jillian and I have to discuss pressing charges—or not. If we don't, I suppose he could disobey the officers' orders and come back, looking for you. And he opened your door and recognized some of your things."

Mike swallowed hard. "I must not have shut it tight when I ran out of there. You said there was another room you could move me to?"

Kate stood gazing at him for a long moment. Her estimation of Mike Schuman had just ratcheted down a notch or two. He was scared of his cousin, and he wanted to keep hiding from him. He didn't seem to care that he'd caused emotional trauma to at least a dozen people.

"Yeah, we can move you if you want. But first, I'd really like to know what's behind this."

"Okay, I'll come downstairs with you. You go first and make sure the coast is clear."

"All right, but come out of there. I need to make sure this is shut and no one else sees the door open."

He started to leave the sanctuary but turned back. "Oh, I almost forgot." Two steps took him across the tiny room to a shelf, where he retrieved a square wooden box.

"What's that?"

"Take a look. It's some sort of compass. I think

it's really old. I was going to ask you about it."

Kate frowned and took the box from him. She opened it and peered down at a brass-rimmed compass about six inches across.

"Huh. I've never seen it before."

"Really? It was behind those books over there." He nodded toward the shelf.

"I'll have to ask Jillian about it. I think I'll just leave it here for now."

"Sure. I won't tell anyone about it."

"Thanks."

Mike stepped into the lounge, and she pushed the library shelving gently. It swung back into place with a reassuring click.

Kate turned to the stairway and walked down with measured tread, thinking about the past half hour. At the second-floor landing, she glanced into the game room. A couple and another man sat in the lounge chairs, talking calmly.

She continued to the ground floor and went to the lobby doorway, where she scanned the hall and dining room and beyond, to the living room that overlooked the bay. No one was in sight. She waited until she heard Mike's steps on the landing above. He paused and moved on down the steps.

When he appeared on the curved stairway above her, she said, "Everything's fine. Come on down. Do you want coffee?"

"That sounds good."

He came down the last few steps, and she pointed to the office doorway behind the lobby desk.

"In there. You can shut the door. I'll come in from the hallway. Do you take cream or sugar?"

"Just cream. Thanks."

She strode to the dining room's coffee station, grabbed a tray, and fixed mugs for both of them. A few Danish pastries and muffins were left from breakfast in the clear, boxed-in shelf unit, and she picked up the tongs. It was nearly suppertime, but she figured they could both use a sugar boost. At least, she could. With a variety of pastries on a plate and some napkins, she picked up the tray and carried it carefully out into the hall.

The elevator doors opened, and she nearly dropped her burden. Mrs. Stein got off smiling, and Kate relaxed.

"Oh, Kate, I'm glad I ran into you. About the picnic basket for tomorrow . . ."

"Yes?"

"Jeffrey's on a cheese kick. Would it be possible for you to put in a cheese sandwich for him? Just cheese, but no meat?"

"Of course. Does he like mayonnaise, or lettuce, or . . ."

"A little mayo, and mild cheese. That's it."

"Sure. Ham and cheese okay for the rest of you? Or we have sliced turkey, tuna, and peanut butter."

"Ham and cheese sounds great. Thanks."

Kate nodded. "I'll fix it first thing in the morning."

Mrs. Stein headed for the dining room. Kate was glad she'd raided the pastry shelves when she did. She decided she'd better unlock the front door for now. Balancing the tray carefully, she did that then opened the office door and went in.

"Oh, that looks good." Mike rose and took the tray from her and set it on the desk. "Thanks! I was actually kind of hungry. Did you make these muffins?"

"I did make that batch. The Danish came from a bakery."

"Well, you're a super muffin baker, I'll testify to that." He picked up a blueberry one and the milky mug of coffee.

Kate sat down and took her cup of black brew. "Before you bite into that, give me some answers."

He made a wry face and sank into a chair opposite her. "Right. Well, see, I borrowed some money from Peter."

Kate gaped at him. "All this fuss is over a debt between cousins?"

"Well, it's a little more complicated than that."

Jillian crouched beside Carl, pushing down on his shoulder to make sure he stayed low behind her car. She strained to hear anything. At first she

257

heard nothing but distant traffic sounds. Then a door closed and footsteps crunched on the snow.

Carl stirred, and she pressed on his arm. "Shh!"

The footsteps hastened, and a moment later, a man ran past the car, heading for the road. When he was four or five yards beyond the Taurus, he flung a look over his shoulder. Jillian pushed Carl down flat on the ground. *Lord, help us! Help us!*

The footsteps sounded again but grew fainter. She dared to glance toward the road and glimpsed the man's form dashing past the snowbank Eric had left near the entrance to the driveway.

"He's gone." She sat up and tugged at Carl's sleeve. "Are you okay?"

"I think so. Who was that? Did you see him?"

"Help!"

She jerked upright at the muffled cry and listened. "Did you hear something?"

Carl stood shakily beside her, leaning against the car.

"Help!"

She could barely recognize the muffled cry.

"That's Eric!" Carl scrambled around her and staggered toward the house.

"Wait," Jillian called, her heart racing.

Carl hesitated, and she caught up to him. "Let me call the police first."

"But Eric—"

"I know. This will only take a second." She was already hitting Rick's icon.

"Jillian?"

"Yes. I'm at the Roofners' house. We think Eric's been shot. When we drove in, we heard what sounded like gunfire, and a man ran out of the house."

From the road, she heard an engine start. That truck down the road. Why hadn't she paid more attention?

"He's getting away, Rick. Black pickup!"

"Got it. Keep safe. We'll be right there."

"We're going in to see if Eric needs help."

He didn't tell her not to do it, so she tapped to end the call. "Carl, let me go in first."

"No. He's my son."

From the house came another plea for help, more of a moan.

"Come on." She could move faster than Carl, and she took advantage of that fact, running toward the porch.

The front door wasn't locked, and she threw it open. Peering into the dim interior, she yelled, "Eric?"

"Help . . ."

He sounded far away—or very weak.

She hauled in a deep breath and strode through the living room in the direction of the voice.

Eric lay on the floor in the kitchen, sprawled on the beige and brown tiles.

"Help me." His desperate eyes met hers for an instant, then he squeezed them shut.

As she rushed to his side, Carl came in behind her and flipped the light switch. She squinted in the glare and turned her attention to Eric. Blood soaked one leg of his jeans. He still wore his light gray jacket but had unzipped it. A dark stain bloomed on the right side of his abdomen.

She yelled over her shoulder, "Call an ambulance!" Rick may have already done so, but she wanted to be sure. "Eric, can you speak to me?"

His lashes fluttered, and he looked into her eyes. "J—" He fumbled to clap his left hand to his side and whimpered.

She knelt on the floor. "Help is on the way."

Eric nodded and shuddered. "Is—is Dad okay?"

"He's fine. Who did this, Eric?"

He panted a couple of times before looking up at her again. "He was wearing a mask."

"A ski mask?" Jillian frowned. Behind her, Carl shakily talked to the 911 dispatcher.

"D-Dad?" Eric turned his head, searching for Carl.

"You father's calling 911." Jillian laid back his jacket and noted the spreading stain under his fingers. It morphed into a grotesque design on his T-shirt. Breathing was an overwhelming task for her. She couldn't imagine how hard it was for Eric.

Peeling off her jacket seemed logical, and she wadded it up and applied the mound to Eric's abdominal wound.

He sucked in a breath and groaned, fumbling to grasp the fabric.

"I'm sorry. I don't know what else to do." She threw a glance toward his leg. That wound was bleeding too. A lot.

Carl said, "Ambulance is on the way. What else can I do?"

"Get me something absorbent. Towels—anything."

Half a long minute later, he came to her side with both hands full of clean dish towels.

"Careful," Jillian barked. "I don't want you to slip and hurt yourself."

Carl edged back, away from the blood pooling on the tile near Eric's leg.

"Put a couple of those on his leg and apply pressure." Where were those EMTs? She yanked her bloody jacket from Eric's hands and shoved a wad of dish towels in its place.

He moaned and lay still.

"Hang in there, son," Carl said.

He crouched beside Jillian. They waited, both panting from exertion. A siren wailed in the distance.

"They're coming," she gasped.

Carl adjusted his towels against his son's thigh. "Is he . . ."

"I think he passed out," Jillian said, but she wondered too. Had Eric fainted because of the pain? Or had he lost too much blood already? *God, help us!* Aloud, she said, "Pray, Carl."

Chapter 19

Mike Schuman's mouth worked for a moment before anything came out. "Okay, see, I was planning to buy a house three years ago. I was married, and my wife wanted it really bad. She kept begging me to get us out of our apartment. So I asked Peter for a loan."

"To help with the down payment?"

"Yeah. But—"

Kate's cell rang, and she pulled it from her pocket. "Sorry." She glanced at the screen. Jillian. Should she take it or ignore it? "It's my sister."

"Go ahead. My story can wait."

Kate just bet it could. He was probably hoping she'd forget all about it.

"Hey, Jillian."

"Kate, Eric's been hurt."

"What? Is he—"

"The ambulance is here, and they're taking him to Bangor. Someone came to the house and shot him. He's got some nasty wounds. I was just bringing Carl home when it happened, and he's very upset. I'd like to drive him up there, to the medical center. Do you mind?"

"I—I guess not." Actually, Kate felt useless

263

and once again cast aside. "I could ask Don to come—"

"No, one of us needs to be there in case Mike Schuman's cousin comes back."

"He was here! I'm sorry, I should have called you. Rick came, and they arrested Peter Schuman."

"Rick's just driving in," Jillian said. "Craig and Geordie got here before him. So, is it all right if I take Carl and go to Bangor?"

"I guess so. Yes, of course." What was the matter with her? Carl needed her sister! "And Rick can fill you in on what happened here."

"Okay. I'll call you when we get to the hospital."

Kate signed off and looked at Mike. "She's taking a friend of ours to the hospital. His son was—was badly injured." No sense spilling everything to this guy. He was a stranger, after all.

"I'm sorry." Mike looked truly sympathetic, which caused her a pang of regret. Why couldn't he be the man she'd hoped he was?

"So, back to the story," she said. "You borrowed some money from Peter."

"Right." He looked away. "I was going to use it for the house, I really was."

"You mean you didn't?"

"It took a long time to convince him to make the loan, and then, before we could close on the house, Lindy walked out on me. So, of course I didn't want to buy a house with her not there, right?"

Kate frowned at him. "Tell me you gave the money back to Peter."

He looked away, his face souring. "If I had, would he be hounding me now?"

"I'm guessing not." How could she have thought this man was in the right?

"I didn't mean to renege on the loan," Mike said quickly. "It just—well, I had some bills to pay, and they gave Lindy a chunk of alimony, and before I knew it, the money was mostly gone."

"That's a lot of debts," Kate said.

"Yeah. I guess I was looking at it as a kind of consolidation. So, I only owed Peter, and not half a dozen other people."

"What did Peter say?"

His mouth skewed.

"What? You didn't tell him?"

"Not right away. But when he found out I didn't buy the house . . ."

"Of course he wanted his money back."

"Yeah." Mike huffed out a breath. "Only I'd decided to go on a ski trip with this buddy of mine, and—"

"What? You spent what was left of his money on a *ski trip?*" Kate's screech grated on her own nerves, and she pulled in a deep breath. "How long ago was this? Did you say three years?"

"Yeah. Three years on Friday." He paused and glanced at her, as if expecting a response.

"Are you going to pay him back?"

"Not planning on it."

"Why not?"

"Well, see, the statute of limitations on debt collection is three years. So if I don't give him anything by Friday, the debt is cancelled."

Kate scowled, thinking about it. "That doesn't seem right. For one thing, I thought the statute of limitations was six years, not three."

"Not where I'm from. In New York, it used to be six, but they changed it, and now it's three."

"Really?" She wasn't sure she believed him, but she wasn't going to argue over it now. His explanation made her wonder if he had enough left in his bank account to pay his two-week hotel bill. "Uh, what exactly do you do for a living, Mike?"

"I'm a dental hygienist."

That surprised her. She couldn't remember meeting a male hygienist, but she supposed that reflected her small-town, conservative background.

"So . . . are you on vacation, or what?"

His very handsome eyebrows drew together. "Yeah, I had some time coming, and I thought this was a good time to use it."

"I see." But she wasn't sure she did. Something

still didn't add up. She'd ask Jillian. Her sister might have more insight. "Why didn't Peter come after you before this? Why now?"

"Uh . . . I had told him before that I'd pay when I could, but, uh, somebody might have told him about the deadline. That statute of limitations thing."

"Somebody?"

He seemed unable to look her in the eye.

"So, okay. What now?" she asked.

Mike huffed out a breath. "Peter will be upset that the police took him in. I don't think he has a record."

"Well, he does now, and that's his own fault."

"Yeah, in a way."

"In every way. You're not the one who yelled and pounded on people's doors, and you're not the one who called the cops."

"True." His frown lifted. "Thanks, Kate. I should have thought of that earlier."

"Well, it's probably not over. For you, I mean." She pursed her lips. "The police asked if we want to press charges. I'll have to talk to Jillian about that."

"Could they keep him in jail?"

"I don't know. It might just be a misdemeanor thing. Or maybe he'll have to pay a fine." She shrugged. "Anyway, Rick said they won't let him go right away. You should go to your room and get some sleep."

"I guess you're right." He watched her closely for a moment. "What's the matter?"

She let out a sigh. "This whole thing. You've hidden here for the last two weeks—"

"Not until Friday."

"All right, almost two weeks, and you've bothered a whole lot of other people."

"Peter's the one who did that. You just said so."

"Because of you," Kate said. "We assumed you had a legitimate reason for hiding, and that we were doing the right thing by keeping him away from you."

"You were."

Kate frowned but said nothing. After several seconds, she stirred. "Would you like more coffee?"

"No, thanks." Mike eyed her for a moment. "Would you like me to leave? Leave the inn, I mean? Tonight?"

"We don't mind your staying, so long as our other guests aren't disturbed. And if you want a different room, I believe Scout Finch and Jeeves are vacant right now."

"Jeeves? As in the butler?"

"Gentleman's gentleman, but yeah. Oh, and the guest in the Virginian Room checked out, but that's the one Jillian wants to redecorate, so it might be best not to put you in there right now."

"Hmm. Where are those rooms? What floor?"

"Jeeves is down here on the first level, and

Scout Finch is the one that shares the bathroom with your room on three."

"I don't think I'd feel secure on the first floor. There's not another secret room down here, is there?"

"No." She closed her lips tightly. No way was she telling him about the one on the second floor. He knew enough of her family's secrets.

"Well, I guess I'd take the other one then. Scout Finch?"

"Yeah. From *To Kill a Mockingbird*. I'll code another key for you. Just move your stuff in there and lock the door between the vanity area of the bathroom and the main part of the bath. Leave the key to Rip Van Winkle in the room, and the maid will pick it up when she cleans. Oh, and if you hear someone moving around in there, it will be the maid or else me or my sister. If we can help it, we won't reassign the room you have now."

He swallowed hard and nodded. "Guess that's the best you can do."

Kate frowned. The best they could do. Right. What did he want, a penthouse with a bodyguard at the door?

She went out to the front desk, unlocked the drawer where they kept the key cards, and quickly did the coding. The front door opened, and her heart slammed as she looked up to see who was there. Craig Watkins strode into the lobby.

"Sergeant! What brings you here?"

"Since Jillian and Rick are tied up, I thought I'd drop by and update you."

"Thanks." Kate looked over her shoulder. Mike Schuman stood inside the office doorway, watching them fretfully. "Would you please excuse us, Mr. Schuman? I need to speak privately to Sergeant Watkins." She held out the new card.

"Sure. I'll go move my stuff." He took it and went out the door that led to the hallway.

"That's the guy who's caused all the commotion?" Craig asked.

Kate nodded. When she heard the elevator doors open and close, she relaxed a little. "Come sit down. Would you like coffee?"

"I'd love it, but I'd better not stay that long. I need to get back to the station."

"Rough day?" she asked.

He hesitated. "I just came from breaking up a big fight at the Chappells' house over some carved duck decoys." He held up both hands. "That's all I'm saying, and it's probably too much."

Kate couldn't help smiling. Her sister had told her about the decoys. "I don't know how this town could survive without you guys. Come in here, where we can have at least the impression

270

of privacy." She led him into the office and closed both doors then turned to face Craig. "Okay, so exactly what went down? Jillian said Eric was shot."

"That's right. She stayed with Carl at the bookstore while he closed up and then drove him home. When they got there, they heard gunshots and saw a man run out of the house and down to the road, where he'd left his truck."

"Wow. He went to Eric's house and shot him?"

"Yes. Up until now, the violence has been confined to the store."

"So you think it was the same person who shot Stanley Chappell?"

"We have no proof. But of course it's possible it's the same man who killed Mr. Chappell—not to mention the driver who ran down Carl Roofner."

"It seems like too much of a coincidence that those things happened at Carl's store and then at his house." Kate scowled at him, waiting for confirmation.

"I agree. So we sent Eric to Bangor in the ambulance, and Jillian and Carl are following in her car."

"Do you think she's safe?"

He hesitated.

"Did one of your officers go with them?"

"I sent Geordie in the squad car. I need Rick

here to investigate. Eric will no doubt have surgery. Rick will go up later to talk to him. No sense sending my best man up there to cool his heels for several hours."

Kate nodded, frowning. "Did Eric say anything?"

Craig hesitated. "He said the shooter wore a ski mask."

"Of course he did." Kate met his gaze. "Jillian and I have both heard Eric arguing with someone on the phone and she's seen him refusing to take calls."

"So, you think Eric knows the person who shot him?"

"Don't you?"

"It's a good possibility. And your sister will probably tell you this anyway, so I'll say it. When the man ran out of the house and passed her and Carl, where they were hiding behind Jillian's car, he wasn't wearing a ski mask."

Kate stared at him. "She saw his face?"

"Just for a second, but we're going to have her look at some photos later."

"So, Eric was lying?"

Craig gritted his teeth. "I wouldn't go that far. It's possible the shooter had on a mask and tore it off as he left the house."

Kate blinked but couldn't think of anything to say.

"He saw Jillian's car when he came outside,"

Craig said. "Just be glad he didn't turn and shoot at her and Carl."

"Absolutely."

"When Eric's able to talk again, Rick will press him on that. Because if we can I.D. the shooter, there's no point in Eric lying about it."

"What's Eric's prognosis?"

"I don't know. He was bleeding heavily, and it's a long ride to Bangor."

"Why didn't they take him to Bucksport? I guess he needed the facilities in Bangor?"

"I'd say the EMTs felt it was best to take him directly there."

"So it's really serious. He could die."

Craig frowned as though reluctant to give an opinion on that. "He had two wounds, at least. One in his leg and the other in his abdomen."

Kate winced. "I suppose Jillian will call after she gets to the hospital."

"I'm sure she will. The medical personnel will update Carl. I expect Geordie to call in too, as soon as he gets any solid information about Eric's condition."

The desk phone rang, and she snatched it up. "Novel Inn."

"Hello. I'd like to make a reservation."

Kate grimaced in Craig's direction and said into the phone, "Of course, can you hold just a second?" She muted the call. "I have to take a reservation."

"I need to get moving anyway."

"Thanks for coming by, Craig."

He nodded and headed for the lobby door. When he reached it, he paused and turned back. "You call me if anything weird goes on here."

"I will. Thanks." Now, that was the kind of man her sister should hang on to. The kind of man she wished Mike Schuman had turned out to be. She mustered her most pleasant voice and pushed the button on the phone. "There now, what days did you want to stay with us?"

Jillian handed Carl one of the paper cups of coffee she held and sat down beside him on a waiting room chair. Geordie Kraus paced farther down the room, having already downed a cup of coffee and refused a refill.

"Do you think we'll hear something soon?" Carl asked. His face was pale, and his voice wavered.

"Well, it's only been an hour since they took him in." Jillian sipped her drink and tried not to make a sour face. The top-notch coffee they served at the inn had spoiled her.

A couple of times she saw Geordie talking on the phone, and one of the hospital's security guards came in and spoke to him briefly. Finally, the doctor came in and went straight to Carl.

"Mr. Roofner, your son is out of surgery. It went fairly well, and I expect he'll make a good recovery. But he'll need a lot of rest, and then physical therapy."

"Can I see him?"

"They're getting him settled in the recovery room, and he's not awake yet. I'll have a nurse come get you when you can go in."

"Thank you. Doctor, how long do you think he'll stay here?"

"Several days at least, maybe a week or so. We'll see how the healing process goes, shall we?"

Carl nodded.

Jillian could almost hear his mind creaking through all his worries and problems. She put her hand on his shoulder as the doctor left the room.

"Come sit down, Carl. You're worried about the store, aren't you?"

"Yes, but not as much as I'm worried about Eric." Carl sank onto a vinyl-covered chair. "Oh, Jillian, what should I do? Should I sell the store?"

"I don't think you should make any major decisions until you see how quickly Eric gets better. If he can't work on starting his own business for several weeks, or even months, then you probably need to keep the Book Rack going."

Carl sighed. "If I have to keep closing it, I'll be in the red. And if that man comes back—" He turned to face Jillian, his features taut. "First Stan, now Eric. And he tried to get at me. What is going on, Jillian?"

"I don't know." She stroked his arm rhythmically, hoping to soothe him. "The police will find out. Meanwhile, don't forget I told you about Hannah Reece this afternoon. She needs a job. Her father, Don, is our nighttime desk clerk. He's a terrific worker and very reliable. I've met his daughter, and I like her. She might make a good employee for you."

"I don't know." Carl's eyes crinkled. "If I have to be up here a lot for the next few days . . ."

"You could give her some instruction and work with her half each day, then come up here for a few hours. Carl, I can go to the store some, too, and you wouldn't have to pay me. I could stay with Hannah while you're gone, if you're concerned about her being alone in the store."

"I am, but . . ." He eyed her anxiously. "Hannah?"

"Yes, Hannah Reece. I told Don to have her call you, but of course, she can't get through to you while you're away from the store. But I could call Don and get her number. She could be at the store when you open in the morning, or even a half hour earlier. You could do an interview, and if you feel she's a good candidate, have her work with you tomorrow morning. Unless you need to be here, of course."

Carl took a shaky breath. "That might work. Would you be there?"

"I can be."

"Thank you. But I need to know Eric's stable first."

"Yes. The doctor sounded optimistic."

"He didn't give many details, though."

Jillian's heart ached for the older man. They sat in silence until Geordie came over.

"Mr. Roofner, the sergeant asked me to go to the recovery room and stand watch over Eric tonight."

"You'll be here all night?" Carl's brow furrowed.

"Well, for several hours. Then a county sheriff's deputy will relieve me. But we'll have an officer on duty constantly until we're sure Eric is safe."

"Thank you."

He left the room, and Jillian said softly, "Carl, would you like to pray together for Eric? I know you've been praying ever since it happened, but . . ."

"Will you, Jillian?"

"Of course." She took his hand and prayed quietly, earnestly, for Eric's life.

When she opened her eyes, a nurse in a blue uniform was entering the waiting room. She looked around, spotted them, and walked toward them with a smile.

"Mr. Roofner?"

"Yes." Carl stood shakily, and Jillian jumped up in case he needed steadying.

"Your son's coming around. If you want to

come with me, I'll take you in to see him."

"Thank you. Can Mrs. Tunney come too?" Carl asked.

The nurse looked at Jillian. "Are you family?"

"No, I'm Carl's friend. I drove him here."

"I may need her," Carl said. "Please. She's a big help to me."

"It's not our usual policy."

Jillian clamped her lips shut and grabbed her belongings, along with Carl's coat, and followed them down the hall and through the imposing double doors.

Chapter 20

When Jillian walked through the inn's front door at five minutes to ten, Kate sat at the desk. She tapped her phone when she saw Jillian and pulled out her earbuds.

"Just listening to an audiobook."

Jillian nodded. "Everything quiet?"

"It is now."

"I guess I missed the big show, huh?"

"Yeah." Kate grimaced. "Mike's in Scout Finch now, and I put the Rip Van Winkle Room on Mindy's list for cleaning tomorrow."

"Okay."

"How's Eric?"

"He came to, but he was in a lot of pain, so they gave him more painkillers. Carl and I sat with him for a couple of hours, but he was asleep when we left. Geordie Kraus is still up there. He said he doubted the police will be able to question him until tomorrow."

"So, he was gut shot?"

Jillian's lip curled in distaste. "Don't say that in front of Carl. But yeah, he took one bullet on his right side, lower abdomen. It just missed his kidney. The other wound was to his left thigh. I thought he was going to bleed out right there in the kitchen, but the ambulance arrived fast."

"Man. What did you do?"

"Put pressure on the wounds with towels and prayed." She held up a bulky plastic bag a nurse had given her. "My jacket's beyond repair."

The doorbell rang, and they both turned toward the glass front door. Don Reece stood outside and gave them a wave. Jillian strode over and opened up for him.

"Hey," he said. "Am I late?"

"No. Come on in." Jillian walked with him to the desk, where Kate still sat. "Don, we told you about our guest, Mr. Schuman, didn't we?"

"Is that the 'Do Not Disturb' guy?"

"Yeah," Kate said. "His cousin's been back, making trouble. We called the cops on him, and they've got him in a cell right now."

"Wow, I miss all the action." Don set his messenger bag on the desk. "What else do I need to know?"

"Mike Schuman has moved out of Room 9 and into Room 8." Kate spread her hands. "We don't expect any more trouble tonight, but if anybody comes around asking for him, call Room 8 and tell him the extra pillow he asked for will be right up."

Don frowned at her. "Is that some kind of a code or something?"

"It means he's supposed to hide."

"Call us on one of our cells if that happens," Jillian added.

"Okay. Do I call the cops?"

Jillian looked at her sister.

Kate shrugged. "Only if the person won't leave or starts making noise, I guess."

"Got it."

"Oh, and I'm supposed to meet Carl at the Book Rack in the morning," Jillian said. "I called Hannah after I talked to you. She's going to meet us there at eight thirty, half an hour before opening time. If Carl likes her, I'll stay with her and open the store. Carl will drive himself to Bangor to be with Eric."

The next morning, Jillian awoke still tired. She barely remembered a snippet of a dream, in which she was working in the bookstore and wearing a Kevlar vest.

She joined Kate in preparing breakfast for their guests and was surprised to see Mike Schuman enter the dining room ten minutes before they officially opened. Nearly everything was set up, but still . . .

"Good morning," she called cheerfully as she set a covered dish of hot link sausage into the warmer tray.

"Hi." He glanced around at the otherwise empty room and chose a coffee mug. "Thought I'd grab something to eat before the crowd descends."

"Help yourself. We don't usually put the

omelets and bacon out until the last minute—but it's the last minute."

He chuckled. "I have to say, the food here is excellent. I know I've been a pain for you, but thank you for putting up with me—for helping me. Your brother was very understanding too."

"We try," Jillian said. She pulled off her oven mitts. "Kate told me about your problem with your cousin. Is something like that really worth this feud with him? Couldn't the two of you just sit down and work something out?"

"That wouldn't be a good idea right now."

"Why is that?"

"Because, as I told Kate last night, when the statute of limitations runs out on this debt, I won't owe Peter anything. I don't want to talk to him until that happens, which is Friday."

Lord, show me how to respond.

"Mr. Schuman—Mike, I don't think that's the way it actually works."

"What do you mean?"

Jillian swallowed hard. "I don't think the debt just goes away. The statute of limitations means he can't sue you for it anymore—can't take you to court over the debt. But you'll still owe it to him. He can put collectors onto you and demand repayment for the rest of his life."

He stared at her for a moment. "Huh. Is that just here in Maine?"

"No, I don't think so. It's pretty much everywhere. Have you paid him back anything at all?"

"Nope."

She nodded slowly, trying to remember what she'd learned in the past, when a friend was going through the stress of trying to collect an old debt. "I'm surprised he didn't come after you before this. I think you should talk to a lawyer about it, one who knows the law in your state."

"Maybe." His eyes shifted.

"Go ahead and get your breakfast." Jillian gave him a fleeting smile. "Talk to someone who knows. And then maybe you can patch things up with your cousin. Because losing a friend over something like that—well, it's not worth it."

"We've never got along very well."

"Then why did he lend you the money?"

"I . . . I don't know. It took a lot of convincing."

"And you promised to pay it back, right?"

Mike looked away. "I did tell him I'd pay when I was able."

"Maybe he was trying to have a better relationship with his cousin," Jillian suggested.

"I can't imagine it." Mike frowned and picked up a plate.

"My sister and I get along really well. We have occasional disagreements, but we've always managed to talk them out. And my brother—sometimes he's put out with me. But after we cool off, he's always willing to make up."

With a scowl, Mike opened the sausage warmer

and took the tongs. "Peter's not that way."

"Are your parents and Peter's still living?" she asked softly.

He looked off across the room. "My father died recently, and my mom five years ago. Peter's folks are gone too."

"I'm sorry," Jillian said. "We lost both our parents in an accident last spring."

"That's rough." Mike put several sausage links and a blueberry muffin on his plate.

"I know it's not really my business, but a sibling—or a cousin—is a wonderful thing if you make it that. I can't imagine how devastated I'd be if I lost Kate or Rick now."

"That's good for you, but it doesn't work in our family." He picked up his mug and headed for the door.

"Wait! Don't you want . . ."

He was gone. She shook her head and went back to the kitchen. In the doorway, she met Kate, who carried a bin of cheese omelets.

"Was that Mike? Did I miss him?"

"Yeah. I wanted to talk to him about forgiveness and how God can help him and his cousin, but we didn't get that far."

Kate's face drooped. "Did you tell him what you told me last night? About the statute of limitations?"

"Yes. He wasn't happy about it. I suggested he sit down with Peter and try to work things out.

Maybe try to have a better relationship with his cousin."

"Yeah. After all, Peter did loan him a huge amount of money."

"Well, I hoped we'd get around to a productive discussion, but it didn't happen."

"I'm sorry. You know, I thought he was such a great guy, but my estimation of him took a huge hit yesterday."

In the hallway, the elevator opened.

"I know." Jillian picked up her oven mitts. "But he's not interested in even trying to reconcile with Peter."

Kate looked past her. "Here are the Steins. You'd better get the bacon out. I'll tell them their picnic basket is ready."

They worked steadily for an hour, then Jillian took off her apron and hung it on a peg near the back kitchen door.

"I've got to go get ready. I'm meeting Carl and Hannah at the store in half an hour."

Kate set down the tray of dirty dishes she'd just bused from the dining room. "Okay. I'll take care of any stragglers and finish the cleanup. Say, Jill—"

Jillian turned back with her hand on the storeroom doorknob. "What?"

"What do you think about Mike? I mean, really. Should we ask him to leave?"

Jillian sighed. "It's only two more days. I

285

did suggest he get himself a lawyer, but I don't suppose two more days will matter much, now that I've given him a heads-up."

Kate opened the heavy-duty dishwasher and started loading plates and silverware. "I can't stop thinking about it. Friday morning, I want him out of here, and his bill paid in full."

"Yeah, I've been thinking about that too."

Kate's lips squeezed into a thin line. "We have no guarantee his credit card company will honor the payment."

"It's not like the card was refused," Jillian said. "But you're right, we don't usually have guests who stay two weeks and owe that much."

"Maybe Rick could check his credit record."

"Wouldn't that be a conflict of interest, since Rick's a part owner in the inn? But I guess we could ask Craig about it. And stop waving those forks around, or you'll stab someone."

Kate shoved the handful of flatware into a compartment in the dishwasher. "I really don't want us to be out two weeks' fees."

"I can't think about it right now. If Rick comes by, you can ask him, okay? I have to run."

Jillian hurried out the back and down to the carriage house. She changed her clothes quickly and ran a brush through her hair. Eyeing her image in the mirror critically, she decided she'd pass as far as the bookstore clientele was concerned. After pulling on her old jacket, she grabbed her purse, and hurried out to her car. On the way at last—or not.

She braked when she reached the inn's parking lot. The police department SUV Rick drove most workdays was parked in front of the lobby. She glanced at the clock and threw the transmission into park.

In the lobby, Rick stood before the desk talking to Kate.

"What's going on?" Jillian asked.

Rick turned to her. "Hi. I'm not staying. I just wanted to tell you about a bulletin we got at the station. But then Kate started telling me about Schuman. Do you want me to ask Craig about it?"

Jillian considered it. "I think we should wait. We don't know anything's wrong."

Kate nodded. "I guess we can do that and not borrow trouble. Now what was the bulletin that brought you here?"

Rick glanced at Kate and back to Jillian. "Jacob Reynolds's wife is dead."

Jillian frowned and looked at Kate, but her sister seemed to be just as much in the dark as she was.

"Who's Jacob Reynolds?" Kate asked.

"You know. The guy you two tailed in the park."

"We didn't know his name," Jillian said quickly. "Craig said he'd do some checking on him, but—"

"Wait. His wife is *dead?*" Kate's voice rose, and her gaze drilled into her brother.

Rick nodded. "Craig heard it from the state police about twenty minutes ago. Jacob called it in to the Kennebec County Sheriff's Office."

"Kennebec County?" Jillian tried to picture it. Craig had said the man lived in Waterville. Maine's capital, Augusta, was there too.

"He lives on the outskirts of Waterville," Rick said. "The local police logged the call on the database the state police use, because the S.P. were up there asking questions about this Reynolds guy a few days ago, thanks to you two. And Detective Seaver, from the state police, called Craig."

"Wow. Maybe our little stint as private investigators did some good," Kate said.

Jillian made a sour face. "How is it good if the guy's wife is dead?"

"Because we already had a tentative link between Reynolds and Eric Roofner," Rick said. "We had no proof he was the one Eric was supposed to meet, but it was a possibility. The state police are already questioning Reynolds, and as soon as Eric can talk again, we'll ask him about this guy."

"But . . . was the wife shot?" Jillian asked.

"No. If she was, we could try to match the bullets to the ones that hit Eric. But this is a case of blunt force trauma."

"You mean, somebody bashed her over the head," Kate said.

Rick let out a big sigh. "Something like that. We've got a long way to go on this one, I'm afraid."

"Do you think Carl is safe?" Jillian asked. "I dropped him off at his house last night, and I'm headed for his store. I'm supposed to work at the store today with Don's daughter, Hannah, while he goes to the hospital."

"Hmm." Rick's eyebrows drew together.

Kate gazed at Rick. "What about the bookstore? Will Hannah and Jillian be safe there?"

"It might be better not to open it today," Rick said.

Jillian bridled at that. "Carl's losing money. He can't keep the store closed this much and break even."

Rick nodded slowly. "Be careful. Really careful."

"Can you stop in and check on us?" Jillian asked.

"I'm headed for Bangor to talk to Eric, but I'll speak to Craig about it. He's going to get some good pictures of this Reynolds character for you to look at. He may be the man you saw at the park—or at Roofner's house yesterday. It seems to fit what's happened. But we don't have conclusive evidence yet. Meanwhile, we'll make sure an officer goes by the store a couple of times today. You call right away if anything seems funny, okay?"

Many of the downtown stores didn't open until ten in the winter, but Carl stuck to his 9 a.m. opening time, except for the one day he was in the hospital. Jillian parked around the corner and approached the Book Rack at eight twenty-five with misgivings.

If Rick was uneasy about the bookstore reopening, they all probably should be. In light of the recent violence there and at the Roofner home, it might be best for Carl to cut his losses and close permanently. She hated that thought.

Hannah Reece pulled into an empty parking space a few slots away from the store's front door. Jillian paused and waited for her. Hannah climbed out of her ten-year-old Civic and grinned when she saw her.

"Jillian! I'm so glad you're here. Dad thinks I have a pretty good chance of landing this job."

"I do too. Carl really needs someone right now. If he okays it, I'll stay with you while he goes to be with his son at the hospital."

"I'm ready." Hannah bounced a little as she walked.

As they neared the door, Jillian said, "Did your dad tell you about the crazy things that have been happening here?"

Hannah sobered. "Yeah, and I saw it on the

290

news. We'll be safe, won't we? I mean, you wouldn't be here if you thought we were in danger, right?"

Jillian paused with her hand on the door. "We'll need to be cautious."

"Dad says whoever the shooter is, he got the people he was after."

"I don't know about that. But we'll be on our toes." She pulled the door open, wondering how many brave souls would dare to enter the Book Rack today.

Carl looked up from where he was arranging books on the sale table.

"Good morning."

"Hi!" Jillian strode toward him with a smile. "This is Hannah Reece, the young woman I recommended."

"Pleased to meet you," Carl said.

Jillian eyed his drawn face. Even though he smiled at Hannah, he looked worn out. She made a quick decision not to bring up the Jacob Reynolds matter. If the police thought he should know, they could tell him in Bangor.

"Did you sleep last night, Carl?"

He shrugged. "Some. Not as much as I'd have liked."

Jillian put a hand on his shoulder. "Are you sure you want to drive all the way to Bangor by yourself?"

"Yes. I want to be there for Eric. And I want

to hear what he says about what happened yesterday."

She nodded. "All right, then let's get to it, shall we?"

"I thought we'd meet out here." Carl glanced toward the door. "It's probably best to have someone out front at all times, where we can see the door."

"Good thinking."

"I put a couple of folding chairs by the counter. I thought we could sit there and talk, if you ladies don't mind."

"It's fine with me." Jillian turned to Hannah. "Ready?"

Hannah nodded eagerly. "I brought you my rather slim resumé, Mr. Roofner."

"Good, good." Carl led the way to the counter and took a seat on the stool behind it.

Jillian took one of the chairs and turned it slightly, so she could easily look toward the door without shifting much. Hannah pulled off her jacket and sat down in the other chair, facing Carl. She opened her tote bag and took out a folder, from which she extracted a sheet of paper and slid it across the counter.

"I got on at the dollar store last summer, but business has been slow since Christmas, so they laid me off about two weeks ago."

"And do you have future plans?" Carl asked.

"I'm starting to think I might want to go back

to school later," Hannah said, "but not yet. I'd like to work a while longer. I don't know what I'd study, so it seems like a waste of money until I know that. I'm trying to save up, though. My folks aren't rich, and I'd have to help with the tuition, for sure."

Carl nodded, surveying the paper. "I see you've put down your supervisor at the dollar store as a reference."

"Yes, she offered to recommend me. She told me they were pleased with my work, but they couldn't keep on so many part-timers at just a few hours a week."

He pursed his lips. "I can't pay much." He named the hourly figure, and Hannah smiled.

"That's more than I expected."

"If it were too much, I wouldn't have offered it." Carl stood. "Jillian, perhaps you could instruct Miss Reece on how our cash register works while I go out back and give Ms. Barton a call."

"Certainly." Jillian raised her eyebrows in Hannah's direction, and they both rose.

As Carl walked down the center aisle toward the back room, she pulled the folding chairs aside. "Carl showed me the ropes a few days ago. This system is easy as pie. You shouldn't have any trouble, with your experience at the other store." She sneaked a glance at her phone. "Ten minutes until opening."

"Do you think he's going to hire me?" Hannah's eyes gleamed.

"Unless your old supervisor says something negative."

"She won't. I was always on time, and I worked hard."

"No worries, then." Jillian showed her how Carl accepted cash and credit cards. "I never saw him take a check. I think he would, if it was someone local, but maybe we should ask him."

"Who writes checks anymore?"

"Right. Now, let's take a quick run through the store." She showed Hannah the layout by section. "We have to keep an eye on kids—once in a while, parents will leave them in the children's section while they go look at something else."

Looking around the store, Hannah pushed back her auburn hair. "Okay, I know it won't happen, but just for drill, what should we do if someone walks through the door with a gun?"

Stomach clenching, Jillian tried to keep her voice even. "Get down behind the most solid thing available. If you're toward the back, try for the back door. But stay low. I'm keeping my cell in my pocket, in case I need to make a quick call. I have my brother at the top of my contacts. And pray."

As Hannah nodded soberly, Carl came from the back room.

"Well, young lady, Ms. Barton gave you a good

recommendation. I'll need you to fill out a form later, but if you and Jillian are ready to begin work, I'll head for Bangor now." He looked at Jillian.

"I believe we are."

"Great. Thank you so much for doing this. I called the hospital, and they said Eric's awake and had a light breakfast."

"Wonderful." Jillian stepped forward and gave him a brief hug. "Carl, do you need any help cleaning up at home?"

He gave her a sheepish smile. "I think I got most of it last night."

In dismay, she cried, "After we got back from Bangor? But it was so late!"

"I know, but I couldn't go to bed and leave it like that."

She nodded, picturing the bloody tiles in his kitchen. Under the circumstances, she wouldn't have been able to leave it and go to sleep either. "I'm so sorry."

"Thank you." He nodded at them both. "Now, I'll be off."

Chapter 21

Rick paced the hospital hallway, waiting for the doctor to finish examining Eric. He'd brought Dave Hall along to take over for the officer guarding Eric's door and sent him for coffee before starting his shift. At last the doctor emerged from the patient's room and focused on Rick.

"He's awake and alert, Officer. You can speak to him now, but he's due for more pain meds in half an hour. I suggest you wrap it up by then."

"Thanks. Is he going to be okay?"

The doctor hesitated. "That depends on what you mean by 'okay.' He has a long recovery ahead, and he may have some residual effects. But I expect him to be able to walk and function fairly normally in time, if that's what you mean."

Rick nodded soberly. "That's a lot for him and his father to take in."

"Yes, it is. I intend to sit down with his father when he gets here and have a frank discussion about Eric's needs—therapy and so on. But to be honest, the woman he says found him and helped him until the EMTs got there saved his life."

"That was my sister."

"Well, if she hadn't come along when she did, he'd have bled out in minutes." The doctor eyed him keenly. "I'm told that his father was also attacked recently. Do you know who's behind it?"

"We're working on it."

The doctor grunted and walked away.

Rick let out a breath. He loved solving crimes, but interviewing victims was not his favorite part of the process. He strode into Eric's room and was glad to find the young man was the only occupant of the two-bed room.

"Eric, how you doing?"

"Hey, Officer Gage." Eric blinked and touched the button that raised the top half of the bed until he was sitting nearly vertical.

Rick pulled over a chair and sat down facing him. "I guess you know what I'm here for. Can you tell me what happened yesterday?"

Eric sighed and gazed at the opposite wall. "I was at the store. My dad and I were talking. Then Mrs. Tunney came in. She's the one who was there the day Stan was shot."

"She's my sister."

"Oh, yeah, that's right." Eric scrunched his eyes shut for a moment. "I'm on pain meds."

"Yes, I know. I won't keep you long. I just need to get an idea of what happened after you left the store."

"Okay. Yeah. Let's see . . . Jillian said she'd bring my dad home, so I went on back to the house. I loaded up my Ski-Doo because I hoped I could get out for a ride this morning. Then I went in and started cooking some chili for supper. Then someone knocked on the door."

"And you let him in?"

Eric hesitated. "Well, yeah."

"Was it someone you knew?"

Eric's lips twitched. "Not really. He had on a parka and a ski mask. Black ski mask."

Rick leaned closer. "Eric, you said last night that the man was wearing a ski mask. So it's hard for me to understand why you'd let in someone wearing a mask unless you recognized them and trusted them."

"Well, I . . ."

"You were shot in the kitchen, Eric. Not in the front room, where the door is. I don't think that guy went around to the back door, because the path hadn't been shoveled. I looked."

Eric's eyes darted about, seeming to search for anything but his face.

After a moment, Rick said, "And I'll tell you another thing, buddy, my sister says that guy was not wearing a mask when he came out of the house."

"She saw him go out?"

"Yeah. She and your father had just driven in. They were out of the car, and they heard the gun go off. Jillian pulled your dad down behind the car. So, I'm thinking maybe she saved both your lives last night."

Eric swallowed hard. "I'll have to thank her."

"Yeah, you will. Now, give it to me straight. Did you know the person who came to your door last night?"

Eric stared at the opposite wall. "I'd seen him before."

"So you *do* know him."

They sat in silence for a moment, and Rick said, "Why did he shoot you, Eric? You know it wasn't random."

His face twisted. He seemed unable or unwilling to meet Rick's gaze.

"Come on," Rick said. "You know more than you're saying. You're holding out on me." He waited then added, "We can help you."

Eric shook his head. "Nobody can help me."

"Has someone been threatening you?"

No response. Rick almost felt sorry for him, but he knew this was his best chance to get some answers. If Eric stayed silent now, he might never tell the full story.

"Look, Eric, if you're in debt, or if someone wants revenge on you, you need our help. It's too big for you to handle alone."

Eric stared up at the ceiling.

Rick considered the incidents of violence in and outside the bookstore. "Stanley Chappell's death," he said softly. "The hit-and-run on your father. Now this. It's all connected, isn't it?"

How could he jolt this man out of his stubborn

silence? Rick thought about his conversations with Craig about his sisters' escapade at Higgins Park, followed by the news they'd heard last night. The man Jillian and Kate had followed had gone home last night and found his wife dead.

"The surgeon who operated on you yesterday removed a bullet from your leg."

Eric turned toward him, his mouth open.

"We'll see if we can match it to a gun used in other crimes. It was a handgun, right?"

Eric nodded, and Rick took that as a good sign. At least it was some form of communication, even if it was minimal. He decided to lay it out there.

"Jacob Reynolds's wife was killed last night."

He let it hang there between them and watched closely. Eric's eyes widened, and he clenched his teeth.

"Tell me what you know, Eric."

"He did it himself."

At last! Rick pulled in a deep breath. "Why do you say that? You were nowhere near his house in Waterville. What makes you think Reynolds killed his wife?"

Eric jerked his head away.

"Come on, Eric. I know that you know Jacob Reynolds. And you know something about why he's been violent lately."

No response.

"You were supposed to meet him at Higgins

Park a week ago, but you didn't show. He waited a while, but when you didn't come, he took off."

Eric turned slowly toward him, his face drained of color. "How—"

"One of our officers reached the park just after Reynolds left. Where were you? Were you scared to meet up with him?"

"I did go to the park, but I was late, and I saw a cop car there, so I drove on by." He looked up at Rick. "Was that you?"

"No, it was my sergeant. Why did Reynolds want you to meet him there?"

Rick thought he wouldn't answer, but after a few seconds, Eric jerked his head in a nod.

"I'm not sure. Probably to threaten me again. But I finally told him I'd meet him, because he wouldn't leave me alone. He kept calling me over and over. Even when I was at the store with Dad. I was afraid if I didn't go, he'd do something else bad."

Rick nodded. They would get his phone. There'd be a lot of evidence there. "Why did he keep calling you, Eric? We need to know, before somebody else gets killed."

"I . . ." Eric grimaced and clenched a handful of the sheet. "I figured it would be crazy to meet him. If he believed me when I said I wouldn't do what he wanted, he'd hurt me. Or somebody else. And I couldn't tell him I would do it."

The pieces shuffled in Rick's brain, but it still wasn't adding up. "Do what?"

"I don't even want to say it."

Their eyes met. Rick said slowly, "He wanted you to do something in exchange for him killing Stanley, or what?"

"No, no! Stan was an accident. I'll never fogive myself."

Still not making sense. "You were in Clifton when Stan was shot. You didn't kill him."

"No, I would never hurt Stan. Or my dad. You've gotta believe me!"

"Your dad." Rick sat back in the chair as the jigsaw puzzle took shape. "He was supposed to kill your father, and he got Stan by mistake."

"Yes, but I never told him to kill Dad. I wouldn't!" Eric held out both hands in supplication. With a wince, he touched his bandaged side.

"Then why did Reynolds try to do it?"

"It was all his idea, and I said no. He'd been complaining at a snowmobile meet the week before about his wife being a drag. He wanted her gone. I griped back a little about my dad, how he kept me tied to the bookstore and wouldn't let me do what I wanted. So he came up with this plan."

"He'd get your dad out of the way, and you'd take care of his wife."

"Exactly." Eric's eyes widened. "But I didn't—it was all him."

"How well did you know this guy?" Rick pulled out his notebook.

"I didn't. We met for the first time that day."

"What day, and where was it?"

"One week before—before Stan was . . . It was in Carrabassett Valley. See, I belong to a snowmobile club, and we go to different places where there are trails, meet up with other clubs. I'd never seen this guy before, that I remember. He had a nice machine, and we started talking."

"A snowmobile."

"Yeah. We had a couple beers together over lunch, and he started spewing about his wife. I wanted to get away from him, but I thought I'd be polite, you know?"

"So you started bad-mouthing your father."

Eric looked away. "Yeah, I guess so. Dad and I disagree about the future of the bookstore, and I said a few things about that. But I didn't want him dead! Or Stan either. When Jacob suggested he'd take care of my problem if I'd help him with his, I didn't know what he meant at first. He had to spell it out for me."

"What did you say?"

"I was sick. I couldn't believe he really meant I should kill someone. I tried to backpedal. I said no, no, I didn't want to go to that extreme, but he'd got it into his head that this was perfect.

We had no connection before the rally. He . . . he even offered to do his part first. I told him no, don't do that. I don't want my father dead."

"What did he say?"

"He just laughed." Eric's mouth skewed and his eyes shimmered.

The door opened, and a nurse came in with a paper cup in her hand.

"Time for your medication, Mr. Roofner."

Eric accepted the pills. Since he was closest to it, Rick handed him the container of water from the bedside table. Eric sipped from the straw and handed the water back to him.

The nurse looked at Rick, eyeing his uniform. "He needs his rest now, Officer."

"Okay, I'll be right out. I promise." Rick stood and pushed his chair aside.

She eyed him doubtfully but went out.

"Tell me the honest truth," Rick said. "If you said no, why did Reynolds carry on with it?"

"I don't know. He must have been desperate to get rid of his wife. But I swear, I told him to forget it and walked away. I thought it was done. And then . . . the next week I got the call from you, telling me to come home and get to the store. When Stan was shot. I thought—" Eric's face crumpled. "At first, I thought he'd killed Dad."

Rick gave him a moment to regain his composure. "So, Reynolds didn't go to the rally in Clifton."

"No."

"But he knew you would be there?"

"I might have mentioned it the week before."

"So he knew you'd have an alibi for your father's death," Rick said.

"I guess so. He'd said something about making sure each other was covered when we . . . when we did our part. That was what made me realize he was serious, and how dangerous he was." Eric grimaced and reached to lower the bed.

"I have to leave," Rick said. "Just tell me, why didn't you call the police?"

"At first, I kept telling myself he couldn't really mean it. Then nothing happened for a few days, and I thought he'd dropped it. Or found someone else to make plans with. But then . . . Stan. And he started calling me . . . over and over."

The calls he ignored or tried to deal with when Kate and Jillian were nearby. Rick sighed. "It didn't occur to you that your father was in danger? Or Reynolds's wife?"

Eric huffed out a breath and shook his head. "They say . . . hindsight is 20:20 . . . you know?"

"We're going to get him," Rick said. "Not just for Stanley's murder, but for attacking you and your father."

"You don't know it was him."

"We know it was him at your house last night, right?"

After a moment's hesitation, Eric nodded. "I'm sorry I lied. It was him."

Rick exhaled in relief. He hoped Jillian could confirm that when she saw photos of Reynolds. The truck she'd seen on the snowy road was a signpost too, but he had Eric's word now. He clenched his jaw. "If he did kill his wife, we'll get him."

"I hope you do." Eric closed his eyes.

Rick watched him for a few seconds. If Eric wasn't dozing, he was a good faker. He walked slowly out into the hallway. Dave Hall sat in a chair just outside. He stood as Rick closed the door.

"Did you get anything?"

"Yeah." Rick frowned. Jacob Reynolds had been taken in for questioning last night in Kennebec County. Was he still in custody? Rick put his hand on Dave's shoulder. "You look sharp, buddy. Nobody goes in but medical staff and Carl Roofner, you got it? Nobody."

"Got it."

"A state trooper should be here to relieve you at noon. Don't you leave this spot until then—not for a second. No coffee, no restroom." He eyed Dave sharply. "Do you need to use the men's room now?"

"No, I did that while you were in with him. I'm good."

"Okay. This guy is not out of danger yet, and

neither is his father. I'm heading for Skirmish Cove. The sergeant and I need to have a confab and update Detective Seaver. I'll see you later."

Rick stopped in the lobby to speak to a security guard, asking him to make sure Carl Roofner made it safely into the hospital when he arrived. Then he hurried out to his SUV. Best to give Craig a call before he set out, to put him on the alert.

"Sarge, it's Rick. Is Jacob Reynolds still detained?"

"No, they let him go while they continue the investigation. He stayed in a hotel in Waterville last night, since his house is an active crime scene."

"Can you get someone over to the bookstore? This isn't over yet." Quickly, he filled Craig in on what Eric had told him. "Now, the way I see it, Reynolds is mad at Eric for not fulfilling his part of what he thought was an ironclad agreement. And it's possible he's found someone else to do the job for him. But he could still be determined to see Eric dead."

"And maybe Carl too," Craig said.

"Yeah. I think he went after Eric yesterday out of revenge for reneging on the agreement. If he's heard Eric's still alive, he must be steamed."

"Yeah, Reynolds still wants to get back at him for sure," Craig said.

"That's what I think. And Carl may be the

answer to his rage. If he takes Carl out, it will prove in some twisted way that Reynolds was faithful to their pact when Eric wasn't."

"I'll get a man right over to the bookstore to stay with Carl."

Rick's throat went dry. "Carl's supposed to come here to see Eric this morning. He may be on the road, and I gave the hospital security a heads-up to watch for him. But Jillian and another woman were going to open the store for him."

"I'll call right now and see who's there," Craig said. "And don't worry—I'll go to the store myself. But, Rick, there's one more thing."

"What?"

"Seaver told me they found a key fob belonging to Eric Roofner outside the Reynolds house last night. It has keys to a Ski-Doo on it. And Reynolds's machine is a Polaris. They're saying maybe Eric killed Mrs. Reynolds yesterday afternoon."

"What does Reynolds say? Does he have an alibi?"

"He didn't get home until late last night— almost midnight. He claims he was out drinking with several buddies. The troopers are chasing them down now for their statements."

Rick's brain raced. "Eric was shot around five thirty last night. When did Mrs. Reynolds die?"

"The medical examiner says it was before that.

Possibly as early as two or three o'clock. No later than five."

"Eric was at his father's bookstore most of the afternoon. Jillian went over—I don't know—maybe four o'clock? Eric went home then. I'll bet Reynolds went to the house to steal something of Eric's to plant as evidence in his wife's murder."

"We've got to get everyone's statement," Craig said. "Reynolds lives over an hour away from the Roofners."

"You're right," Rick said. "It doesn't add up. Reynolds was either sloppy or desperate."

The second hour of the Book Rack's business day was coming to a close, and Jillian was pleased. They'd had a sprinkling of customers browsing the aisles since she unlocked the front door at nine, and several had made purchases.

"How is Carl doing?" became the standard greeting from those who knew him. Jillian was a bit surprised no one asked about Eric. But then, the shooting hadn't made the local news last night. She wondered if Craig and Rick had deliberately kept the incident quiet.

Her satisfaction was short-lived. Just after eleven, a woman she recognized as a reporter for the *Bangor Daily News* breezed in, looked around, and headed straight for the counter, where Hannah was ringing up a couple of books. Jillian intercepted her.

"Hello, Marlene."

"Oh." The reporter stopped, eyed her for a moment, then smiled. "Hello. You're the inn-keeper, aren't you?"

"Yes, Jillian Tunney. You did a feature article when my siblings and I reopened the Novel Inn last spring."

"That's right. How's business?"

"It's been great. I'm filling in for Carl Roofner today."

"Oh. Mr. Roofner's not here?"

"No, he had a family emergency."

The smile was back, but more guarded. "That's why I'm here. I got it from the police log this morning. Apparently, there was another shooting in Skirmish Cove?"

"There may have been," Jillian said carefully, conscious that every word she uttered could be on tomorrow's front page. She was surprised that Marlene would check the police log in such a small town. The report must have made it to the Bangor P.D., and she learned it from her contacts there. She gulped, wishing she hadn't mentioned Carl's family emergency. "It didn't take place here at the store."

"The state police spokesman I talked to didn't name the victim," Marlene said. "I hope it wasn't Mr. Roofner? He's such a nice man."

"No, it wasn't him."

Marlene's eyes narrowed. "But you said he

had a family emergency. Is that connected to the shooting?"

Jillian swallowed hard. She wasn't sure how much she ought to reveal. Pulling in a deep breath, she thought, *I stood up to Peter Schuman. I can stand up to Marlene Cohen too.*

"I think you'll have to speak to someone with the police department for anything on the victim, if that's what you're asking."

The landline rang at the counter. Hannah picked up the receiver and gingerly pushed a button. After her initial greeting, her eyes widened. She beckoned to Jillian.

"Excuse me, please," Jillian said to Marlene.

When she reached the counter, Hannah passed her the receiver mouthing, "Police."

Jillian put the phone to her ear and turned halfway around. As she'd feared, Marlene had followed her and made no pretense of not listening.

"Hello? Jillian Tunney speaking."

"Jillian, it's Craig."

She relaxed and smiled. "Well, hello. What's up?"

"Everything all right at the store?"

"It's fine. We're doing a brisk business." She stepped aside as a man approached with a paperback thriller in his hand.

Marlene had the decency to move out of his way, and Jillian took the cordless receiver away from the counter a few steps, toward the Maine books, giving Hannah space to work.

"Good," Craig said. "Rick called me from Bangor, and he's concerned that someone could be planning another attack."

"What? No." Her adrenaline surged. "What should we do?"

"I'm coming right over. We don't have anything solid, but Eric gave your brother some information that's got us a little on edge. I'll fill you in when I get there."

"All right. Thanks."

Hannah was done with the customer, and Jillian handed her the phone with a smile. "Nothing serious. Just Sergeant Watkins checking on us."

"That's nice," Hannah said, putting the phone back on its base.

"He's coming over," Jillian added, hoping Marlene wouldn't read too much into that.

The reporter smiled. "Oh, good. Maybe I can get some details from him."

The next fifteen minutes dragged. Jillian helped a customer locate the newest issue of *Crochet* magazine and stayed near the counter while Hannah straightened books and toys in the children's section. Marlene wandered about, pausing here and there to pick up a book and read the back cover copy.

Jillian's pulse surged every time the door opened, but each person who entered was a harmless shopper. The postman, Luke Shibles, came in, and she took a handful of envelopes from him with a smile.

"Say, you're not the usual clerk here," Luke said. "Who's running the hotel?"

Jillian chuckled. "My sister. I'm just helping out. Carl had a family emergency."

"Oh. Too bad." Luke nodded and left without any further inquiries.

Relief washed over Jillian. She wouldn't like explaining—or avoiding doing so—with Marlene in the store. Luke probably had to keep a schedule. He never lingered long at the inn either.

She looked around, and her heart lurched. Marlene had Hannah cornered in the Young Adult section. She wished she'd had a chance to tell Hannah to zip her lip around the reporter.

Striding toward them, she caught Hannah's eye, and the young woman stopped talking. Jillian pasted on a smile.

"Hannah, Carl said he left a shipment of new magazines out back—two boxes. I wondered if you could bring out one of those so we can shelve them." She'd actually planned to put the chore aside until later because it would be a meticulous task, but she was in favor of anything that would get Hannah away from Marlene.

"Sure." Hannah gave an apologetic smile to Marlene and headed for the back room.

Marlene pulled in a deep breath, eyeing her

keenly. Jillian got the feeling she was in for a rebuke, but the front door opened at that moment. She turned toward it. Never had she been so glad to see Craig, resplendent in his uniform.

"Ah, Sergeant Watkins is here." She left Marlene standing there and hurried toward him. She met him in the aisle, between outdoor books and cozy mysteries. "Craig! Thanks so much for coming over." She lowered her voice. "We've got company from the *BDN*."

He glanced past her then returned his gaze to her face. "How much does she know?"

"She's heard about Eric. I wouldn't tell her anything, except that it did not happen here at the store."

"Okay." He looked past her again and nodded soberly. "Ms. Cohen. What brings you to Skirmish Cove?"

"I imagine the same thing that brings you to this store. May I ask you a few questions?"

"Of course. I can't guarantee I can answer them all, since we have an ongoing investigation regarding this store."

"Would you like to sit down out back?" Jillian asked. Letting a reporter grill a police sergeant on the sales floor couldn't be good for business.

Craig surprised her. "I'd rather stay out here where I can keep an eye on things, if you don't mind."

"Of course."

Craig drew Marlene toward the far wall, where there were no customers at the moment, and Jillian was grateful for that. She spotted two women heading toward the checkout and strolled toward the counter. Having Craig in the store lowered her blood pressure, despite Marlene's presence. Maybe he could give the reporter a few sound bites and she'd leave.

"Hello," she said cheerfully.

"Hello," one of the women said.

"Oh, you must be planning some day trips." Jillian scanned the price on a book titled *Maine Day Hikes*.

"My grandchildren are coming for a week in May, and I want to be ready," she replied. A second book she'd selected was an illustrated book on Fort Knox, a short distance away in Prospect. It was supposedly the best-preserved granite fort in the country, and Jillian had always loved taking her daughter there and had chaperoned many school field trips to the site. "I hope you have a wonderful visit with them."

The second woman's picks ran to cooking magazines, and they chatted about those for a minute while Jillian ran her credit card through. When the two left the store together, she let out a big breath and glanced at the clock. Two and a half hours of business, and nothing amiss had happened. She felt like calling Carl and giving him a report but quashed that notion. Carl had enough to think about at the hospital. If he wanted updates, he'd call.

She went to help Hannah with the magazines.

"So, we take out the old issues?" Hannah asked uncertainly, gazing down at a copy of this month's *Country Living*.

"Only the ones on the list Carl gave us—oops. I left the list at the counter. Most of them sell out, and he said he leaves the back issues of the puzzle mags and some of the others, because people may come in and buy the back issues. But some need to have only the latest issues on the shelf. I'll get the list."

At last, they'd finished the carton and had placed outdated periodicals they'd removed in the box.

"Should I go get the other box?" Hannah asked.

Craig and Marlene appeared to have finished their interview, and Craig was edging toward the counter as though trying to get away from Marlene. At the moment, the only other customer in the store was a woman leading a toddler by the hand toward the children's section.

"Let's wait on those. You can put this box out back, though."

Jillian walked toward Craig and Marlene. "All finished?" she asked.

Craig brightened immediately. "I think so. Sorry I can't give you more, Ms. Cohen. Maybe in a day or two." His phone whirred, and he took it from his pocket and looked at the screen. "Excuse me, please. It's business."

Jillian had caught a glimpse of his phone and the name "Rick" on it. Good—her brother was checking in. She hoped he was almost here.

Clearly Marlene wasn't happy with Craig's dismissal. As she closed her notebook, a frown wrinkled her brow, making her look older than her true age—or perhaps, Jillian reflected, it let people see her true age beyond the cosmetics.

"I'd like to see the alley where Mr. Roofner was hit last week."

Jillian's chest squeezed. She looked at Craig, hoping he could bail her out of this one. He had turned aside and was talking on the phone in a low voice.

"I'm sure you can find it," she told Marlene.

"May I use the rear entrance?"

"Oh, we're . . ." She was about to say they weren't supposed to allow customers into the back room, but she'd just offered to let her interview Craig there. "Well, it would probably be better if you went outside. If you go to the end of the block, to Bay Street, you can walk around behind the stores and see it."

Marlene lifted her chin, giving her an icy glare.

The glass of the front door shattered, throwing shards into the store. At the same moment, the calm atmosphere exploded in a deafening *pow! Pow! Pow!*

Chapter 22

Before Jillian could catch her breath, she was knocked down, hard. A phone spun past her face, across the floor.

"Take cover," Craig shouted in her ear.

She stared at him stupidly for an instant, light-headed and confused, then looked toward the counter. It was the most solid fixture in the store. Rising to her knees, she crawled hastily behind the end farthest from the door. Craig bailed in behind her, encircling her waist with one arm and pulling her back even farther. As they moved, another burst of gunfire sounded, and a woman screamed.

"Lie down!" Craig moved toward the end of the counter and poked his head around, leading with his pistol. All was quiet for a moment—or was her hearing muted by the blast?—and then he yelled. "Stay down! Anyone in the store, shelter in place!"

Jillian's heart seemed to have stopped functioning, but now it pounded. Where was Marlene? And Hannah? She tried to remember if there were other customers before the shots were fired.

Craig crawled out from their refuge. She wanted to grab his belt and hold him back, but

318

he was doing his job. He was a police officer, and when the need arose, he would rise to the occasion.

He scooped up his phone from where it had come to rest under a shelf unit and then ran out of her field of vision. His footsteps retreated in the direction of the door.

Jillian thought she heard him talking, but she wasn't sure. She listened for more gunfire, but all was quiet for a moment. Then a moan reached her.

She crawled to the edge of the counter and peered out into the open area of the store. Icy air poured through the glass door. The entire panel had shattered, leaving the frame gaping, with only a few jagged bits of glass hanging around the edges. Jillian could barely pull in a breath. Had Craig jumped over the shards and out through the gaping hole?

Marlene Cohen lay on the rug by the discount table, writhing and groaning. Jillian fumbled with her pants pocket and managed to extract her cell and punch in 911.

"What is your emergency?"

"The Book Rack store in Skirmish Cove. There's been a shooting just now. A police officer is chasing the shooter, but we have a person injured. At least one. There may be more."

She looked frantically around the store, not hearing the dispatcher's voice as the woman went on to ask her more questions. How many people were in the store when the shooting erupted?

Hannah! Where was Hannah? She'd gone to the back room with the carton of outdated magazines. Was she safe?

Flicking a glance toward the front door, Jillian knew the shooter was gone. She refused to think what might happen to Craig. Marlene was her most urgent concern, but as she ran toward her, she yelled, "Hannah? Are you there, Hannah?"

She caught a flicker of movement to her right and whirled toward the rear of the store. Hannah's white face peered over a shelving unit next to the door of the back room.

"J-Jillian?"

The relief made her stomach lurch. "Are you okay?"

"I think so. Are you?"

"Yes. I'm calling an ambulance for Marlene. Check if anyone else needs help."

She sank to her knees between Marlene and the table loaded with marked down books.

"I—I think I'm sh-shot," the reporter gasped. With her right hand, she squeezed her left shoulder, and blood seeped between her fingers.

"Hold it tight. Put pressure on it." Jillian remembered the phone she held and put it to her ear.

"Are you there?" a woman's sharp voice demanded.

"Yes, yes, I'm here."

"What's happening?"

"We have at least one person shot. She appears to have a shoulder wound. Her arm, that is. Upper arm. It's bleeding a lot."

"Is she conscious?"

"Yes."

"Help is on the way."

"Th-thank you."

"Stay on the phone with me," the dispatcher said.

Jillian looked up as Hannah jogged toward her. She crouched beside Marlene.

"Is she okay?" Hannah's blue eyes darted wildly about the store.

"Well, she's shot, but she'll make it. Is there anyone else?"

"There's a mom and her little boy in the children's section. The mom's holding her kid and doesn't want to come out."

"I don't blame her. Can you check the back room for a first aid kit? I don't know if there is one. Bring paper towels from the—No, wait. I'll get it." Jillian thrust her phone into Hannah's hand. "Talk to the dispatcher. I'll be right back."

Fetching something to help Marlene was easier than talking right now. Jillian ran to the back room and into the small restroom. She knew there were paper towels in the restroom, but was there anything like gauze on the premises?

She took a quick survey of the tiny room and gave up. With her hands full of paper towels, she ran back out into the store. Hannah was still on the floor beside Marlene, and Jillian peeled off several paper towels and shoved the rest at Hannah. Clumping a few into a pad, she nodded. Hannah removed her bloody hands from Marlene's shoulder, and Jillian laid the absorbent towels over the wound.

Marlene clamped them down with her hand. She seemed lucid, but her face was white, and she was shivering.

Movement behind her sent Jillian's heart skittering, and she whirled toward the sound. Two policemen came in through the door—Craig and Geordie—stepping cautiously over the broken glass. Behind them, several bystanders stood on the sidewalk, peering in at them.

"Thank God you're here!" she ran toward the two men. "We called 911, and they're on the way."

"I did too," Craig said. "Are you sure you're all right?"

"Yes, and so is Hannah, and the customer who was at the back with her child. Marlene seems to be the only one hurt."

As she spoke, Geordie joined Hannah and Marlene.

"Yes, two officers are here now," Hannah said into the phone. "We still need the ambulance."

Jillian gazed at Craig, feeling numb. "What happened? Did he get away?"

"We got him. I spotted the car you took the photo of at the park—Jacob Reynolds's car. He was heading for the highway. Geordie and a couple of state troopers joined me, but it was your brother who got him. Rick was almost back to town. He made a U-turn and cut Reynolds off."

Jillian let that sink in. "Is Rick all right?"

"He's fine. I can't say the same for his vehicle."

She swallowed hard.

"The state police are handling it with him out at the scene. I should get back out there, but I wanted to check on you." Craig took a breath and touched Jillian's shoulder. "Maybe you should sit down."

She shook her head. "I'm okay. You said Reynolds. It was him, then?"

"We've got him for sure on this, and I'm confident we can pin the other attacks on him too. He thought he had a deal with Eric, to kill Carl in exchange for Eric killing his wife. But Eric didn't want any part of it, and Reynolds got angry. Very angry."

"Wow. So—he killed his own wife and then came back to get Eric?"

"That's what we think. Stan Chappell was a mistake. Reynolds thought he was Carl."

Jillian huffed out a breath, trying to make sense of it.

"Where's this customer you mentioned?" Craig asked.

"Come on." Jillian led him to the children's area, in the far back corner. As she walked, she breathed a prayer of thanks that the mother and toddler weren't injured.

A woman of about twenty-five held her little boy on her lap, stroking his back and whispering, "I've got you. It's okay." The child was sobbing, and the mom looked up at them with a haggard face.

Jillian approached them and stopped a couple of yards away. "I'm so sorry you were caught up in this. Are you and your son all right?"

"Yes," the woman said. "But he—he wet himself. Is there a restroom? Maybe we can clean up a little."

"Of course," Jillian said. "And this is Sergeant Watkins. He'd like to speak to you when you're done."

Craig extended a hand to help the woman up.

"Thanks. I'm Lori Monahan." She managed to stand up still holding the child.

"This way." Jillian led her to the back room and showed her the restroom. As she reentered the sales floor, a siren wailed nearby.

"EMTs are here," Geordie called, from where he was still crouched beside Marlene.

"It took 'em long enough," Marlene said through clenched teeth.

"I'll go out and bring them in," Craig said. "That glass is a hazard."

He wheeled and went out without opening the door.

"Should I sweep it up?" Jillian asked. "I don't want to disturb any evidence."

"They'll have to get a gurney in here." Geordie frowned, surveying what looked like mountains of shattered glass. "We need to cover that door too."

"I think I could walk out, if someone can help me get up," Marlene said. Her left sleeve and the front of her blouse were saturated with blood.

Geordie kept his hand on the makeshift bandage. "Better let them look you over before you get up. You've lost a lot of blood, and you may feel woozy when you stand."

Hannah had stepped away toward the local history section and told the dispatcher, "Yeah, they're here. Okay, thanks." She handed Jillian the phone.

Jillian made sure the call was ended and stuck the cell in her pocket. Craig appeared at the door with a uniformed woman carrying a medical bag. He steadied her as she stepped over the glass. He pointed toward Marlene.

Geordie came over to join them, looking to Craig for direction. "What do you think, Sarge? Should we clean up the entrance?"

"If Jillian can get us a broom and dustpan and

a box or a trash bag, we can start, but we need to watch for shell casings and anything else that could be pertinent. Ordinarily I'd say leave it until we have a chance to search everything carefully, but that's dangerous the way it is. Ask the EMTs what they think."

Geordie headed for the blood-stained area of floor that had become their emergency room.

Craig gazed intently into Jillian's eyes. "How you doing?"

She realized she was shaking and thinking how hard it would be to clear away all the broken glass and get the blood off the floor again.

"I'm freezing. Oh, Craig!" Before she knew it, she was enfolded in his arms.

"Hey, it's okay."

"I kn-know." She gasped. "Sorry. I don't usually lose it like this."

"You were perfectly calm when you needed to be. Now's a good time to let it out."

Jillian sobbed and clung to him for a few seconds then pulled away, swiping at her tears with her sleeve.

"Hannah seems to be okay too," he said.

"She's a brick. Kept her cool and did everything right. But what about that Mrs. . . . Mrs. Monahan? And her little boy? They must still be in the restroom."

"I'll go make sure they're okay. You sit down."

Craig guided her to the stool behind the counter. "Is your coat out back?"

Jillian nodded.

"I'll bring it to you. We need to get you home."

She looked over at Hannah, who was pulling on her gloves.

"Hannah, I thought we'd be safe. I'm so sorry."

"It's not your fault."

"Maybe not, but I should have realized there could be danger. I wanted to think it was over."

Hannah shrugged, which only made Jillian feel helpless. Everyone was concerned about her, but who was taking care of Hannah?

"You should be the one sitting down and being waited on." Jillian eyed her critically. "Your dad will probably skin me alive for getting you into this."

"I'm okay. And I'll handle Dad." Hannah gave her a doubtful smile. "I've just been praying— you know—in my head—ever since it happened."

"Me too."

"Sergeant Watkins says I can go home. One of the officers will find me if they need to ask me any more questions." Hannah grimaced. "We might have to testify in court, but he said it would be a while." She looked around. "First day on the job. I guess it could be my last."

"You'd want to keep working here?"

"Well, sure, if that guy is in jail for sure."

"I'll call you later when I know more," Jillian said.

Hannah nodded and left through the smashed front door.

Craig came back a few minutes later with her jacket and a foam cup of coffee. "This was all brewed out back, so I brought you a cup."

"Thanks." She took it.

"I told Mrs. Monahan she can take her son home. I think Geordie's got things here under control long enough for me to take you to the inn."

She started to protest. After all, her car was just outside. But having Craig drive her the short distance seemed a whole lot better. She set down the cup and pulled her coat on. Craig caught the collar and held it while she got her arms into the sleeves.

"How's Marlene?" she asked.

He smiled. "She wants to call her editor and dictate a first-person account. I told her to wait at least until they get the bleeding stopped. They're taking her to the hospital in Bucksport."

"I dread reading tomorrow's paper."

They waited as the EMTs maneuvered a gurney inside, and then they stepped onto the sidewalk. Everything seemed too bright out there. Another uniformed officer was directing pedestrians to the other side of the street, so they'd avoid the store entrance and the ambulance and police cars.

A cold, salty breeze nearly took her breath away.

"Carl might have to close the store," she said as they walked to Craig's squad car.

"I guess that's a possibility. He'll have to sort it out." Craig used his remote to unlock the passenger door and opened it for her.

Jillian's cell rang as she settled into the seat, and she peered at it. "Kate. She must have heard something."

"Tell her you're all right, and you're on your way home," Craig said.

It wasn't exactly a suggestion, but Jillian didn't mind. Going home was precisely what she wanted to do most.

Chapter 23

Two weeks later

"Zeb's got a whole string of flags flying," Kate said as she entered the inn's kitchen through the back door.

Jillian looked doubtfully at the pan of cream filling she was stirring. "Guess I'd better go take a look. I haven't seen him since Stanley's funeral. But not until I'm done with this."

Kate came closer and leaned in to get a good whiff. "Mmm. Is that for the cream puffs?"

"Yes, tonight's dessert. Not very fancy, but . . ."

"Everyone will love them."

Jillian decided she was right. Rick's whole family was coming for supper, and so was Craig. They'd eat in the inn's dining room because the carriage house's eating area was too small.

"I think it's done." The mixture smelled temptingly of vanilla, and the texture felt right. She knew it would set up firmly after it cooled.

"Well, I'm not sure what Zeb wants," Kate said. "YZ and then three more flags. That means it spells something, right?"

"Uh, yeah. It means what follows isn't a code. So, what followed?"

"I don't know. Something and then two of the same."

Jillian turned off the burner and set the pan to one side. "Two of the same?" She frowned at her sister.

"Yeah."

Suddenly it clicked. "Lee. His nephew's there. I should go over and say hi." She reached behind her to untie her apron strings. "Come with me?"

"What? No. I'll watch the front desk."

"But . . ."

"What is it?" Kate asked.

"Nothing, just that I had the feeling last time Lee was there that Zeb wanted to fix us up."

Kate's face furrowed. "Lee is, like, at least fifty. Probably older. Not in your generation, let alone your decade."

"Well, I'm not exactly young." Jillian sighed. "He's nice, but there's just no way. Not with him living in Portland and—"

"And Craig Watkins living three miles away," Kate said with a smart-aleck grin. "Go on. Just don't stay long."

"I can't. I have to fill those cream puffs and cook the chicken. And I wanted to check in on Carl at the bookstore."

"I'll stop in and see him this afternoon," Kate said. "Hey," she called when Jillian had nearly reached the back door. "Take that compass thing with you and show it to Zeb."

"Oh, yeah." Jillian shrugged into her jacket and paused in the storeroom to pick up the wooden box Kate had mentioned. On the side porch, she gazed up at the flagpole that showed above the treetops. Yup, Zeb's signal spelled YZLEE. She jogged toward the bridge, glad this week was warmer than last. Maybe February would be kind to them this year.

When she reached the snug little house on the bluff, she noted a red SUV in the yard. The door was opened by none other than Lee Wilding, Zeb's nephew. He wasn't bad-looking, with gray at his temples and telltale streaks of it in his beard. He grinned at her and swung the door wide.

"Jillian Tunney! What brings you here?"

As if he didn't know. He'd probably prodded his uncle to run the flags up the mast.

"Hi, Lee," she said. "Great to see you." As they walked into the tidy living room, she nodded to Zeb, who sat in his favorite chair. "Hi, Zeb. I brought something for you to look at. I'm hoping you can tell me a little bit about it."

"Oh?" He eyed the square box she set on the coffee table in front of him.

"It's a compass, but it's too big to carry around in your pocket. I figured you'd know a lot more than I did." As she opened the lid, Zeb and Lee both leaned in for a good look. The brass-rimmed instrument glittered, and the needle floated for a few seconds, then stilled.

"That is a beauty, lass. It's from a ship's binnacle."

"Wow. Really? What's a binnacle?" Jillian sank down on Zeb's sofa, and Lee took a chair opposite.

"It's the housing for a compass. Goodness, you need sailing lessons. Maybe Lee can take you out on his boat this summer."

She shot Lee a quick glance. "Oh, I doubt I'll get down to Portland. We keep pretty busy at the inn."

"I might run up here when the weather's good," Lee said.

Jillian decided to ignore that. She wouldn't mind an outing on a sailboat, but she didn't want Lee to think she fancied him.

"Now, where did you get it?" Zeb asked, intent on the compass.

"Remember I told you about the guest who was hiding from his cousin for a couple of weeks?"

Zeb laughed. "I remember. You let him hide in—" He darted a glance at his nephew and went on quickly. Jillian was glad he didn't mention the secret room. "Don't tell me he found it?"

"Yes. It was behind some things in—in that room. After he checked out, Mindy and Kate gave it a thorough cleaning, but they didn't find anything else unusual. Kate and I can't remember ever seeing it before, and we wondered if you had. I'm thinking maybe Dad left it in there."

"Well, now, your father was a good hand at picking up curiosities. Still, you'd think he'd have shown me this."

"Yes, I would think so," she said.

Zeb lifted the compass carefully from the box and turned it over. "It's old."

"How old?"

"Maybe a couple hundred years."

"Really? Fantastic! We should put it in the Hornblower room, near the telescope."

"First, you get it insured," Zeb said.

"Do you think it's valuable?"

"Could be." Zeb frowned, looking down at it. "Pretty thing. Take it to the Penobscot Marine Museum, over in Searsport. I can give you the name of a fellow there who could tell you more than I can."

"Thanks!"

"Say, did you get your money from that fella?" Zeb asked.

"Oh, yes, his credit card went through just fine." The memory of Mike's meek offer to leave early to alleviate the tension almost made her tear up.

Zeb nodded. "I knew you were a little concerned when you found out he owed his cousin."

"No worries. And he left an impressive tip for Mindy."

"Have you heard any more about his dust-up with his cousin?"

"No, not a word. I hope they can work things out. Kate and I decided not to press charges for the ruckus Peter made, hoping it would put them in a better mood." Jillian stood. "I really should get back. We're having company tonight, and I'm cooking dinner."

"Oh, too bad you can't stay," Zeb said.

Lee stood. "Yeah, I'd love to hear more about the guest who found the compass."

"Your uncle Zeb can fill you in. Good to see you, Lee." She made her escape with the compass in her hands and dashed back across the bridge and through the trees.

That afternoon, Kate walked briskly into Skirmish Cove's business section. As she approached the Book Rack, she smiled. The plywood was gone and a spotless new glass door stood in its place.

Carl was restocking the suspense section when she walked inside, and Hannah stood behind the counter, directly under the second camera Carl had installed, cashing up a customer's purchase, which looked substantial from Kate's vantage point.

She strolled through the aisles and came up beside the owner.

"Hello, Carl."

He turned and smiled. "Kate, glad to see you."

"How's Eric doing?"

"Better, now that he's home."

"Good. Jillian asked me to tell you she'll pop over to see him this afternoon and take him some scones."

"I'm sure he'll appreciate that. Tell her to go around to the back. We've been leaving it unlocked, since it's hard for Eric to get up and answer the door." Carl's face still carried a worried cast.

"Surely he's safe now."

"I believe so, but both of us will probably keep on being cautious."

"Yes, so will I." Kate glanced toward the counter. "I see Hannah's settled in."

"Hannah is wonderful. I couldn't ask for a better assistant. And I've hired another clerk who's coming in afternoons this week. If all goes well, I'll put her on a regular part-time schedule. But Hannah is now full time. We're working out the details of a contract for her—sick days and so on. I've never had to do that before, but I feel she's worth it, and—well, I *am* getting older."

"Oh, Carl, you're not old."

"Thank you for that, but I am slowing down. I've felt it these last few weeks."

"You've been under a lot of stress."

"Yes, but it's more than that. I've accepted the fact that Eric doesn't want to take over running the store. When he's able, he's going to start a new job."

Kate straightened and eyed him closely. "Really? Where?"

"Do you know Blaine Holt?"

"Doesn't he own the garage on Maple Street?"

"That's the one." Carl slid some books over on the shelf and inserted a new one. "He's going to give Eric one bay to use repairing motorcycles, ATVs, and snowmobiles."

"Wonderful!"

"Eric thinks so. If it works out, it will give him a chance to save some money toward his own business. I've known Blaine a long time. He'll be fair with Eric. But he won't put up with any nonsense, either. They're going to give it a trial run this summer. They'll decide in August whether or not to continue the arrangement."

"His nephew's still working with him, isn't he—Mickey?"

"Yes, he's still there. But they get a lot of inquiries about repairs on recreational vehicles. Blaine said if it worked out, he'd encourage Eric to start his own business."

Kate nodded slowly. "I hope it goes well."

"So do I. It's already given Eric an incentive to work hard at his physical and occupational therapy. He knows he needs to be fit to take it on."

"I'm pleased that you've found a way to meet both your needs. And if you need someone to fill

337

in here for a few hours, don't hesitate to call on me or Jillian."

"Thank you. You girls have already been such a help."

Kate smiled at being called a girl. At almost thirty-four, she wasn't called that by many people besides her siblings.

That evening, Jillian walked Rick and his family to the door. Her sister-in-law, Diana, embraced her.

"Thanks so much for the meal, Jillian. It was wonderful." She turned to hug Kate. "You too. Next time you come to our house."

"It's a deal," Kate said.

"Aunt Jillian, thanks for showing us the secret room." Joel's grin was huge.

She put a finger to her lips. "You're welcome, but remember, it's *secret*."

"You know he's a blabbermouth," Ashley said.

Joel turned and punched her on the shoulder.

"Hey! None of that." Rick took Joel's arm and propelled him toward the SUV.

"I know you'll remember," Jillian called after him. She gave Ashley a quick hug. "Come again soon, sweetie."

"Can I help you when you paint the Virginian Room?"

"Yes, you may. Maybe next Saturday?"

"I'll be here! Right, Mom?" Belatedly, she looked to her mother.

"Yes, you may come on Saturday." Diana squeezed Jillian's hand and followed the others to the vehicle.

Craig had lingered inside, and when Jillian went through the lobby, she found him at the table with a cup of coffee before him. Everyone had helped bus the dishes after dessert, so the table was clear. She could hear the clinking of china from the kitchen.

"Guess I'd better go help Kate load the dishwasher."

Craig reached for her hand. "She said she can handle it and we should snatch a minute while we can."

"Oh, I like the sound of that. Bring your coffee into the living room." She'd have to do something special for Kate later.

The curtains were open, and the moon shone over the bay, highlighting a few boats with a ghostly sheen. The inn's guests rarely used this room but preferred the lounge and library above.

"Looks like we have the place to ourselves." She led Craig to a settee facing windows.

"It's always peaceful here." He sank down beside her.

Jillian chuckled. "We both missed the big to-do when Peter Schuman came looking for his cousin. I'm told it was anything but peaceful that day."

"Yeah, maybe I should have said every time I've been here."

"Maybe it's you who brings the peace."

Why had she said that? Craig looked deep into her eyes, and her heart thudded.

"Sorry," she said. "I didn't mean . . ."

What didn't she mean.

"Jillian . . . may I?"

She knew what he meant. He wanted to kiss her, not for the first time.

"I don't think you need to ask anymore," she whispered.

He kissed her and then pulled her closer. Jillian slid her arms around him. Somewhere in the background, the house phone was ringing, but Kate would grab it in the kitchen.

"Oh, sorry," Kate said a moment later.

Craig jumped away from Jillian then gave her an apologetic glance.

"What is it, Kate?" Jillian brushed a hand over her hair.

"Uh, somebody wants to reserve six rooms for the first week in May. Party of ten, but six rooms."

"Okay." It would take a while for her pulse to slow down, but Jillian tried to sound professional.

"That would fill us to the max with the reservations we already have," Kate said. "And that's if the Phileas Fogg Room is available."

"It will be ready by then. Book it."

"Okay. Just wanted to make sure. Sorry." Kate glided out of the room.

"She's good at sneaking up on people," Jillian said.

"I'll say." Craig hesitated then said, "Guess I probably should go."

"Don't stay away too long."

His smile lit his whole face. "How about Saturday night? I've got the day shift, but if nothing goes wrong, I'll be off at four."

"Great."

"I'll call you before then. If there's something you'd like to do, let me know."

She walked with him to the front door. He leaned down for a final kiss. The beam of a car's headlights swept over them as a guest pulled into the parking lot.

Jillian pulled back. "Guess it's not as peaceful as you thought."

"Not quite, but it's worth it."

About the Author

Susan Page Davis is the author of more than one hundred books. Her books include Christian novels and novellas in the historical romance, mystery, and romantic suspense genres. Her work has won several awards, including the Carol Award, two Will Rogers Medallions, and two Faith, Hope, & Love Reader's Choice Awards. She has also been a finalist in the WILLA Literary Awards and a multi-time finalist in the Carol Awards. A Maine native, Susan has lived in Oregon and now resides in western Kentucky with her husband Jim, a retired news editor. They are the parents of six and grandparents of eleven.

Visit her website at: https://susanpagedavis.com.

Center Point Large Print
600 Brooks Road / PO Box 1
Thorndike, ME 04986-0001 USA

(207) 568-3717

US & Canada:
1 800 929-9108
www.centerpointlargeprint.com